I0598800

The Predator Analysis

Kepos Chronicles
Book 4

Erica Rue

ISBN-13: 978-1-945994-74-6

Editing by Jessica Hatch of Hatch Editorial Services

Cover Design by Sanja Gombar, fantasybookcoverdesign.com

Published by Tannhauser Press
tannhauserpress.com

This is a work of fiction. Any similarity to real persons or events is coincidental and not intended by the author.

Visit ericarue.com for more information.

For Wayne Roy

I'm sorry I didn't finish in time for you to read it, but your support throughout my life, and especially your encouragement of my writing in recent years, meant more than you knew.

The Predator Analysis

1. DIONE

The ship's grating alarm blared. Dione was practically vibrating with the unpleasant sensation. She slipped out of bed and shivered in the cold that seeped into the ship from the black void outside. Unlike the *Calypso*, the clunky old colonizer never really got warm. Still, the vessel had gotten them off Kepos and moving back in the direction of home.

She limped over to where her leg brace lay on the floor of Brian's cabin. A few months ago, one of the dragons on Jameson's nightmare island had torched her calf. The brace allowed her to walk almost normally, and she took pain meds when it got bad, but she was improving. Slowly. Which was the pace at which she moved these days. Nevertheless, she committed herself to daily physical therapy exercises and was grateful for the amount of strength she'd recovered.

"What is that awful sound?" Brian asked. Dione was already in the doorway of his cabin, ready to find out.

"It's an alert," Dione said, pulling her brown hair into a messy ponytail. "I think we've reached Campos."

Home. They were finally going home.

After a minute, Dione paused to catch her breath and give her leg a rest. They'd left Kepos a few weeks ago for the outer colony on Campos. There, they could call home using the near real-time, or NRT, comms array, and a faster ship would come to take them to Lavinian, her home planet and a well-protected core world. *Home, home, home,* she thought with each step.

Brian followed her down the corridor. The colonizer wasn't built for speed and its jump tech was old, so it couldn't jump as far or as frequently as the *Calypso,* which meant the trip to Campos, the closest planet to Kepos with an NRT comms array, had taken nearly two weeks.

She checked the time on her manumed. "We must have slept through the final jump." The tone of the alarm didn't feel right. It was ominous. Despite her misgivings, she could hardly contain her excitement at the thought of calling home and reassuring her dad and uncle, and Lithia's parents, that they were all okay.

Dione led the way down the corridor, hesitating for just a moment in front of Zane's cabin. She half expected to meet Bel and Zane in the hallway, but maybe they were eating breakfast. She shivered but kept moving, her steps clanking unevenly against the metal grates of the floor as she favored her left leg. The colonizer was only one segment of a three-part ship. One section Dione, Brian, and his father, Oliver, had left behind on Jameson's nightmare island because it was infested with dragons. The middle segment they left with the Ficarans and Aratians, who planned to use its fabricator to ease tensions and rebuild after the Ven attack on Kepos. The third segment, which they'd repaired and flown from Kepos, was much bigger than the three dozen crew needed. Most of the cabins were unused, and the empty corridors felt eerie.

Her manumed vibrated, and she looked down at her wrist. A message.

"Lithia?" Brian asked.

"No, Bel. They're already at the bridge. Come on."

They climbed up a ladder to reach the third level. Their segment of the colonizer had five levels in total. Command was on the third level. Most people were staying in cabins on the second. On the fourth level was the officers' mess, which was where they had been taking their meals and having meetings.

With no explanation, the alarm shut off. Dione relaxed her shoulders, relieved. The noise had made her feel sick.

She smiled as they passed a confused Ficaran.

"Morning," Brian said, nodding.

"What's happening?" the Ficaran asked.

"Not sure yet," Brian replied. "We're going to check it out."

About two dozen or so Ficarans and Aratians had chosen to leave Kepos, and Brian and his parents were among them. Their other passengers, a handful of former Green Cloak traitors, had not been given free reign of the ship. Instead, they were restricted to the fourth level. Brian was wary of them even though they had shown no signs of renewed interest in harming people. All seemed to regret their involvement in helping the Vens storm the Aratian settlement back on Kepos.

They found the bridge more crowded than usual.

Bel stood next to Zane, looking over the professor's shoulder at one of the readouts. Oliver, Brian's father, sat in the captain's chair, reassuring a few Ficarans who had also made their way to the bridge.

"What's going on?" Dione asked.

"We've almost reached Campos," Oberon replied.

Professor Elian Oberon looked tired. He had looked tired since she'd rescued him from the Vens on Kepos, and she wondered if he would ever return to his old self.

"That's a good thing," Dione said. "Why is everyone so grim?"

"The Vens beat us here." Bel's voice was low. Her dark brown hair was down today, hiding the spiral scar on her cheek.

"That alarm was a proximity alert," Oberon said. "We passed by a ship that's floating adrift." He pressed an icon. On the display screen appeared a small ship in a slow spin with no sign of power.

"The Vens?" Brian asked.

"They boarded the ship," Oberon said. He pressed a few more icons, and the display switched to a still image showing hull damage. "It's consistent with the marks the Vens left on the *Calypso* when they attached their docking ramp. We haven't gotten any response to our hails. We assume the ship was fleeing the colony and that everyone on board is dead."

"What about the colony? Is anyone there responding to hails?"

"No," Zane said. His grim expression almost made his blue eyes look gray. He was nearly as tall as Brian, but he was lanky where Brian was muscular, and his black hair was cropped short where Brian's came down to his shoulders.

Why had the Vens attacked? Were there any survivors? Was the NRT comms array still working? Had the Alliance come to evacuate them? Dione had a million more thoughts and questions, but she held her tongue. The people around her probably had the same questions, and there was only one way to get the answers.

"When are we going to the surface?" she asked.

Bel and Zane exchanged a look, and Oberon's gaze flashed down to her leg brace.

She rolled her eyes. "Don't bother. I'm going to go."

"Dione, we don't know what's down there. There could be Vens, still alive and mending."

"Oberon—"

"You're staying here," Oberon said, using his long-forgotten teacher voice, a tone he'd rarely used on her back at StellAcademy. "It will be a quick trip anyway."

Apparently he thought she'd obey without question now that they were back inside the Bubble. She tensed in anger, about to disabuse him of the notion, but pain shot through her leg. She couldn't stop herself from wincing.

"Dione, please." His voice was softer now. "Bel and Zane will join me. We'll only be gone long enough to send a message to the Alliance."

Dione turned to look at Brian, her head tilted in an unspoken question.

"I'm going to stay here," Brian said. "I still don't trust the Green Cloaks, no matter how much remorse they've shown."

"But they're confined to their quarters," Dione replied. "I'll keep an eye out for you. Go with them. I can tell you want to."

He looked past her to his father, who nodded. "All right. It sounds like it will just be a short trip. I assume we're taking the shuttle?"

Oberon nodded. They had taken one of the shuttles, or as the Ficarans called them, Flyers, and docked it inside the colonizer. It had seemed silly to Dione at the time. Why would they need a shuttle when they were just going to Campos to call home and get rescued? She had never stopped to consider that Campos might have been attacked. Her feet were rooted to the spot. What else had happened while they were gone?

"Speaking of shuttles, where's Lithia?" Oberon asked, snapping her out of her thoughts.

Dione frowned. That was a good question, one that she herself should have asked much sooner.

"Sleeping, I think," Dione replied.

Lithia spent a lot of time locked in her cabin. Usually when

Dione knocked, there was no answer. She figured her friend was asleep or just didn't want to be bothered. She'd seemed okay on Kepos after a while, but a few days into their journey, she'd started to hole up more often, skipping meals. She hadn't been very interested in combing through the Ven datacore with them.

"Let her rest then," Oberon said.

Dione looked behind her at the door to the bridge. "I'll go check on Lithia after you leave."

And then Oberon wasn't addressing her anymore. He was addressing the people going down to Campos. "I don't want to waste any time," he said. "We'll go long enough to send a message and maybe gather some supplies. It's cold at the colony, so grab your warmest clothes, then meet me by the shuttle."

The landing party hurried past her as she limped along toward Lithia's cabin.

2. LITHIA

Lithia pressed the bottle to her lips in the dim light of her cabin. She was wearing two pairs of socks, but her toes were still numb with cold. The *vigo*, a stimulant the Keposians used to stay awake while on watch, tasted bitter, but she couldn't risk falling asleep. The nightmares were worse in space, and the bitter drink was the only thing that kept them at bay.

It wasn't just the nightmares, though. Everything was worse in space. A few months ago when they'd been on the *Calypso*, she'd loved it. The silence, the vastness, the freedom! Now, she missed the warmth of the sun, the buzz of bugs in the trees, and even the laughter and cries of playing children, reminders that life continued all around her.

Her cabin aboard the colonizer was small, barren, and lacked the warmth of the *Calypso*. Dione's cabin was right next door, but she wasn't there. She was never there. Every night she headed over to the opposite side of the ship where the boys' cabins were to spend the night with Brian. Knowing Dione, there was a high probability they were just sleeping.

Bel was always over there, too, with Zane. Adults and families were in the larger, officer-style quarters near the bow. There were a just a few people left in her section, and they probably didn't care why she woke up screaming. They didn't care that she was alone.

The *vigo* wasn't even working right anymore. Aratian watchmen used it to stay awake, and one had shared it with her when she'd joined Cora, her cousin, to hunt down the treacherous Green Cloaks. They'd given her a few bottles as a thank-you gift. Or going-away gift. She wasn't sure.

She took another small sip, but when she tilted the bottle back, there were only a few drops left. After only a couple of weeks in space, she was flying through her supply.

Maybe if she got up and moved around that would help. Anything for a change of scenery. She'd spent so much time staring at the ceiling of her cabin she could tell someone from memory how many bolts there were and the different shapes and patterns she could form by mentally connecting them. She pulled on a light StellAcademy jacket and blue sweatpants and ventured out into the corridor.

Today a loud, discordant alarm had pulled her from her nightmare early. She'd ignored a message from Bel telling her to come to the bridge. They were probably at Campos or something. No need to get excited too early. Until she was at home in a warm bed, full from a home-cooked meal, she would be skeptical. Nothing had gone to plan. Nothing.

Breakfast will help, she thought.

Normally, she looked forward to meals, but ever since getting into space, the food hadn't tasted the same. Still, it was a habit, and she heard her mother's voice in the back of her head. "Eat something. You'll feel better afterward." *We'll be home soon, Mom*, she thought. *Then you can scold me in person to eat.*

"Hey! Lithia!"

She looked up, only just realizing she had been staring down at the floor as she walked, avoiding the cracks where the floor grates met like she was still a little kid running down the sidewalk.

She forced a smile. "Dione," she said, nodding in greeting.

"Where are you headed?"

"Breakfast."

"Can I join you?" she asked.

"Sure. What was all the noise about this morning?"

"We've reached Campos."

Lithia felt a trickle of relief spill from the dam she'd built to hold back her optimism. She would see them again. Mom. Dad. Grandpa Min. Even her brother, Max. She flashed a genuine smile this time. "Great! Have you talked to them? Did they call a fleet ship yet? When are we going home?" The look on Dione's face was answer enough, and the trickle of relief evaporated with Lithia's smile.

"Things aren't going as planned," her friend said.

Lithia braced herself for what was coming. They reached the mess hall, which contained just a few people. No Green Cloaks, thankfully. The Keposians delivered their meals to their cabins. Oliver had agreed to take some of the surviving Green Cloaks with them. Lithia had not been thrilled by this decision, but the Aratians and Ficarans wanted the Green Cloaks near them even less than she did. Lithia braced herself for the news.

"The Vens attacked. No confirmed survivors."

Lithia did her best to keep her face neutral, but she could feel the hope that had been building inside her during their approach to civilization leaving her body, like a violent decompression. The exhaustion from too little sleep coupled with the stimulants in the *vigo* made her feel hollow, but this was something worse. She was less than empty. The news had crushed her like a tin can.

"I'm sorry to be the bearer of such bad news," Dione said, filling the lull in the conversation. "The others are going down to the planet to use the NRT comms array."

"And they didn't invite me?"

"I thought you were sleeping in, but you still look exhausted. Are you sure you're okay?"

"I'm fine. It's just so cold on this ship. I don't sleep well."

"From what Oberon said, the colony is colder than the ship. I'll get you some hot coffee," Dione offered.

Her friend returned with two mugs, then left her again to get some breakfast. The Keposians had happily volunteered to take on the cooking duties. Dione returned with scrambled eggs, toast, and melon. The eggs were well-seasoned, which made them easier to eat when Lithia wasn't hungry. Energized by her half-eaten meal, she was able to slip back into her perky persona. Old Lithia. Pre-Kepos Lithia.

"The melon was delicious," she said, knowing it was the right thing to say rather than feeling it. "I hope Bel and Zane bring back some candy bars from the planet." She looked around once more. "Where's Brian?" The two were inseparable. If she'd had the energy, Lithia would have given Dione a hard time about it.

"He went down to the surface with the others to send a message with the comms array." Dione looked down and focused on coating every corner of her toast with an even layer of butter.

"You wanted to go. They left you," Lithia said.

"Because of my leg."

"Well, they left me too. You're barely limping anymore. You'll heal, Dione. I know you will." *One of us has to, and I don't think it can be me.*

"I hope. At least we're back inside the Bubble."

"For whatever that's worth. Looks like the Alliance failed to protect the Bubble in the case of Campos."

"Hopefully the others will find some answers."

Lithia took a bite of her own toast. Unlike Dione, she'd smeared the butter on carelessly before taking a bite. The toast was dry and salty, and Lithia chewed for a long time, trying not to think about what toast was supposed to taste like. Instead, she tried to coax back that trickle of optimism. There was still the comms array. Help would arrive soon, even if the colonists here were dead. She ignored the voice in her head that asked why help hadn't come in time to save Campos.

Dione waited until Lithia had finished her last sip of coffee. "I'm going to head to the bridge and wait to hear back. Want to come?"

Lithia's first instinct was to say no, but old Lithia would have happily joined her. That's who she would be today. Old Lithia.

"Sure," she replied. She ate her last piece of fruit, bussed both of their plates, and prepared to follow Dione to the bridge.

Anything was better than counting the bolts on her cabin ceiling again.

3. BEL

They had just landed when Bel got the message from Dione: *Bring back a chocobun for Lithia. She needs cheering up.*

Lithia needed more than a chocobun, but Bel would grab one if she could. The chill hit her as soon as the shuttle door opened. The colonizer had been cold, but Campos was utterly frigid. Bel opened her mouth to sigh, and a wisp of white mist escaped her lips. She wrapped her arms around her body and stepped out into the port. She tried not to look too closely, but it was hard to ignore the carnage around her. She could see bodies clearly not dressed for the outdoors lying near ships.

Some ships had their doors open but had failed to lift off. She looked back at the others who were observing the same things.

"How far is the comms array?" Bel asked with a shiver.

"Five kilometers. Too far to walk, but we can take a car," Oberon replied, gesturing to the nearby street.

Bel looked where he was pointing and saw more bodies and several abandoned cars. The cold had one benefit. The bodies had been preserved and, as a result, didn't smell. This colony was much larger than her own had been, large enough to have a few jump-capable ships. Despite the carnage, she realized with a breath of hope that some people must have escaped. Still, the frozen death that lay scattered around the landing zone told her that the Vens had won here in a meaningful way.

"Didn't they have protection?" Brian asked. "There must have been thousands living here."

"If they did, it wasn't enough," Zane replied, his words catching in his throat.

Bel put a reassuring hand on his back. Seeing a scene like this inside the Bubble was disturbing. She dropped her hand down to her side and followed Oberon to the street and into an empty car. The ignition chip was still in the slot. Oberon turned it on and input their destination. He followed the car's directions to the comms array. It was eerie to hear the computer's voice, chipper and warm, in the face of the disaster that surrounded them.

There were a few places Oberon had to go off the road to avoid obstructions like cars and bodies. Occasionally, she saw a large, green corpse. The Vens had come in overwhelming force, and the colonists had been completely unprepared.

The car stopped, and she looked up at the building that housed the array. Its walls were dark and sleek, and a few of the windows were broken. The structure itself was large and prominent. They must be close to the city center. In front of the doors, she saw several heaps of green. Her chest tightened, and she hoped that after two weeks, the Vens would stay dead. The visual reminder that the Vens had done this reignited the rage inside her that never quite went out, but the anger did nothing to keep the chill in the air from numbing her nose and fingertips.

"There are more Ven bodies here than anywhere else," Bel observed.

"I think the colonists were trying to send a message, and the Vens found them," Oberon said. The first door he tried opened, and he disappeared into the darkness. The lights came on inside the building automatically, and Bel followed. Zane and Brian were checking the Ven bodies on the ground, and once they were satisfied, they, too, stepped inside.

Bel's heart was pounding. She didn't think any Vens were lurking in the shadows, but the occasional flickering light and the faint stench of rot filled her with dread. Inside was warm. The heat was still going, and she was grateful that she could feel her fingers again. The walls were pockmarked with bullet holes. This was where much of the resistance had been concentrated. It made sense to Bel. This building was by far the largest and sturdiest of any they had passed on the way. In addition to housing the comms array, it housed the local government.

She skimmed a notice about permit requests as she followed Zane down the hall. Intersections were labeled with plaques and arrows like every other government building she had visited. The stench grew stronger. When they rounded the corner, Bel flinched at the smell of several corpses draped across the floor and the sight of crates that had been lined up as makeshift barricades. Bel didn't look too closely as they picked their way to the room that housed the NRT array.

The comms room consisted of several workstations arranged in front of the jump chamber, which took up the back third of the room. Slick, white panels covered the floor, walls, and ceiling, and the chamber was protected on its open side by a wall of glass. Well, it had been. The glass was now mostly in shards on the floor. Even Bel's untrained eye deemed the situation hopeless, and Oberon's hunched shoulders and Zane's groan confirmed her suspicion.

"It must have been destroyed in the fight with the Vens,"

Oberon said. "The jump chamber has been compromised, and the drones are useless."

"Can we fix it?" Bel asked.

"No," Zane cut in. No explanation, no hope, just no.

From what Zane had explained to her earlier, Bel knew that the array worked much like the emergency beacon they'd cannibalized to repair the Icon, only faster. Messages were recorded on very small drones, which got jumped from one array to the next until they reached their destination. The microdrones themselves didn't have jump drives and relied on the drives at dedicated communications facilities to transport them. This method of jumping—sending an object along a network of arrays—had been tried to move ships, but it failed. Only microdrones, the size of small bugs, could be successfully jumped in this way.

"Zane's right," Oberon continued. "There's no way to repair this damage, and with the chamber compromised, the microdrones aren't going anywhere."

"Did they get a message off before that happened?" Zane asked.

"Give me a minute," Oberon said. He sat at one of the workstations and began typing.

Bel felt Zane's tension and stepped closer to lace her fingers through his.

"Looks like several messages were sent out with emergency priority," Oberon said.

Zane crossed his arms.

"Was there a reply?" Brian asked.

"There was a request for details, then confirmation that a Fleet ship was dispatched."

"Then what happened?"

There was a pause while Oberon swiped through some

information. "The fleet ship was delayed on its way. It arrived after the improvised evacuation and battle were over."

"So they failed to save Campos, and then they just left it like this? This is no way to treat the dead," Zane fumed.

"Campos is an outer planet. It takes time to get all the way out here," Oberon replied. His tone was factual rather than defensive, which she appreciated.

Bel squeezed Zane's hand. She didn't begrudge him this anger, but it felt misplaced. As much as she shared his concerns about the Alliance, she couldn't lose sight of the real threat. The Vens. It was always the Vens. "Maybe they had to respond to another call for help."

"Either way, I agree, Zane. It's disconcerting that they would evacuate rather than provide aid. I worry…" Oberon trailed off and closed his eyes for a long moment.

Bel knew what he was holding back because that same fear sliced through her heart. "You worry about how bad it must be everywhere else for the Alliance to behave this way." Her words were quiet, but they echoed in the silence of the jump chamber.

Brian was bent over another workstation. "Look at this."

"What did you find?" Bel asked.

"I think I know where the colonists went," he said.

Bel read over his shoulder. It was a comms log. There were several messages sent to the Alliance interspersed with calls to places called Lorentia and Tagam. The Alliance had responded, but Lorentia and Tagam had not. At the very end of the list was another name. Doran. Campos had sent several messages until it received a response.

"The Alliance wouldn't arrive in time. Lorentia and Tagam didn't answer. I bet those who could went to Doran," Zane said.

While Oberon studied the list, the creases in his forehead grew more pronounced. "Lorentia and Tagam are colonies in this general vicinity that have NRT comms arrays. I don't know anything about Doran."

Bel hugged her stomach. If the Vens had attacked those two planets, they desperately needed to be stopped. They had been growing bolder in the months preceding their original StellAcademy research trip, but now they appeared to be out of control. Maybe the Alliance could seek out the Sugians, and they could work together to defeat the Vens once and for all. The Vens might see the Sugians as a shell-sucking nightmare from ancient ghost stories, but the Sugians just might be humanity's salvation.

4. LITHIA

The others had returned from the surface and reported immediately to the bridge to share the grim news. Lithia clenched her jaw to keep her teeth from chattering. She was sitting next to Oberon, staring at their proposed course on one of the bridge's displays. They were dimmer than the *Calypso*'s and flickered slightly whenever anyone bumped the console. "No comms. No rescue ship," she said. *No hope*, she thought.

She looked at the map in front of her and did a few mental calculations. "Doran? That's another week, at least."

"Eight days," Oberon said. "It's the closest option." Doran had an NRT comms array, but there was a catch. It was an independent colony and did not generally welcome visitors.

"Based on the logs we found, it seemed like the people who escaped were heading to Doran," Brian said.

"Then we go to Doran," Dione said. "Do you really think they'll help us?"

"I hope so," Oberon said. "These are difficult times, and I like to think that even those who keep to themselves will be more welcoming than usual."

"Difficult times can also bring out the worst in people," Zane muttered. "They don't like visitors, but at least the Campos refugees called ahead. We don't know how they'd react to unannounced visitors."

"There's always Lorentia and Tagam," Lithia said.

"I don't want to go to a colony that didn't respond when Campos called them in desperate need," Bel said. "What if those two colonies have been destroyed by the Vens already?"

"Then we won't have to ask permission to use their NRT comms array," Lithia muttered. The others ignored her, and Dione switched gears.

"We need to warn the Alliance about the Sugians, in case they don't know," Dione said.

"More like convince them to get the Sugians to take care of our Ven problem," Bel replied. "If the Sugians really have caught up to the Vens, that will be good news for us."

Dione snorted, and Lithia rolled her eyes at the two of them. She'd already heard this argument a dozen times. The give-and-take continued, but Lithia tuned it out. *Eight days*. Lithia felt like the walls were closing in. *Eight days*. She needed to get out of there, so she slipped away and moved toward the door.

Brian, the only one who noticed, raised an eyebrow. "Where are you going?"

She could pretend she was sick, but that was too close to the truth. No need to get everyone fawning over her, asking if she was okay. An idea popped into her head. "I'm going to help make lunch," she said. She'd helped do some of the cooking back on Kepos in the months they were repairing the colonizer, and it seemed like the perfect break from counting her ceiling bolts.

"Can I come?" Brian tilted his head toward the arguing pair.

"You can, but—" She grasped for a reason to make him stay.

"But I should probably stay here and break this up. You're right."

"Have fun."

"You too."

That was a tall order considering the news. She'd been counting down the days until they reached Campos. She'd had plans. They'd call home, Dione's dad would send some fast and fancy ship to get them, and they'd be home in no time. While they waited, she'd be able to send a message to her parents. *Exchange* messages with her parents, and even her annoying little brother, Max. They would have been safe and sound on an Alliance colony, their odyssey over.

Instead, their safe harbor had been destroyed. The people had evacuated or been killed. How many other worlds had the Vens targeted during their stay on Kepos? Were the Sugians on their way, and who was right about them: Bel, who hoped for Ven-killing allies, or Dione, who was just as wary of them as she was of the Vens?

She entered the ship's galley to find Mary, a young Ficaran woman with fair skin, blue eyes, and light blond hair. "I'm here to help with lunch. Anything simple I can do to make your life easier?" Lithia asked.

Mary recovered from her surprise quickly and pointed to a bowl of root vegetables next to some weird contraption.

"Lunch is almost ready, but you can cut the vegetables for tonight's stew. I've already set the slicer to the right thickness. Just put one of these in the top," she said, picking up a thick, round vegetable that looked like a bright green potato. "Then turn the handle. Perfect cubes." She smiled.

"I didn't know perfect cubes were necessary for stew."

"They're not, but I haven't found any knives in this galley. Just fancy tools like that."

Lithia nodded. "I guess having drawers full of knives on a spaceship isn't a great idea."

She got to work slicing up the veggies. She had to switch arms every few minutes, but the task was calming. The click-click-tink of the device was rhythmic, reminding her of a song that had been popular around the time they left Lavinian, and she started humming along. *No need to butcher the lyrics along with the vegetables.* In no time, she had finished cutting up the vegetables, and without the beat, the song faded from her mind, leaving a void where it had been.

"Need anything else?" she asked, bringing the filled bowl over to Mary, who was five spice jars deep into seasoning the stew base.

"More canned tomatoes from the storeroom, or whatever it's called on this ship," Mary said, never looking up from her work. "Two jars ought to be enough."

"Got it," Lithia replied. That was easy enough. Then she could get back to… lying awake in her room, staring at the ceiling? Assuming she could stay awake. The *vigo* wasn't working very well anymore, and she had to drink more and more to stay awake. She was running low, even though the Aratian who gave it to her had promised it would last her months.

Just get the tomatoes, she thought.

The storeroom was neatly organized. Different foods were contained in small, well-labeled lockers. She located the tomatoes and turned to leave, but a well-secured crate of bottles made her hesitate. They were separated from the rest of the food. What was inside them?

The crate reminded her of her own, filled with bottles of *vigo*. Hers were mostly empty, but these were full. Untouched.

She brought the tomatoes to Mary.

"Thanks," the woman replied.

"No problem. I knocked over a small tin of something in there. Maybe tea. I'm just going to go back and clean it up before I leave."

"Okay," Mary replied, still focused on the stew.

She would investigate the crate. If it was *vigo*, she could just substitute one of her empty bottles for a full one. The glass was dark. No one would notice for a while.

Lithia closed the storeroom door behind her and carefully opened the crate. The bottles were sealed, just as hers had once been. She opened one and took a sip, welcoming the bitter taste she'd become accustomed to.

Just as she was closing the bottle back up, the door suddenly opened. She scrambled to put the bottle back where she found it and turned to see Brian looking down at her.

"Lithia?" he asked. "What are you doing in here?"

"I was helping Mary. She asked me to bring her tomatoes, but I knocked something over and came back to clean it up."

Brian looked around at the clean floor. "What'd you knock over?"

Why is he acting so suspicious? she wondered. "Honestly," Lithia said, rising to her feet, "I have no idea. Half of these things are new to me. At least in their uncooked forms." She threw up her hands and gestured to a basket full of nuts.

Brian chuckled. "Those are *gora* nuts. Need any help?" he offered.

"Nope, I'm all done," she said, relaxing a little. "What are you doing in here?"

"Oberon asked for an inventory list. Looks like we've got another week or two ahead of us, but he wants to make sure we're stocked up well beyond that, just in case."

"In case the Vens have killed everyone on Doran too?" She had intended to sound sarcastic, but it fell flat. She sounded scared instead.

"Are you okay?" Brian asked.

"I'm fine, just frustrated by the news. You heard them. The comms array is busted."

"No, you're shaking," he replied.

She looked down at her hands, which were trembling. This happened sometimes if she needed to drink more *vigo*.

"Yeah, I'm fine. Just cold. I'm always cold on this ship."

"Let's take you to the med bay."

"No, really. I'm just going to get another sweater from my cabin."

"The others are on their way to lunch if you want to come back and join us."

"Yeah, sounds good," she replied.

She got back to her cabin and shivered. It felt colder inside than in the corridor. She pulled her thickest sweater over her head and pulled her last bottle of *vigo* from its hiding place. She took a small sip, savoring its bitterness, then a swig, before putting it back. She had to make it last. There were two more weeks ahead of her, and she only had this last bottle left.

When she returned to the mess hall for lunch, Dione and the others were there.

"Lithia!" Dione waved her over. "We've got a surprise for you."

Bel slid over a small package, decorated in large, bright blue letters: "CHOCOBUN. *The* Chocolate Experience."

Lithia grinned, feeling genuine happiness at the small gesture. She ripped open the package and took a giant bite, ignoring the meal Mary had prepared.

Her smile disappeared, though, as she began chewing.

"What's wrong?" Dione asked.

"Nothing." Lithia forced the corners of her mouth back into a smile again and struggled to keep them there, as if she were carrying the sky on her shoulders. She took another giant bite. Lithia chewed and swallowed, sagging in her chair. She thought it had just been the unusual foods from Kepos, but this confirmed it. Chocobuns were her absolute favorite food. But this chocobun? It tasted like nothing. Everything tasted like nothing. Maybe that's why the bitterness of the *vigo* didn't bother her.

Dione and Bel had picked up the Vens versus Sugians argument again, and Lithia was so, so tired of it. She hadn't been down to Campos with Bel to witness the destruction, but she could imagine it. Streets filled with bodies; lives interrupted, then ended. She knew what Vens were capable of. It was hard to stop her mind from wandering down these dark paths, especially when the alternative was listening to her friends argue.

"We need to focus our research on the Sugians!" Dione said, throwing up her hands. "I can't do this alone."

"I'm not going to help you. Anything that eats Vens is an ally in my book," Bel replied.

"Dione, just drop it. I'll help you." Brian stepped in as the voice of reason.

"Drop it?" Dione asked.

Lithia felt the argument grating on her. Why didn't Dione get it? The Vens had to be stopped, whatever the cost. So what if the Sugians were ugly and terrifying? She shuddered as she conjured the image in her mind. Pale skin covered a thick body and four powerful legs. Horrendous fleshy flaps covered the beak the Sugians used to pry apart Ven plates just enough to slip their feeding appendage inside. Once they injected the right blend of enzymes, they could begin to ingest the soupy, nutritious innards of the Ven. Bel was right. Sugians ate Vens. That was all that mattered.

"Yes, Di, just shut up already. You're clearly not convincing her, so just run on back to Brian's cabin, snuggle up under the blankets, and do a little reading together, or whatever it is you all spend your time doing these days."

Dione's face grew red. "I didn't know you felt that way."

"Of course I do. I want the Vens dead and gone almost as much as Bel," Lithia said, picking at the half-eaten chocobun on her plate. "Get out of your own head, Dione, and then use it."

Dione slowly looked around, her eyes pausing briefly on Zane, the only one who had yet to speak, but she didn't engage him. *Smart choice. He's not going to back you up, that's for sure.*

"All right. Message received." Dione pushed her chair back and left, not bothering to wait for Brian.

Brian stood and gave them a nod. "Later."

Lithia could tell he got it. He knew why they were all so hostile to the idea of picking apart the Sugians' capabilities and intentions.

She didn't want to know anything else about the Sugians. They killed Vens. She wanted to believe that the Sugians would eat all the Vens, and they'd live happily ever after.

Lithia took another tentative bite of the chocobun. It was sweet but tasteless, and she couldn't bring herself to finish it. The others' conversation lowered to a dim hum, and somehow, despite the room buzzing with people, Lithia was alone.

5. DIONE

Dione felt Brian following at a distance behind her, but he didn't say anything. She was grateful. Words were failing her right now, which was not a common occurrence.

She wanted to throw something, but considering she had ended up outside Brian's cabin out of habit, rather than her own, she would have to control that impulse once she got inside. She stood staring at the door, listening to Brian's approaching footsteps. Once he got close, she could smell him too. At first she'd thought he smelled like Kepos, but in reality, Kepos smelled like him.

She waited as he opened the door, then followed him inside. He wrapped her in a warm, calming embrace, but calm was not what she wanted. She pushed him away, sat down on the cold, hard floor of his cabin, and pulled her knees to her chest. She'd jarred her leg when she sat, and she leaned her head back against the wall as she waited for the pain to dull.

"Talk to me," Brian said.

"It feels like they're all ignoring the elephant in the room."

"They are," he agreed. "Ask yourself why."

"I get that it's easier to believe that the Sugians will save them all, but it's so naïve. Especially for someone like Bel."

"She's lost the most to the Vens, though," he replied.

"So she has nothing left to lose to the Sugians?" came Dione's sharp reply.

Brian rolled his eyes. "No, but she wants the Sugians to be a control on the Ven population. I've heard you guys debate invasive species and pest control enough to understand you see this differently on a fundamental level."

"That's putting it mildly. I'm just tired of being the only one who thinks the Sugians might be a curse rather than a blessing."

"You're not alone. I'm with you. And I would go easy on Lithia right now. She's not herself. The fact that they disagree with you makes you second-guess yourself. People half as smart as you promise miracles with one hundred percent confidence. Stop doubting yourself. You've got a reasonable concern, so do what you always have."

"Ask the professor?" Dione asked.

"Research it to death."

Dione looked up at him, his earnest, brown eyes staring back at her. He was right. She got up off the floor and joined him on the bed. Her tablet was already here since they'd been using it to watch movies every night. Brian had a lot of pop culture to catch up on. Before she could open the files on the Sugians, her manumed buzzed with a message.

She frowned.

"Is everything okay?" Brian asked, mirroring her concerned expression.

"Yeah, it's Zane. He's sent me a list of articles related to the Sugians from the datacore."

"He must share your concern about the Sugians," Brian said.

"But he doesn't want to contradict Bel," Dione sighed. This list would make things easier, though the sheer quantity of links made the task more daunting than ever. "I guess this is as good a place as any to start the research."

"Let's get started then."

"Sorry. I've got to go check on my parents," he said, "but I'll be back. Love you." He kissed the top of her head before leaving without waiting for a response. His casual declaration of love distracted her, but she brushed it off. He had probably just meant to comfort her in her distress. With some effort, she shifted her focus back to Zane's message. The Sugian research called, and soon the mystery consumed her.

6. DIONE

She was the last one to reach the mess hall, and the others had already started eating.

"Got you a bowl," Brian said, tapping the seat next to him. His dark, wavy hair was tied back, and his brown eyes, full of concern, glanced down at her injured leg. An unclaimed bowl of hearty vegetable stew marked her spot, and the steam infused with Aratian spices wafted up and warmed her as she sat down.

"Thanks," she replied, settling in and carefully stretching out her bad leg under the table.

Dione took a bite of the stew and glanced up at the others. Zane was nearly finished with his, Bel and Brian were making steady progress, and Lithia's bowl was nearly as full as her own. Instead of holding her spoon, she cupped the sides of the bowl, pressing her fingers against it as if to maximize the surface area.

"You okay, Lithia?" she asked, taking another bite.

"Yeah, just cold."

That explained her death grip on the warm bowl. Dione wasn't buying the excuse, though. Lithia had been spending more and more time in her cabin as the days went by, and Dione hoped they'd reach Doran soon. It would take another couple of months to reach Lavinian in the colonizer, but only a week or two, maybe less, if her father sent a ship for them. Lithia had endured a lot at the hands of the Vens. They had learned from their preliminary searches through the datacore that the Vens were terrorized themselves by a deadly predator, the Sugians. Her friend picked up her spoon again, ladled out a large chunk of root vegetable, and then devoured it.

"So, Dione, did you find anything interesting?" Bel asked.

All five of them been searching through the Ven datacore, at least the part that Sam had translated. Sam was the human-turned-AI on Kepos who had controlled the Mountain Base and the powerful Icon weapon along with it. Bel had downloaded the datacore from one of the Ven ships before the Icon had destroyed it, and the information was almost overwhelming.

Dione set her spoon back down. "Yeah. I don't think you're going to like it, though."

"Zane and I found something with a lot of potential," Bel said.

"Potential? What do you mean?" Dione asked.

"If our goal is to figure out how to stop the Vens, I think we've found the key."

"That's fantastic. What is it?" Dione's heart beat faster.

"We found some references to a Ven plague a few centuries back," Bel said. "It spread through a couple of their Citadel ships, back when they had a lot more than their current two. It made them easy prey."

"It also made the Sugians sick. It was a huge disruption to their cycle, and it's the reason for their small numbers now," Zane added.

"Small numbers?" Lithia arched an eyebrow. "There are

hundreds of thousands of them. And who knows how many Sugians."

"There are billions of us," Dione replied. "Even just on Lavinian."

Brian sucked in a breath, as if startled by yet another reminder of how big humanity really was. He had lived most of his life believing that Kepos was the only human-inhabited planet in the galaxy. Or at least that's what the Keposians had been told by the colony's founder, Jameson. Many of them, including Brian's father, Oliver, had held on to doubts.

"That's how you know we're the prey. Lots of us to feed all of them," Dione added.

"The Vens don't feed on humans. They just murder us for practice. Or fun. Probably both," Bel snapped back.

"But the Sugians might."

"Might what? Murder us?" Bel asked.

"Might feed on us. There's a reason they follow so far behind the Vens." Dione was about to reiterate her theory that the Sugians stayed behind after chasing the Vens off in order to consume whatever life existed on that planet or system.

"Not this again," Lithia moaned. She dropped her spoon, which clattered against the table, and leaned back in her chair. "Please, let's just not have this argument right now. We can't prove whether or not the Sugians stay behind and feast on the inhabitants of whatever planet the Vens just attacked. The data is missing, and we'll never know."

Bel set her lips in a firm line, but she didn't press the point. She had been excited about the Sugians ever since she'd come up with her Ven hypothesis, that they were originally prey. She was in favor of anything that would put a stop to the Vens, even if the cure was worse than the disease.

"It's not just the Vens we have to worry about," Dione said, glancing down and taking a slow breath. "I've been focusing on the Sugians. Here, listen to what I found." She began to read:

> There was a time when the shell was enough.
> But Fate was Hungry, and that Hunger came to find us.
> That was the time when our empty shells were scattered
> like pebbles on the shore, sucked dry of life.
> Our shells grew thicker, our claws sharper,
> and for a time, there was peace.
> But Hunger never stops.
> When we could no longer thicken our shells or sharpen our claws,
> we thickened our walls; and for a time there was peace.
> But Hunger never tires.
> When we could no longer thicken our walls,
> we built new shells made of metal.
> We left our home to search for a new one,
> but without the right shells, peace could not last.
>
> Our first new home was taken.
> We were plucked up like juicy feasts.
> So we made ourselves hard and unappealing before finding our
> next home.
> They reaped us there too,
> like meadow grass before the teeth of a thousand bulls.
> We did not settle again.
> Our homes are the citadels that chase the stars.
> Our homes are the clans whose marks we bear.
> But one day, our shells will once again be enough.

Dione looked up when she finished reading the passage. It was one of many new things she'd discovered about the Vens and Sugians in the past two weeks they'd been on the colonizer. "It's ancient. The Ven who wrote this is centuries dead."

"How could poets become monsters?" Bel asked.

"All poets are monsters," Lithia quipped.

Dione rolled her eyes at Lithia, but she understood Bel's confusion. "My best guess? Centuries of selective breeding, genetic manipulation, and a cultural shift so extreme it's hard to fathom. I never thought I'd feel bad for the Vens, but—"

"Don't," Bel said. "The Vens from that myth, if they ever truly did exist, haven't existed for centuries, probably longer. Zane and I found descriptions of Ven castes. They developed them on the ships as they had to prioritize limited resources in space. The Warrior Caste is the largest, with different clans having more or less power. They have a limited number of Workers, who are rejects of the Warrior Caste."

"What happens to the ones who don't make it as Warriors or Workers?" Lithia asked.

"I assume they kill them," Bel replied.

"You're probably right," Dione agreed. "In their attempt to escape annihilation, the Vens have killed and doomed several other civilizations, either directly or by leading the Sugians to them."

The Vens and Sugians seemed trapped in some sort of predator-prey cycle. The Vens found a new world; honed their fighting skills; stole technology, especially genetics-related research, that could enhance them. Then they tried their luck against the Sugians in combat once they showed up. Whatever lifeforms the Vens had just terrorized, the Sugians stuck around to gorge themselves on. At least, that was what Dione suspected, based on the Ven records. The proof wasn't definitive. Bel, who had her own biases based on her experience, was skeptical, and

Dione didn't like the idea of the Vens being victims either.

She had enough Ven attack highlight reels in her memory to fuel nightmares for months. She hated the Vens and only wished that the Sugians had finished them off long ago, before they'd left their home planet. Before they'd attacked the *Calypso*, invaded Kepos, and taken so many innocent lives, human or otherwise. The Vens were a menace, and the galaxy deserved to be free of them, no matter what had turned them into monsters.

7. BRIAN

Brian considered the Green Cloaks his responsibility. They were all Aratians, not Ficarans like him, but the farther they got from Kepos, the less that distinction seemed to matter. He made a point to do at least one meal delivery shift a day, so, equipped with his bag of food containers, he made his way up to the fourth level where the Green Cloaks had been quartered. The Green Cloaks had let the Vens into the Aratian settlement, and then a few of them had attempted a coup of Aratian leadership after the Vens had been defeated.

Brian had eventually come to feel some sympathy for them. They'd been lied to by the Farmer. Then Elijah had manipulated them to help him overthrow the Aratian leadership.

He hadn't been thrilled that they'd been brought along in the first place, but they were exiles from Kepos. Wary at first, they'd brought food in pairs, but the remorse that the Green Cloaks all displayed was so sincere, even Bel had believed them. She still didn't like them, and Brian didn't blame her. He didn't like them either, but that wasn't why he was here, giving them meals. They were, for better or worse, his responsibility, at least until they got to Lavinian. He wasn't sure what would happen there, but Dione had assured him that they would find a place. And in a city so large, how could they not?

These people had a chance for a fresh start, which was all they had been looking for when they joined the Green Cloaks. These people had been deceived so many times, but for all the sympathy he felt, a smoldering anger lingered. The fire might be out, but whenever he saw them, it was as if he raked the ashes to reveal a few more live coals glowing underneath.

Brian knocked on the first door. "Jill," he said, "I've got your lunch." A plump woman with messy blonde hair answered. "No nuts, just how you like it."

She flashed him a genuine smile. "You remembered. Thank you. Most people don't."

Jill was talkative and lonely, so they chatted for a few minutes. Oberon had insisted the Green Cloaks receive access to any and all information they wanted about the Alliance and Lavinian, and Brian's own father had agreed. It had been a good idea. Jill and the others were full of questions and amazed observations. After so much confusion and deception, they were finally able to access an incredible scope of information. For a few of them, shame was an understatement.

Asher especially had surprised him. Asher, whose father Elijah had been the leader of the Green Cloaks, was eager to start a new life.

When Brian got to Asher's room, he waited for a full minute before the boy answered the door. At fifteen, he was the youngest Green Cloak. There had been some debate about whether or not to leave him on Kepos due to his age, but there had been more than a few threats against his life. Even though he was a boy, his father had tried to organize a coup and take advantage of the destruction left by the Vens. After Elijah's death, people had needed a place to direct their anger, and they'd chosen a teenager. Even Brian had struggled to keep perspective.

"Here's lunch," Brian said.

Asher took the container. "Brian?" he asked, hesitating in the doorway.

"What's wrong?"

"I've been thinking." The younger boy looked down at the container in his hands. "Do you think I'm wrong to love my father? Even the other Green Cloaks hate him."

"He was your father," Brian said. "You know what he did was wrong, but no one can tell you how to feel. It's okay if those feelings are complicated."

Asher didn't look satisfied, but what words could satisfy that question?

"Thanks."

Sorting out his own feelings about Victoria had taken a lot of time, and Brian still didn't know where exactly he'd come down. She'd been a role model and mentor to him at one time. He had respected and admired her. Then she'd been forced to make hard decisions about running their settlement. Eventually, she'd become so harsh and stubborn that his old mentor was barely recognizable. His situation wasn't the same as the one Asher was going through, but he thought he understood the boy, just a little.

Brian continued passing out the meals, making small talk when it was initiated and getting to know these people that he was still trying to forgive.

Their actions had cost lives, and forgiveness for that was not easy.

8. LITHIA

Lithia shivered under the blankets in her bed. It was the middle of the afternoon in ship time, but there was no place on board she'd rather be. She'd tried to ration the *vigo,* but she was out of the stimulant. They wouldn't reach Doran for a few more days, and now she had no way of keeping the nightmares away. A voice nagged at the back of her mind.

What about those bottles in the storeroom?

Lithia pulled the covers over her head. She could feel the effects of the drink piling up, but this was temporary. A stopgap measure. She could self-medicate with *vigo* just long enough to get to Doran. Once she was back home, her parents would know what to do.

Lithia dragged herself from the meager warmth of her bed and ventured out into the ship. One thing she appreciated about the galley and the mess hall was that they were the warmest areas on the ship. The galley was especially nice, considering big containers of stew had been cooking all afternoon. Mary was nowhere to be seen, which made sense. Everything for the evening's meal had already been prepared.

Lithia strode past the galley and found herself at the storeroom in no time. She didn't creep or slink. That sort of behavior looked suspicious. She had long ago mastered the art of looking like she was exactly where she was supposed to be, even when she was breaking the rules. She entered the storeroom and removed the small satchel she had brought. She used it at school to carry her books and tablet, but today it only contained her tablet and an empty, opaque bottle that once held *vigo*. The bottles were identical, and unless someone picked it up or looked very closely, no one would know that the second bottle in the back row was empty.

She made the switch in moments, then turned and grabbed a *polla*, the smooth, purple fruit that her cousin, Cora, had loved, out of the basket. That was her cover story for being here in case anyone saw her leaving.

Lithia exited the kitchen and proceeded through the mess hall. She was nearly at the door when Oberon saw her from his table and waved her over.

"Lithia," he said. "I haven't seen much of you since we left Campos. What have you been up to?"

Lithia nodded and shifted on her feet in the hope that he wouldn't notice the bottle-shaped bulge in her bag. "Watching movies. Reading. Shivering in my cabin."

He chuckled. "This colonizer *is* much colder than the *Calypso*."

Lithia shrugged. "Just a few more days, right? Please tell me that Doran is warm."

"It is, at least where the comms array is."

Lithia turned to leave, but Oberon stopped her. "Wait." Her stomach dropped. He knew about the bottle somehow. "Where'd you get that *polla*?" he asked. "I didn't see any left out."

"Storeroom."

Oberon frowned. "You're not supposed to just take things

from there. We're keeping close track of inventory, and you can't just take whatever you feel like. We need to stay organized. We've still got a few more days until we reach Doran, but space travel can be unpredictable. We need to be mindful of our supplies."

She held back a bitter laugh. She knew all about the dangers of failing to be mindful of her supplies and how unpredictable their journey home had become. She didn't need him to remind her, but she put on a well-practiced look of modest contrition.

"Sorry, professor," she said. "Won't happen again."

The annoyance in his eyes softened into something else. "Lithia, are you okay? You look tired."

"Yeah, I'm fine. Just ready to be off this ship and back on solid ground." Lithia was eager to get away with her stolen goods, but she could tell Oberon had something else he wanted to say.

"I know you experienced things on Kepos that no one, especially a student, should have to experience. All of you did. I wish I could go back—"

She cut him off with a raised hand. He was just as lost as the rest of them, wasn't he? "I know, Oberon. Me too. Really, I'm fine, just ready to leave the Vens behind me and go home."

Should she just tell him the truth? Break down into tears, hand over the *vigo*, and ask for help? She shifted again, feeling the weight of the bottle grow heavier. The strap was beginning to dig into her shoulder. She quickly dismissed that idea. She was fine. Plus, Oberon looked as messed up as she felt. He was a biology nerd like Dione, and though he might enjoy his summer fieldwork, that was a far cry from fighting off the Vens. She'd been doing okay until she ran out of *vigo*. She could last another few days, and then she'd be able to talk to her parents. Then they'd be able to help her. They were doctors. Oberon was just a teacher, and for the first time, she could see her own pain echoed in his eyes.

"Do you want to talk about it? About what happened when we—when you were left on the Ven ship? Or about the scars on your arms from those Ven mothers?" She tried to be sincere, but too late she realized that her questions hadn't come from a place of care. They'd come from her own pain.

"Not especially, no." He crinkled his forehead and leaned back, peering at her even more closely.

See? You're fine too. Everything is fine.

She was halfway to the door when she heard Oberon call her name again, but she pretended not to hear. She kept walking toward her cabin, and he didn't follow. She was glad. Once she got back, she locked her cabin door and prepared to spend the night alone and, with any luck, in a dreamless sleep. She'd only drink a little. Just enough to take the edge off and dull the nightmares. It was only for a few days.

She stared down at the bottle. The *vigo* was an unfamiliar drink. She had been able to tell herself that it was basically strong coffee, but she felt the toll her erratic sleep schedule was taking on her body.

But the nightmares aren't healthy either. She pulled off the lid and took a sip. *Plus, this is temporary.*

9. DIONE

Dione was growing to hate jumps in the colonizer. They seemed to take longer, and the numbness lingered in her limbs for several seconds afterward, just like it was doing now. She flexed her fingers and arched her back, ignoring the pins and needles in her bad leg. Unlike most of the jumps they'd made in the past few weeks, instead of empty space, the view screen now displayed a planet covered in swaths of green and blue. The bridge was crowded with people. Bel and Zane stood near the back, but they were attentive. Lithia leaned against a workstation to Oberon's left. On the right a handful of Ficarans, including Brian and his parents, stood tall, eagerly staring at the new world before them.

They shared their amazement through quiet observations.

"It's just like Kepos."

"No, it's greener than Kepos. Bigger too."

"How can you tell it's bigger?"

Dione sat at another workstation in the back in between Lithia and the Ficarans. Oberon, the de facto captain of the colonizer, sat in front of the console in the center of the bridge. "Let's say hello and see if anyone's home," he said. He prepared a message, but before he could send it, a light on his console began blinking. An incoming message. The professor played it.

An authoritative male voice gave the brief, audio-only message. "Leave immediately."

Dione wasn't surprised by the cold welcome. The colony on Campos, like many other colonies, was Alliance-sponsored, but this one was independent, owned by some tech corporation.

"We can't," Oberon replied. "We need to recharge our jump drive."

"Use your emergency jump function to leave orbit. Get as far away as you can and recharge there." The man's broad accent made him hard to follow, or perhaps that was just the speed of his words.

Oberon shook his head, a futile gesture over audio. "This is an old colonizer. It can't do that."

"Who the hell are you people? Why did you come here in a colonizer? Our facility is private, and no colonization has been authorized here, I'm sure of that."

Concern wrinkled Oberon's brow. "Who are you?"

"You came here, knocked on my door, and you're asking who *I* am? Leave orbit or you'll regret it, that's who."

Dione swallowed. The words felt more like a warning than a threat.

"We don't mean any harm. We need help, but if you're unwilling to give it, we'll leave as soon as we've charged up."

A bitter laugh crackled over the speakers. "You think *I'm* going to hurt you? You got it all wrong, my boy. Trouble is on its way. You never answered my question. Who are you, and why are you so far out in a clunker of ship during a bloody war?"

War? He must mean the Vens. By the looks on her friends' faces, Dione knew they were thinking the same thing.

"Oh, just tell him, Oberon," Lithia snapped from the back of the room.

Dione watched the internal struggle play out on Oberon's face. He didn't like the way this man was speaking to him, but the potential threat the Vens posed if they were on the way was unparalleled. He looked around the room at all the different people depending on him.

The voice grew impatient. "I don't have time to squabble with backwater fools. I've hatches to batten down. Either tell me who you are or get as far from our orbit as you can without jumping."

"We were on Campos, and we were hoping to send a message through your array." It wasn't a lie, but it still wasn't the whole truth. "What happened to the other ships from Campos that came here?"

"We passed on their message, and they went on their merry way. That was weeks ago. Why are you just getting here?" The voice sounded suspicious now. "Forget it. I haven't got the time to play guessing games with you. Send me your message, and I'll pass it along."

Oberon heaved a sigh and sent along the message he'd prepared that identified who they were, a vague explanation of what had happened, and a request for assistance.

A few minutes later, they got a reply from the impatient man. "I don't believe it. You're from the *Calypso*? Turn on the visual. I won't be bothering Marius with this without proof."

Marius? Oberon's message was for Dione's father, Marius Quinn, but why was this man on a first-name basis with her dad?

"Sure thing," Oberon replied. With the tap of his finger, he was now sending video to the grumpy man on the planet. "I'm Elian Oberon. Nice to meet you." Dione pressed her lips together to hold back her smile. He was using the overly kind tone of voice he typically reserved for freshmen who tested his patience. He'd once confided in her that amping up the kindness was his way of coping with the frustration.

"It's him, all right," said a new female voice. "Hair's a bit longer, but it's him. If anything could bring Marius here faster, it's this."

"What about the kids?" the man demanded.

"Before I show you anything else, I'd like to see and know to whom I'm speaking." His voice was calm and deliberate, and Dione could see why. All of a sudden, the professor had the upper hand. He had information these people wanted.

There was some grumbling, and Dione thought she heard the woman giggle, but then the view screen showed a man and a woman.

"Hello, Elian, I'm Michele." A beautiful woman with light brown skin and brown hair smiled at them. She gestured to the man next to her. "This is Kai." Despite being grumpy, he was attractive for an older man. His skin was fair, his eyes were bright blue, and his cheeks and chin were covered in black and gray stubble that matched his hair. He was probably in his late forties, at least a decade older than the woman.

"Thank you," Oberon said, gesturing for Dione and the others to come closer so they would be in the frame.

Kai looked each of them over, but his gaze settled on her. "That's all four, Marius's daughter included."

"Despite his curt greeting," Michele said apologetically, "he was being truthful. We'll send his message, but if you can leave—"

Oberon shook his head. "This ship needs half a day before it hits the minimum energy threshold for a jump. We're not in the *Calypso* anymore. We can stay here in our ship if you can't accommodate us."

Michele and Kai exchanged a meaningful look.

"We can't protect them," Kai said firmly. He turned back toward the monitor. "We can't protect you. They're coming here. We've got hours at most. We can shelter the five of you, but if the Alliance doesn't show up in time, it won't matter."

"Who's coming? The Vens? Because we've survived more than one Ven attack while we've been gone." Oberon rubbed one of his forearms where two of his Ven clan scars were. "We might be able to help."

Confusion contorted Michele's features, but Kai gave a dark chuckle.

"Oh, that's a good guess, but it's not the Vens who're on their way here today. When you left, the Alliance only had one vicious alien species to fight. Now, there are two. The Vens might have attacked Campos, but they're not the ones on their way."

"The Sugians," Dione whispered. "They're already here."

10. DIONE

Dione felt a little nauseous, and Kai frowned at her proclamation. "No, but they will be, and soon. How did you learn about them if you've been out of contact for so long?"

"It's a long story," Oberon said, "that we apparently don't have time for right now."

"Right. I'll send you the coordinates for where to land, and then Michele will collect the five of you."

"Wait," Oberon said. "There are a lot more than five of us now. We found a colony, and some of the people there joined us."

"What? How many?"

"There are thirty-three of us."

There was a brief pause, and then Kai laughed his mirthless laugh. "And you're sure you can't jump out of here? Because I'm not so much offering you shelter as I am offering you the chance to join us in trying not to die."

"We really can't."

"Beautiful." Kai gave a resigned sigh. "You'll be toast in orbit. The odds aren't good down here, just better. Any of these colonists handy with weapons?"

"Most of them are. That might be a bit of good news, at least," Oberon said.

Michele frowned, and Kai raised an eyebrow at that. "Should we be worried?"

"No. I can explain everything if you'd like."

Kai sighed again. "No time. If they turn out to be holding you hostage and kill us once they get here, it might be a blessing to spare us from the painful, violent death that awaits us at the hands of the Sugians." His tone was light, but worry filled his eyes and pulled down the corners of his mouth. "You can regale us with your stories and explanations once you're down here."

"See you soon," Michele said. Her smile was genuine, but her own brown eyes held the same worry Kai's had.

The next hour was surreal. They left everything that wasn't essential on the colonizer. Word spread quickly to those not on the bridge, including the Green Cloaks, and the ship buzzed with people making preparations. Dione noticed Brian seemed uneasy about the Green Cloaks, but they had been nothing but calm and contrite the entire trip. From his reports, they all showed remorse and sorrow for what they had done.

"What's wrong?" she asked him. "You've got that look."

"I'm worried about the Green Cloaks. What will Michele and Kai do once they find out who they are?"

"They're not going to leave them out for the Sugians, if that's what you're worried about," she replied. "I thought you still hated them."

"A big part of me does, but I also feel responsible for them. Think about it. Because of you, I'm the biggest connection between Kepos and your world. Worlds. The Alliance."

"I understand why you feel that way, but you're not responsible for them," Dione said.

"Someone has to be. They deserve a second chance. I think. I—I don't know what to feel, honestly. Some days, I hate them all. Others, I pity what Jameson and Elijah did to them. What he turned them into. They made choices, and there should be consequences, but I don't think they deserve to die. Not now that they've finally gotten access to actual facts and information."

Dione held back her retort and shrugged. Most of the Aratians hadn't let murderous monsters inside their walls, yet they were as equally uninformed as the Green Cloak traitors. "You should do what you think is right."

Oberon was walking in their direction, so Dione stopped him, wanting to put Brian at ease.

"What are you telling Kai and Michele about the Green Cloaks?" she asked.

"A lie of omission, I'm afraid. Oliver and a few Keposians have agreed to keep a close eye on them, but he doesn't suspect they'll be trouble. They no longer support the Vens, and I don't see a reason why they'd side with the Sugians."

"Thanks," Brian said.

"Right. Better get back to it," the older man said. He hurried past them and out of sight down the corridor.

***

The landing was uneventful, and their disembarkation swift. The colonizer made the few small ships around look like row boats. These people were stuck, too, with no jump-capable ship to carry them to safety. As Dione looked around, questions about who these people were and what they were doing finally popped into her head. Sure, it was an independent colony, which probably meant it was working on proprietary research, but now she wondered why that research was valuable enough to draw an attack from the Sugians.

Michele was already speaking with Oberon. Dione was too far away to hear, but from the gestures, the woman's fast-moving lips, and the numerous SUVs and trucks nearby, she could guess. Then Oberon pointed in her direction, and Michele's gaze fixed on her. A moment later, the two stepped apart. Oberon headed toward the Keposians and directed them to different vehicles. Michele made a beeline toward her.

"Dione Quinn," she said, extending her hand. "I'm Michele. Nice to meet you in person. You and your friends will be riding with me."

Dione didn't have a chance to respond before Michele had moved on to Bel and Zane, then Lithia, collecting them all like a magnet picking up nails. "There's the SUV. Let's not waste any time."

Dione glanced around, trying to find Brian. He was loading his parents into Oberon's vehicle, but he didn't join them. He looked around, his search ending when his eyes met hers. He smiled and blew her a kiss, but hopped into a truck. Lithia was pulling her into Michele's SUV, and the closing of car doors all around them reminded her far too much of gunfire. Because the Sugians were on their way to Doran, a few of the drivers were carrying weapons. She would hear real gunfire soon enough.

Dione settled into the front seat while her friends squished together in the back. As they drove, she stole glances at Michele. "You're not carrying a gun, but some of the other drivers are. Why?"

"It's part of their job description, though it's not usually part of mine. You know very little about this place, which is how we like it, but I'm in charge of the researchers here. The ones with the guns are our usual security. The ones with guns in Alliance gray are our protection detail," she said.

Lithia was staring out the window. "There aren't many of them."

"Until now, we didn't need more protection."

For the next few minutes, they rode in silence along the unlined road. The road was paved, and despite a few potholes, it was well maintained. The windows were down, and Dione took in the dense jungle all around them. The air was warm and thick with moisture, and the gray clouds in the sky warned of a coming storm. Bel rolled down a window, letting in the chorus of birds, monkeys, and other animals she couldn't identify. Dione wanted to ask what kind of research they were doing here, but Michele spoke first.

"It sounds like you've had quite the ordeal while you've been missing. Did you rescue these colonists? How did you survive the Vens?"

"Which time?" Lithia scoffed.

Michele's eye grew wide, but she kept them on the road. "Start with the first, I guess."

Dione waited for Lithia to respond, but her friend had begun staring out the window. Zane and Bel seemed no more eager to tell their story, so she picked it up. She went through the highlights: the Ven attack on the *Calypso*, discovering Kepos, realizing that the Vens were on their way, and the series of battles that followed.

"And you survived all that," Michele murmured when she was finished. "With just a few scars and an injured leg."

"I wouldn't put it that way," Lithia muttered, but Michele didn't seem to hear.

"The leg injury came after," Dione said. *And not all scars are visible.* But she didn't want to get into that right then. "The Vens got thrown off when they lost one of their ships to the planet's defensive weapon."

Zane spoke for the first time. "Why don't you have a defensive weapon here? This is an independent colony, and I'm sure you've got the funds."

"We've never needed it, and our funding isn't as generous as you might think. We're not defenseless, but a weapon like that would have been way out of budget."

Their SUV slowed as they approached the car stopped ahead of them. Beyond, Dione saw a thick, tall wall topped with electrified barbed wire. A heavy gate blocked the road, and the caravan that had spread out during their trip was contracting into a traffic jam as all the drivers waited for the gate to open. Two men with rifles stood in the crow's nest at the top of the guard towers that flanked the gate, and Dione felt their gazes scrutinize the long line of cars. Slowly, the gate opened, retracting into the wall.

Michele followed the vehicle in front of her to a small lot. One of the men in Alliance gray, the soldier in charge, was shouting directions as they stepped out of the SUV.

Michele approached the man. "Colonel Park, any updates?" When the colonel eyed Dione and her companions, Michele continued, "They'll find out soon enough."

Colonel Park relaxed his posture and spoke in a low voice. "They're almost here."

"How long?" Michele kept her voice steady, but Dione saw her swallow.

"A couple of hours, I think. Captain Reyes over there will be our eyes and ears from inside the bunker. She's got her orders."

From the door to the facility, a young woman with olive skin and dark hair pulled into a tight bun waved. She couldn't have been more than twenty-five, but she stood tall and confident next to the door. She didn't fidget like a few of the other Alliance soldiers, even those who looked older.

Zane and Bel followed Michele hurried to the entrance. Dione hesitated. There were a few other buildings inside the walls, but this was the largest. Its thick, sturdy walls rose up five or six stories, though it was hard to be exactly sure without windows. Lithia nudged her.

"Oberon's there," her friend said, pointing at a car that just arrived. "Come on." Dione let Lithia pull her toward the door, but she kept searching the faces in the crowd.

"Where's Brian?" she asked. "And Kai? They were in the same car. A few of the Ficarans are missing too."

Oberon put a hand on her shoulder, letting her know he was right behind her. "They are helping Kai and his men set some snares for any Sugians who approach."

Annoyance burned her cheeks. Brian hadn't mentioned anything to her about it. Fine. That was his choice. "He's going to get himself killed."

"It fits with the theme of this trip," Lithia quipped.

"They lost a lot of preparation time by coming to get us," Oberon said. "Brian and a few Ficarans volunteered to help. Whatever they're doing out there will benefit all of us."

They crossed the threshold of the building, and Michele led their group down a hallway. Dione could smell the sweat and the tension, thick like stifling humidity. The Keposians were whispering to each other, sticking close together. Even the former Green Cloaks were included, though they were clearly their own small cohort near the rear.

Dione read warning labels on thick, gray doors. Nameplates laid stake to various rooms and equipment as Michele disappeared into a stairwell. This was their lab building, not their living quarters.

Why were they sheltering in here?

"Keep moving," Captain Reyes said, and Dione realized she had stopped in the middle of the hallway. Her voice was firm but calm.

"Where are we going?" Dione asked.

"There's a room in the basement we prepped and fortified that we'll be using as a bunker. We've already moved in supplies, but if this turns into a siege, we won't be here long."

"Because of the Alliance?" Dione wondered aloud, inspecting the dark gray uniform the woman was wearing. "More soldiers like you will be coming."

She nodded. "And if they don't arrive in time…" Captain Reyes coughed but didn't finish her sentence, as if she had just realized she was speaking to a child.

"If they don't arrive in time, the Sugians will kill us." Dione shook her head. "I didn't survive multiple Ven attacks and a dragon nest to die in a lab basement."

Reyes cocked her head, and a smile twitched at the corner of her lips. "Dragons, huh? Then let's hope your father makes good time in getting here."

Dione's heart skipped a beat. "Why is my father coming here?"

"To get you," she replied.

"No, that's not really why. Something Michele said made it sound like he was already on his way here. I want to know why." *What were Kai and Michele up to, and what did it have to do with the Alliance?* "And why does an independent facility like this have Alliance soldiers as protection?"

The hint of a smile faded from the captain's lips, and she let Dione's questions die on the air without so much as a refusal to answer.

Dione and her friends had stumbled into something far bigger than she'd originally thought. Why was the Alliance working with a tiny lab at the edge of the Bubble, and what interest did her father have in this place?

11. BEL

Bel followed the others, too lost in her thoughts to pay appropriate attention to their surroundings. The Sugians were not allies. They were yet another terrifying, powerful enemy. How had that happened? How had she been so wrong?

She thought back to her initial observations in the Mountain Base on Kepos when she'd examined the dead Ven. Its hard exoskeleton and rectangular pupils had given her the idea, her Ven hypothesis, but she was still surprised that she'd been right. Maybe that was why it was so disappointing to be wrong now. Instead of saving humanity from the Vens, the Sugians were going to come in and finish up the Vens' leftovers.

Bel surveyed the spacious room, the safest place in the compound according to Michele. Scuff marks and gouges on the floor told her that things had been rearranged recently. A few unmovable machines in the far corner told her it had once been a lab. The corner on the far side, opposite the machinery, had a small pair of doors with restroom signs. Cots—not nearly enough for all of them—lined the walls on the either side of the door. A security station with several screens had been set up on the end nearest the door in such a way that whoever was monitoring the screens would still have a clear view of the only entrance to the room. A line of crates and containers bisected the room, creating two aisles down its length with a few passes for easy movement. Bel could tell from their labels that they contained food, medical supplies, and other gear they might need if they were trapped in here for a while.

When they arrived, they found that rest of the staff were already there, huddling together on the cots, leaning against the wall, or hovering over the monitors. From their casual attire, she guessed they were members of Michele's research team rather than security or military.

Once the door was closed, Captain Reyes strode to the monitoring station and took a seat next to the gray-haired man who pointed to something on one of the screens. Bel turned her attention back to Michele, who was handing out blankets and water to the Ficarans.

"Find a seat wherever you can and sit tight. Restrooms are in the corner, and we'll have what passes for a meal down here in a few hours."

A few feet away, Dione winced as she lowered herself onto a cot and massaged her leg. Lithia joined her and closed her eyes and leaned her head back against the wall. When Oberon and the other Keposians shuffled deeper into the room to find a space, Bel didn't move, and Zane didn't leave her side.

Michele cocked her head. "Is there something else?"

"Has the Alliance tried talking to the Sugians? They're the Vens' natural predator."

"For a group of kids who've been out of contact for months, you seem to know a lot about the Sugians."

"We recovered parts of a Ven datacore," Bel said. "We thought that the Sugians might be able to take care of the Vens. Like how we control invasive species by carefully introducing a natural predator."

"Not this time. The delegation the Alliance sent to them never came back."

"The Sugians killed them?"

"I don't know the details, but it was probably worse than that."

"So they eat humans?" Bel asked.

"How much did you discover about them from the datacore?" Michele asked.

Is she avoiding the question? Bel tried another tack. "Enough to know how they eat Vens. They use their beaks to pry open Ven plating, slip their tongues through, and inject the Ven with enzymes that turn its organs to soup."

"Then you'll understand when I say that it's a bit messier when they feed on humans," she said. "No exoskeleton. It's also not technically a tongue."

Bel grimaced. This was bad news. "The Vens call them the Hunger," she murmured. "I guess I shouldn't be surprised." She'd been so sure that the Sugians would take care of the Ven problem. Her hypothesis about the Sugians' existence had been right, but her hopes of working with them to solve the Ven problem had been very wrong.

That's how hypotheses work, I guess. On their journey, she'd drafted a few letters with her findings and theories to send to Alliance officials, including Dione's dad, but there was no point anymore. "Dione thinks the Sugians stay behind after the Vens leave an area and consume whatever lives there," Bel said.

"I found a few cryptic references in Ven mythology. Nothing solid," Dione said.

Michele shrugged. "I've heard rumors, but I can't say for sure."

She excused herself to talk with Reyes, and Dione stepped closer.

"Bel? Are you okay?"

"Fine," she said curtly. "You get to be right again."

"You think I'm happy about this?" Dione replied, folding her arms across her chest.

Maybe a little. Bel closed her eyes and took a deep breath. "No, I'm just frustrated. I really thought the Sugians would be able to help us, but they're just another threat."

"They might even end up being worse than the Vens."

"If that's the case, then we're screwed," Bel said.

Michele came back to check on them. "I know it's hard to believe, but we're at war. Things are different from when you left. Ven attacks grew at an alarming rate. Then the Sugians showed up, and they didn't seem to care much whether they were attacking Vens or humans. The Alliance knew about the Sugians over a year ago, long before they reached the Bubble. That's when they sent that delegation."

"What? They knew, and they didn't warn people?" Dione asked.

"Apparently only a handful knew," Michele said.

"Where have the attacks been?" Bel asked, bracing herself for the answer she knew was coming.

"Mostly along the Dappled Rim where there are a lot of unprotected planets. But the Vens started attacking outer planets, even Fleet ships. The Sugians are happy to feed on whoever they find, Ven or human."

"Like locusts," Dione murmured.

"How long will we be safe down here?" Bel asked flatly.

"This is the most secure part of the facility. The Sugians would have to breach the walls and the door, then make it down here before they can reach us," she replied.

"You don't need to sugarcoat it for me," Bel said. "I'm not asking because I'm afraid. I'm asking because I want to help. What can we do?"

"Just stay put. Colonel Park and Kai are working together. A few of your people have helped Kai lay some traps outside the walls, and I'm sure he's grateful."

"What about inside the walls?" Zane asked.

"What do you mean?" Michele asked.

"Aside from people with guns, what do you have inside the walls to stop them?" Zane said.

"If the armed soldiers and security team members aren't enough, I'm not sure what more we can do." Michele held out her hands, gesturing to the men and women huddled up on the cots across the room.

"If the Sugians breach the building, how long will we last in this room?" Bel asked.

"Hopefully long enough for the Alliance to show up and rescue us," Michele said. Bel opened her mouth to push back, but Michele held up a hand. "I'll be blunt since you don't want me to sugarcoat it. If they get inside the building, they probably won't use explosives. They rarely do, and we think this is a scouting mission. Like the Vens, they search for technology they can use. The Vens so far have been more interested in genetics while the Sugians are more interested in ship tech, looking for ways to support larger numbers in space."

"Like life support systems? Is that what your team works on?"

Michele gave her a shrewd look. "We've got numerous concurrent projects, but yes, that's one of our areas."

Bel wanted to learn more about these other projects, but Michele kept talking.

"What's more terrifying is how dangerous they are while

unarmed, aside from their natural weapons, like claws. Their ability to camouflage is unlike anything I've ever studied. They'll kill Reyes over there and anyone who still has a weapon first, then the rest of us. They'll have a nice little feast, get what they came for, and leave what's left of our corpses to rot. Or if they find some tech or research they want, they'll call in reinforcements." Michele looked worried.

"Will they find something they want?" Bel asked.

"I hope not." Michele closed her eyes and took a deep breath. "I'm not ashamed to admit that I *am* afraid."

There was a lot to unpack there, and as much as Bel wanted to follow up on what type of projects they were working on, she had a different priority at the moment. "Let us help. You say their camouflage is peerless, so if they do get inside, how can we track them? We can tag them. This is a lab. You must have materials we can use."

Michele was quiet a moment as she scanned the room, then called over a completely bald man with olive skin who looked to be in his forties. "Lars," she said. "Can we rig up something by the main doors to tag the Sugians if they make it into the building?"

Lars raised an eyebrow. He was quiet a moment, just like Michele had been, and Bel could tell he was making a mental list, striking through ineffective options. "We've got some red paint that will do the job. As for a mechanism, I have an idea. If you let me into Rainier's lab and don't mind if I potentially ruin some of his equipment..."

Michele groaned. "Of course you need to ruin Rainier's equipment, of all people. At least he left with the others."

Lars chuckled. "It was the only time I heard him argue that he was nonessential."

Bel exchanged a look with Zane, then asked, "If a bunch of you left, why did the rest of you stay here?"

"Our assignment was too important. We had to finish, and by the time we did, it was too late," Lars said. "Nonessential personnel left a few weeks ago. The ship that was supposed to get us never showed and is presumed destroyed. Marius himself is on the way now because he needs what we've been working on."

"What's your assignment?" Bel asked. Lars was about to answer, but Michele stepped in.

"The kind he's not at liberty to discuss." She stared pointedly at Lars, who took the hint and closed his mouth. Bel doubted he would have told her much, but any clue was better than nothing. "Find someone to help."

"We'll help," Bel said. She looked to Zane, who nodded.

Lars furrowed his brow, which sent a wave of wrinkles up to where his hairline would have been. "No offense, but—"

"We can follow your directions, and we can safely promise never to tell Rainier what you did to his lab equipment."

Lars laughed, then shrugged. "Why not? Come on."

As the trio prepared to leave, one of the monitors started ringing with an alarm.

Captain Reyes cursed. "They've almost reached orbit, ma'am. They'll be here in less than an hour."

Bel was certain there was a reason the Sugians had targeted this facility, and she wanted to know why.

12. BRIAN

Kai drove in silence, but the truck's roaring engine made it hard for Brian to think. The vehicles that carried Dione and his family had already disappeared down the road, yet Kai stopped the car after just a few minutes.

"Here's our first stop," he said. "Grab the box out of the back of the truck, but leave the tarp."

A little farther down the road, Brian could see the other truck that was presumably filled with his security personnel. Brian nodded at the three Ficarans who were in the back of the other car as they got out and got to work.

When Brian had first gone to tell the Ficarans what was happening and that they should gather their things, a few of them had asked what they could do to help. They'd been under siege by the Vens and had some ideas about what they would do differently, namely setting as many traps as possible. Kai didn't have *flaminaria* vials, but considering some of the movies Brian had watched with Dione, Kai probably had explosives that were much more powerful.

Kai stepped off the path into the jungle, and Brian dutifully went to retrieve the box from the truck. A sour stench reached him, and he gagged. He would know that smell anywhere. He wrinkled his nose at the tarp, which covered a bulky heap, but didn't move it. He already knew what was under it, and there was no need to make the smell stronger. He wondered why he hadn't noticed it before, but the port's odors of fuel and hot metal had overpowered this one. He grabbed the box and headed off the path to find Kai.

"Here's good," Kai said. He was fixing a small, metal disc into a nearby tree trunk. "You can make a simple snare, right?"

"Yeah, but it's not going to hold a Sugian. They weigh, what? Two hundred pounds or more?"

"It doesn't have to hold one, just distract it and make it sloppy. I'll be setting the real trap."

"Real trap?"

Kai was already on his knees pulling different tools and supplies out of the box. "Pressure plate rigged with explosives. You make that snare while I work. There's some flex wire in the cab of the truck behind your seat."

Brian retrieved the wire and began to fashion a loop. He'd never tried to catch something larger than a rabbit, so he didn't know if the design would scale. Searching for a suitable spot, he surveyed the area where they were working. Broken twigs, footprints, packed-down leaves. "It will be obvious we were here."

"No avoiding that. If we kill one here, fantastic. If we don't, at least we'll get some warning." Kai pointed at the metal disk he put into the tree, but Brian didn't recognize it.

"What is that thing?"

"Thermal sensor. If there's an explosion here, we'll know it. If a large, warm creature comes by here, we'll also know it, even if the trap isn't triggered."

Brian set up his trap, making adjustments whenever Kai grumbled a suggestion. Soon, they were both done with their work. Brian had expected to be sweating, but the dark clouds made the day cool. He frowned up at them, recalling the storm that had rolled in on the day he'd met Dione and Lithia. He had learned so much since then about Kepos and the worlds beyond it.

"Finished," Kai said. He groaned as he pushed himself up.

Brian stared at the ground where the older man had been working, and it took him a moment to find the outline of the trap. He glanced at his own snare just a couple yards away, clumsily hidden, just like Kai had requested.

Brian looked back to where he knew the pressure plate lay hidden. "How do you know some curious smaller animal won't come by and activate your pressure plate? Are they too light?"

"This stuff," Kai said, holding up a small vial. "Let's just call it Ven essence. This scent will tell every animal on this planet to avoid this area. Except for the Sugians who will start salivating. Assuming they can salivate."

"Should I go get the Ven?"

"I told you not to move the tarp."

"I didn't, but nothing can contain that smell."

Kai chuckled. "That's true. No, the Ven is for a different trap."

Brian grimaced. "Can't wait."

They returned to the truck, which roared to life under Kai's hands. They'd found a few vehicles similar to this at the Mountain Base, but Brian had still preferred to travel by maximute. His heart ached when he inevitably thought of Canto, but the giant, golden dog was in loving hands with Melanie. The truck slowed down again, and he pushed aside the memories of home and the emotions that clung to them. There wasn't much time.

"Have you considered that you're leading them right to you? With all of this Ven essence?" Brian asked.

"They're coming for us no matter what," Kai replied. "Might as well try to figure out from what side."

Brian's manumed buzzed. Back on Kepos, Oberon had given Brian an old manumed that he and Zane had updated as much as possible. They had been using the *Calypso* to anchor their communications network, but once it became clear they'd have to use the colonizer to leave Kepos, Oberon had transferred all of their manumeds to the colonizer's network. Now, he'd been switched over to the Doran network. He read Dione's message and frowned.

Dione: *They're almost here. Hurry.*

"Kai, the Sugians are close. Maybe we should head—"

"I got the update a few minutes ago. We still have a little bit of time. There's one more trap to set."

"With the Ven," Brian said.

"Aye."

They spent the rest of the short drive in silence. When Kai pulled over, they were within sight of the compound.

"What exactly are we doing with the Ven?" Brian asked. "Rigging it to explode?"

"No, we have special plans for it. We're hoping it'll be too tempting a snack for the Sugians to pass up."

"You expect them to eat it? But it must already be rotting."

Kai gave him a bleak smile. "We killed it this morning."

Brian's pulse quickened. "This morning? Did the Vens attack here too?"

"No," came Kai's cryptic, one-word reply.

"I'd forgotten just how bad they smell," Brian replied. Something strange was happening here. Why did they have a live Ven? Did it have something to do with that Ven essence they'd been using?

Kai laughed. "Good. Then there's hope that one day I'll forget that stench too. Give me a hand."

The older man got out of the truck and headed to the bed, pulling off the tarp. With Brian's help, he dragged the Ven into the trees, but this time they stayed close to the road. Kai placed a thermal indicator in a nearby tree and positioned the Ven facedown. "Easy access for the Sugian to feed through the gap in the plates," he explained. Then he called someone over his manumed. "Riley, confirm you have visual."

"Confirmed."

Kai made another call as they headed back to the truck. This time he was urging the other group to head back to the compound as soon as they were finished. Brian was relieved to hear that they were already en route. The walls around the compound were ten meters high, and there were five towers in total, one by the gate and one at each corner. The walls were topped with wire carrying enough electrical current to fry anything that touched them like bacon. The thought was simultaneously comforting and disturbing. The second vehicle arrived right behind them, and Brian turned to see the vehicle carrying his fellow Ficarans. Heat shimmered off the front of the vehicle as it entered the gate, and once they were safely within the walls, he breathed a sigh of relief he hadn't realized he'd been holding in. The gate boomed shut, and the two vehicles parked on the side of the building.

He was proud of his people for doing what was in their power to help, and he hoped their traps would make a difference. Something had been nagging at him for the past several minutes, and now that they were heading inside the building, his brain made the connection. The more Brian thought about the Ven corpse, the more things didn't add up. They hadn't set a trap like before. "How does leaving it out for them to eat help us? If anything, that should have been where we placed the biggest trap, since an actual Ven is the most enticing bait."

Kai looked away, not meeting Brian's eyes. "We're hoping it will be one final indication that they're close. If they're camouflaged, we won't see them coming. We can monitor this Ven for any change in position, and we hope that it's fresh enough to be a temptation."

Brian clenched his jaw and nodded. He didn't know what the man's motive was, but he was certain of one thing. Kai had just lied to him.

13. LITHIA

Lithia had tried leaning back against the wall and taking deep breaths, but dread clung to her body like an oily film. She felt exposed, as if she were welcoming an attack. When the alert sounded, she had expected to feel an adrenaline rush or a wave of panic crashing through her stomach, but she felt the same. Her body had been on high alert ever since they arrived.

There was a lot of chatter and confusion, and the noise seemed to take up physical space in the room. She glanced over at Dione who was sending a message to Brian, warning him that the Sugians were in orbit.

"We've still got an hour or so before they actually reach us," Michele said. "Hurry." She was speaking to Bel, Zane, and the scientist named Lars. Lithia had been following their conversation from where she sat, but she made no move to join them. If they had needed her help, they would have asked.

Shortly after Bel and Zane had left the room, Oberon approached her and Dione with a tall woman whose red hair was plaited in a braid down her back. "This is Dr. Philips," he said. "I asked her if she'd take a look at your leg, Dione."

"Hello, Dione. I hear you suffered a very intense burn a couple of months ago. Do you mind if I take a look?"

"That's fine," Dione replied, removing her brace.

While Dione was getting examined by the doctor, Oberon asked where Bel and Zane went.

"They're going to help Sugian-proof the facility," Dione replied. "They're not going outside."

Oberon pursed his lips but didn't say anything else. It was as if he expected his students to magically fall in line as they got closer to home, but if anything, the opposite was true.

On second thought, maybe Bel and Zane needed help after all. If Lithia was going to be stuck in this room once the Sugians got here, she should stretch her legs while she had the chance.

"I'm going to help them," she said.

"Lithia, you should stay here," Oberon replied. "Michele is calling in everyone who isn't security."

More bodies, therefore less space. Lithia was already standing to leave. The exit was too flimsy, just like every door in this place. It wouldn't hold back a Ven, and it wouldn't hold back a Sugian. Nothing would. The room began to close in on her, and she struggled to breathe. She had to escape. When Lithia reached the door, Oberon put a hand on her shoulder. She shrugged it off and left the door ajar when she ran out.

"Lithia! Wait!" She heard his steps echoing after hers, but she kept running. She jogged up the stairwell, passing a few others headed down, including the Ficarans who had been helping set traps. No Brian, though.

By the time she reached the top of the stairs on the ground floor, she was breathing hard. She could hear Bel's voice, so she followed it. Once Bel, Zane, and the man they were with came into view, she broke into a run again. The doors were just beyond them.

"Lithia!" Bel called after her. "What's wrong?"

Lithia ignored her and pushed open the door to the outside. She inhaled deeply, tasting the living air. The air inside had reminded her of the colonizer. Dull, chemical, dead. Suffocating. Despite the warm humidity, this air was fresh and fragrant. Two of Colonel Park's men were staring at her like they might haul her back inside, so she hurried off.

"Miss!" one cried after her. She glanced over her shoulder. He was following her. Where could she run? What good would it do? How could—

She turned back around in time to see the person she was about to run into. Just before impact, strong hands braced her shoulders, stopping her momentum.

"Lithia?" Brian asked, his brown eyes full of concern. "Where are you going?"

She looked around at the general flow of people, who were all moving toward the main building like water downstream. She stuck out like a stubborn fish.

"I don't know. Nowhere. I needed to breathe, that's all."

"Is everyone else inside?"

"Yes, the Sugians will be here soon. I know I need to go back in. I know. Just give me a minute."

He did. He stood with her, and his slow, steady breaths set the pace for her own. They both stared up at the guard tower by the gate. The man up there was security, not military. He was peering out into the trees beyond the wall. In the minutes they stood in silence, breathing together, the sky grew darker.

"Looks like rain," Brian said, after a few minutes had gone by. "We should head inside."

She expected him to take a few steps toward the door and lead her back in, but he didn't. She looked up at him and realized he was waiting for her.

"Brian, I don't know what you and Kai and the others were doing out there, setting traps or whatever, but it's not enough." She traced her gaze back over the compound's defenses. "The walls, the electrified wire, the guards—it's not enough."

"I know."

Lithia snapped her gaze back at him. "What?"

"You're right. We won't last here forever. But it's not like Kepos, where it was us against the Vens to the death. Help is coming. We just have to hold out until it gets here."

"They didn't get to Campos in time, and Campos was an Alliance colony. This is an independent colony. You really think they'll do a better job saving these random people? Saving us?"

Brian glanced around and led her off to the side, farther away from the people heading toward the main building. He spoke in a low voice. "I don't know what, but there's something special about this place. Something they don't want to tell us. The people here are more important than we realize."

"What do you mean? Did Kai tell you something?"

"No, but he's covering something up."

"Do you think he's a threat?"

"Not to us. Just think about it. There's a small team of Alliance soldiers here even though it's an independent colony. They evacuated most of their personnel, but some stayed. Why? Finally, Dione's father is on his way here. He was on his way even before we showed up. From what she's told me, her father isn't usually this hands-on in his role. Whatever work they've been doing here requires significant attention."

Lithia spent a long silence processing what he'd said. Brian was right. Something weird was going on here, but like Brian, she didn't sense any danger or ill will from Kai and Michele, or even from Colonel Park and the soldiers.

"Well, if we shouldn't be worried about them, I guess it's just the Sugians."

"Dione's father will get here in time. These soldiers aren't going down without a fight, and neither are the scientists. I heard one of them is rigging up some sort of paint trap to prevent the Sugians from camouflaging if they get inside."

Lithia smiled. "Bel's idea, of course. I'll see if they need a hand. I'm not quite ready to go back and lock myself in the basement, but it looks like Colonel Park sent someone to herd us that way." A young man in Alliance gray was beckoning them over toward the doors.

"Are you good to go on your own?" Brian asked. "I want to double-check with Kai that he doesn't need more help."

"I'll be fine. Thanks for giving me the chance to breathe," she said.

"No problem. Better now than once the Sugians actually arrive."

Lithia took one last look at the gray clouds, which cast premature darkness over the compound, before turning back toward the building. Its gray exterior was only a shade or two lighter than the sky, as if it were trying and failing to camouflage itself like the Sugians could. Its windowless facade gave her the impression of a prison, and Brian's observations echoed in her head. This lab was in the middle of nowhere, yet it had numerous defensive features.

She observed the scant number of men and women in Alliance gray and Kai's security green. *There should be more of them.* The thought troubled her. The Alliance had left only half a dozen soldiers here. Brian knew, just as she did, that it wasn't enough to win. Was it even enough to last until Mr. Quinn arrived with reinforcements? The soldier who had beckoned her was only a few years older than she was. Would he die? Many of these people would, just like so many had on Kepos, and an involuntary shudder flickered through her as she remembered the dead-eyed faces and bloody bodies left by the Vens.

Suddenly, hiding in the bunker didn't seem so suffocating. She was tired of fighting. Maybe this time she could just lock the door, close her eyes, and let someone else risk everything. She walked through the open door, her momentary calm replaced by heavy dread that settled in her lungs. Deep down, she knew that, in the end, she wouldn't get to choose whether or not to fight.

14. BRIAN

Brian asked around for Kai, and one of his people pointed Brian in the direction of the NRT comms array building. Kai must have been sending off one last message before the attack.

Before Brian could head in that direction, shouting erupted at the doors.

"Get out of there, Bel. One of them got inside!"

Brian recognized Lithia's voice and saw her back outside, yelling through the doors.

"Zane, you too! They're already inside!"

Oberon stepped forward, his right arm extended toward her in a calming gesture. "Lithia, that's not possible. They're not here yet. When was the last time you slept?"

"I know what I saw!" she replied.

Before Brian could run over to Lithia, one of the soldiers, a burly man in his midthirties, held her. She struggled against him in vain. Oberon and a female soldier approached her, and the woman injected her with something. Soon, she stopped struggling. Brian kept his distance but listened carefully to their exchange.

"Was that necessary, Captain Reyes?" Oberon asked.

"We don't have time to chase her around. The Sugians will be here in less than an hour, and we need all civilians locked in the bunker. She's not the only one who's needed a sedative today. I know it seems harsh, but yes, it was necessary. I'm speaking from experience."

The burly man handed Lithia off to the woman, who picked her up and carried her over her shoulder into the safety of the building. Oberon was with her, but Brian considered going back. Dione would be concerned about him after seeing Lithia carried in like a doll.

He took a step toward the compound when something caught his eye. A large track in the grass. Brian looked around slowly, searching for a second track or anything that might give him a trail, but this track, he realized, was just luck. The surrounding ground was dry except for this small patch. Perhaps a spill had softened it. He examined the partial track again.

Clearly not human. It could be any animal—he didn't know what this jungle held—but he doubted that such a large creature would ever be allowed to roam inside the walls, whatever it was. He would ask Kai, just to be sure, when he found him, but Lithia's outburst just minutes ago made him uneasy. They knew the Sugians were masters of camouflage. Was it so hard to believe that one had escaped their notice?

But they weren't even here yet. It was impossible. The skeptic inside of him was alive and well, though. The only reason it was impossible was because of Kai's conviction that the Sugians had not yet arrived in orbit. Could he be wrong?

Brian headed toward the NRT comms array building, but angry voices coming from the living quarters gave him pause. Kai was arguing with a woman right in front of the door.

"It belonged to my mother," the woman said, clutching a piece of jewelry, maybe a bracelet or a necklace, in her hand. "I wasn't going to leave it."

"I don't care if your mother pressed it lovingly into your hand on her deathbed. These monsters aren't coming to rob us!"

The woman stopped and scoffed. "You sure about that? Because I think that's exactly what they're planning to do."

"But they're not here for baubles." Kai sighed, his voice softening. "Your mother wouldn't have wanted you dead on account of a locket."

The woman smoothed her thumb against the surface of the locket as she spoke. "The way I see it, I'll be dead either way. We haven't heard from Marius in days. He's not coming."

"No response is better than a negative one. He'll be here. We've got humanity's best hope in this war, and now the universe has brought his daughter here. An added incentive."

"I wish I believed that." Her gaze was fixed on the silver pendant, and Brian guessed her mind was full of bittersweet memories. "I know you don't understand, but I just wanted my mother to be with me in the end."

Kai squeezed the woman's shoulder, the anger in their exchange now replaced with reservation, even sadness. The security chief noticed Brian, then called out, "Why are you still out here? Get inside!"

With a rumble of thunder, the gray clouds promised to make good on their threat. Brian had only been on this planet for a couple of hours, but he had seen these storm clouds before.

"I just came to check if you needed help, but I found something."

"I don't need help. I need you inside. I need to find Jenkins, wherever he ran off to, so I can yell at him to get the hell inside.

This is ridiculous."

"But I—"

The man interrupted him. "Does nobody grasp the fact that the Sugians are on their way? Maryn, take him with you. Or you, take her with you. Just get inside!"

Kai stormed back into the building, shouting the name Jenkins over and over.

"Come on, kid," Maryn said to Brian.

"Are there any large animals in the jungle?" he asked, determined to ignore her dismissive tone and at least get an answer to his question.

"Yeah, there are some big cats and a few, large piglike creatures with massive tusks. They can hold their own against the cats. But it's mostly birds, rodents, and bugs."

"Do these cats ever get inside the walls?"

"No, not that I've seen. They stay away from us, even when we're out there. Not that we have much reason to go out into the jungle very often, but there is a nice little waterfall we visit sometimes on days off to relax. I've seen a cat once or twice, but they usually disappear when they hear us coming."

Thunder rumbled again. Brian frowned. "Yeah." His mindless reply seemed to satisfy her, but her words did nothing to allay his fears.

"I wouldn't be worried about the cats if I were you," she said, looking up at the sky and holding out an open palm. The first few drops of rain hit Brian like warning shots, urging him to hurry inside. They rushed into the main building in silence. Maryn headed down the hall, but Brian stopped. Bel, Zane, and an older man were packing up whatever they'd been working on.

"What's this?" Brian asked.

"It's an automated Sugian revelation device," Bel said.

Zane laughed. "It's a few cans of spray paint set up to tag anything that comes in and trips this sensor."

"You really need to get better at selling it," Bel teased.

"I prefer to let my work speak for itself," he replied.

Brian smiled at their banter, and missing his own banter partner, he followed their directions and headed down to the bunker.

Despite looking forward to seeing Dione—though he imagined she would scold him—the deeper he went into the building, the greater his sense of foreboding grew. Heaviness settled over him as he trudged down the stairs, each level like adding a weighty stone to a shoulder pack. He was no stranger to dread, but Maryn's words echoed in his head. They never got a response from Marius. What if she was right and he wasn't coming?

Marius was Dione's father. Of course he would come. But Brian began to fear that he hadn't gotten the message, and that whatever these people were hiding would not be enough to guarantee their rescue.

When he entered, he received a warm welcome from Dione. A hug and a kiss, which were inevitably followed by annoyance that he hadn't told her in advance what he'd planned. She wasn't really mad, though. He could tell.

"How's Lithia?" he asked.

The light in Dione's eyes faded, and she nodded to a nearby cot where Lithia was sleeping.

"I thought she was getting better, but being on the colonizer wasn't good for her. Now here we are again in the same sort of situation as we were with the Vens. They said they didn't give her much, and she'd wake up soon, but part of me just wants her to stay asleep."

Brian nodded, but before he could share anything else, the

soldier who had hauled away Lithia pounded her fist against the table.

"Dammit!"

"What is it, Reyes?" Michele asked.

"We've got our first hit on one of our traps. They're already here."

"Did it work?"

"No kill."

Brian hoped the other traps would be more successful.

15. DIONE

Michele was talking to Kai through her manumed, and Dione was eavesdropping. "Tell the colonel. They're here. Site one."

Dione eyed Captain Reyes with very mixed feelings. She had been the one to drag Lithia back inside and, in Dione's opinion, had been unnecessarily rough when laying her on the cot. On the other hand, she had come over several times to check on her friend. Other than that, Captain Reyes had been diligently monitoring the security feeds alongside one of Kai's men.

"Why is that bad, Captain Reyes?" Dione asked. "We knew it would just be a matter of time."

"Because the trap didn't work," she replied. "And you can call me Reyes."

"That was just one. There are others," Brian said.

It pained her to hear the worry in his voice. He'd helped Kai set the traps. Of course he wanted them to work.

"Michele," Kai said sharply. "Please tell me that Jenkins found his insubordinate way back to you."

Dione had been paying enough attention to know that one of the scientists, Jenkins, had not yet been accounted for.

"He's not here. But he knew what to do. We all did."

"He's a bit absentminded," Kai seemed to reassure himself, "but he's not an idiot. Now he'll have to find his way back in the rain."

"I'm sure he's fine. Is the Ven trap in position?"

"Yes, they'll be there soon, but there are a few more traps along the way."

"Got one!" Reyes said, clapping her hands in a moment of celebration. "Not a kill, but it's limping. Its injuries will make camouflage difficult."

Kai was still transmitting. "Jenkins! Jenks! Son of a—"

Heads swiveled in Michele's direction, and she quickly lowered the volume and put in her earpiece. Dione perked her ears, trying to catch as much as possible, but Michele's face told it all.

"Ma'am?" Reyes asked. "Do you need me for anything?"

Michele placed both hands on the table and leaned against it with her head down. "Lock us down, Reyes."

"Ma'am? Is he—"

"Jenkins isn't coming. Kai has the help he needs. Stay at your post."

Reyes nodded and returned her calculating gaze to the security monitors. "Lockdown complete," she said.

Michele looked up and realized she still had the attention of her accidental audience. "I won't hide it from you. Jenkins is dead. Kai is dealing with the body now."

"How?" a woman called out. "How did he die?"

"We don't know yet," Michele replied.

"What do you mean?" one of them asked. "It had to be a Sugian. They're here already! Why is Kai outside the gate?" The man paused, his expression shifting from deep concern to confusion. "How did Jenkins even get outside? They sealed the place."

Michele took a determined breath and met the man's eyes. "He wasn't outside the compound. He was near the comms array. The array is still working, and Kai was able to send out our last set of messages."

"Any word from Quinn?" someone asked.

Dione jolted at the sound of her last name, but the man had been asking about her father, the one who was supposedly coming to rescue them all.

"No, but that doesn't mean any—"

"We're screwed, Michele. Just admit it. Cowering down here like rats in a hole. How do we even know he likes his daughter enough to take on the risk of coming here?" The man spared a red-faced glare for her. "All the begging he did on the vids? It wouldn't be the first time a political puppet lied."

Brian tensed next to her, and she was thankful Lithia was unconscious. Dione tried to be sympathetic and believe that the situation was bringing out the worst in this man, as perilous situations often did. This man didn't care if he hurt her. He didn't even know her father. Marius Quinn had always kept her at a distance, but she was certain that if it was in his power to save her, he would.

"He knows what's at stake. He promised to help us even before his daughter showed up. He knows what our research will mean for the Alliance. He believed in us when no one else did, and he secured our funding. That alone is enough to ensure his help. Dione's arrival…" Michele evidently decided against finishing her thought out loud, and the silence that followed was quickly replaced by renewed questioning from the others.

Brian took Dione's hand and squeezed it. "You okay?"

"Yeah. One of the doctors here gave me something for my leg, and it feels a lot better."

"That's not what I meant."

"I know." Dione gave him a look, and he seemed to understand because he backed off that topic and brought up one that had caught her curiosity as well.

"Do you know what they were working on here?" Brian asked. "They keep talking about how important it is."

"And it must have been if my dad was coming here personally. He had off-world business a lot, but usually stuck to the core planets. What have you heard?"

"When Kai and I were setting the traps, we set up an actual Ven corpse as bait."

"That makes sense."

"Not the way he set the trap," Brian continued. "For the other traps we used explosives and a liquid scent marker Kai called 'Ven essence.'"

"Gross," Dione said, wrinkling her nose.

Brian nodded in agreement. "The Ven was the best bait, but we didn't set a trap near the body. It was just there within sight of the gate so the guards would be able to see if a Sugian was there. All the traps we set were meant to harm the Sugians, but it was like he wanted the Sugians to be able to get to the Ven without getting hurt."

"You don't think he's working for the Sugians, do you? Like the Green Cloaks wanted to help the Vens?"

"No, definitely not that. They're hiding something from us, though, and I don't know what."

"I guess it's all classified or proprietary." Dione chewed her bottom lip as she mulled over Brian's revelation. "Where did they get the Ven? How long had they been storing it?"

"That's the other thing. It was killed this morning apparently."

"What!" Dione's heart thumped painfully in her chest. "There was a Ven attack this morning? And they didn't mention it? But there's no sign—"

Brian put a hand on her shoulder, and she knew what he was going to say before he said it. "There wasn't an attack. I think they were keeping live Vens on site."

Ven experiments? She wasn't surprised, but keeping live Vens, even just one, was playing with fire. Not to mention the ethical implications. "My father knows what's at stake," Dione muttered, more to herself than to Brian. "They must be working on a way to win the war."

"Against the Vens or the Sugians?" Brian countered.

Dione didn't have the chance to answer. Their conversation was cut short by Michele, who was headed their way.

"Dione," she said. "I wanted to apologize for what some of my people said just now. It was unwarranted."

"No, I get it. Tensions are high. But I do want to know what my father was doing coming here in the first place. I thought this was an independent lab, yet you're working with—or maybe for— the Alliance," Dione said. Michele kept her face unreadable. "You've got six Alliance soldiers. How long have they been here? Why are they here?"

"I can see the family resemblance, especially thanks to this interrogation." She laughed, but Dione didn't join her. She smiled politely, but wouldn't let Michele dodge the question again, not if she could help it. The woman went on. "He was here almost two months ago on Alliance business. He came himself, even though he could have easily sent a proxy. He claimed he wanted to manage the affair personally, but I know he was really hoping he'd find a trace of you and your friends. He spent a lot of time on the array, talking to nearby outposts. He even sent messages to a few of the more isolated colonies that didn't have NRT comms arrays. I've never doubted that he would return in time to help us, but your arrival here feels… auspicious. A good omen. He's the one who brought us Colonel Park, Reyes over there, and the others."

"He knew the Sugians would attack you. Why?"

"I don't think he knew who would attack us, but he knew we might become a target. While I won't lie to you, I can't tell you what our work was."

"I understand." Dione's jaw tightened. *We'll just have to finish figuring it out on our own.*

Reyes called to her from the security monitors. Michele gave Dione a nod, then hurried off. Once the woman was out of earshot, Brian nudged her. "You could have pressed her a little harder."

"I want to uncover a good idea of what's going on, then confront her. It will be easier to judge her reaction than pester her into telling us."

Brian chuckled. "Good thing I don't have any secrets."

Nearby Lithia was stirring, and soon the whole group, aside from Oberon, had converged at her bedside. She sat up, blinking and rubbing her arm.

"What just…" Lithia caught sight of Reyes across the room. "She stabbed me."

"She gave you a sedative," Brian replied.

"It hurt."

"You were freaking out, Lithia. She didn't have a choice."

Dione saw the memory, accompanied by panic, dawn over her friend's face.

"The Sugian. It was here. Inside the building," she said, looking accusingly at Bel and Zane. "And you didn't believe me."

"I was looking in the same place you were, and I didn't see anything. It seemed impossible at the time."

"Well, we're more inclined to believe you now," Zane said.

"Why? I'm not even sure anymore. I… I feel like I'm going crazy. Did you end up seeing it after all?" Lithia asked.

"No, but one of the scientists was found dead. We don't have any details about his death, but it's certainly suspicious," Bel said.

"Don't you think they'd do something if they even suspected it was a Sugian?" Brian asked.

"What more could they do?" Bel replied. "We're all locked away down here."

"But it could be inside the building. That's where Lithia saw it," Brian said.

"I don't think they're putting any stock in Lithia's report," Bel said. "Sorry, Lithia," she added.

"If there really is a Sugian here, what is it doing? Why not just attack us all like it did that scientist?" Dione wondered aloud.

"Not a clue, but it's nothing good." Lithia crossed her arms and shivered. "I was probably just seeing things. I'm sure if there was a Sugian inside the walls they'd say something."

Dione cocked her head to one side. It was unlike Lithia to doubt herself like this, but the bags under her eyes were so pronounced that Dione wondered how she hadn't seen them before.

"I don't think they'd tell us," Brian said flatly. "It's not malice, but they're hiding something." Brian recapped the conversation they'd just had with Michele, as well as their own suspicions.

Dione summed it up. "They were—or are—working on something for the Alliance. Something that would make them a target to the Vens or Sugians, and something that involved having at least one live Ven here."

Lithia's foot tapped nervously against the tiled floor. Bel and Zane exchanged a look. He nodded at Bel, so she spoke.

"When we were helping Lars get stuff from his lab, we got to see some of the facility," Bel said. "Based on some of the things I've seen, and what he said, they do a lot of work with infectious diseases."

"See any nameplates?" Dione asked. "We could look up some of these people if we had enough to go on." It hadn't seemed strange at the time, but Kai and Michele had only given them first names.

Bel shook her head, but Zane went straight to his manumed. "The guy we worked with. Lars Milston," he whispered, not wanting to draw the man's attention. "He's a virologist."

Dione wasn't surprised. Things were clicking into place, and she saw the others were following the same train of thought. "It's a bioweapon," she said. "Highly illegal and unethical."

"Debatable," Zane said. "There's no law against biowarfare when it comes to alien races, unless they passed something in the months we were gone. Seems unlikely."

"Then why all the secrecy?" Dione asked.

"It's probably classified. Considering the Sugians are here, someone might have leaked that information," Zane replied.

"Michele did suspect it was a scouting mission," Dione added

Michele's voice, tense and clipped, drew Dione's attention. Something was happening outside.

"Come on, guys," she muttered. "Let's see what's going on."

Michele and Reyes noticed them approach but didn't send them away. Neither the Ficarans nor the scientists, except for Lars, seemed interested in watching the monitors. Dione didn't blame them. She didn't want to watch, but she felt compelled to.

Reyes must have felt their eyes, and to Dione's surprise, instead of shooing them away, she narrated what they were looking at.

"Gate," she said, pointing to a screen that displayed live video of the gate. Then she pointed to other screens, some full, some divided into smaller boxes. "Different angles on the wall. Front door. Comms array."

"None from inside the building?" Dione asked.

"There are. Here's the front door from the inside. No need to monitor the others right now."

Dione decided not to argue the point. Instead she looked at the cameras. Soon, she saw it. Movement. Reyes saw it, too, and called over her manumed to either her fellow soldiers or the security team, probably both.

A couple of shots were fired, and the Sugian disappeared, camouflaging once more into the trees. This exercise was repeated two more times over the next fifteen minutes.

"Why are they just circling the building?" Lithia grumbled.

"It reminds me of the Vens," Brian said. "They stayed in the trees until nightfall, then attacked."

"But what are they planning?" Lithia asked. "Trying to use up our ammo?"

"We've got quite the arsenal," Reyes said. "We'll run out of soldiers before we run out of bullets."

"That isn't very reassuring," Lithia said.

"When I'm trying to be reassuring, you'll know," came the young woman's reply. Though Reyes's back was to them, Dione could hear the smile in her voice. Dione took comfort in the knowledge that they were well stocked on weapons and ammunition. The colonists had run short back on Kepos when the Vens attacked the Vale Temple.

"As for what they're planning, I'm not sure. They're vicious, but they're not stupid," Michele said, revisiting Lithia's initial question. "They must be waiting for something."

"They're intelligent and resourceful," Dione said. "If they didn't think they could breach the walls, why did they come? Or why didn't they send more?"

No one answered. Their minds were occupied by the next foray and retreat. This time the guard hit one of the Sugians, though it wasn't a vital wound.

"The Ven trap is untouched," Michele said, more to herself than the others. This fact seemed to bother her, and Dione saw an opening.

"You infected the Ven, didn't you?" she asked.

The look on Michele's face all but confirmed it, but Dione pressed on. "That's why you're so interested in a Ven corpse during a Sugian attack."

"What are you talking ab—"

Dione ignored her question. "But why are you so interested in a Ven virus when the Sugians are attacking?"

"I don't know what—"

"I assume you're pretty confident it can't be spread to humans, since Kai himself handled the Ven body. What is it? Viral? Bacterial? Or maybe even a parasite?"

Just when she was about to get answers, Brian derailed her line of questions. "Something's happening. They've changed their pattern so they aren't wandering as far. They're clustering together."

"How can you tell?" Reyes asked. "They keep disappearing into nothing. Plus the rain is falling even harder now."

"They're not making full loops anymore. Watch here," he said, pointing to one of the split screens. Reyes had only been watching a few seconds when it must have clicked for her too.

"Damn it!" A few seconds later she was on her manumed with Colonel Park. Her warning consisted of only two words. "The gate—"

The next moment, the entire room was plunged into darkness.

16. BRIAN

Alarmed murmurs spread throughout the dark room. Dione's fingers found Brian's in the scant light of the various battery-powered devices in their vicinity. A few seconds ticked by before dim emergency lights came on. Next to the door, a red bulb high on the wall flashed periodically to remind them all that something was wrong. His manumed, which had been on the compound's network, was down.

"Kai? Kai!" It was Michele, speaking in vain through her manumed. "Damn. Reyes, get me eyes on Kai and Park."

"Working on it, ma'am," Reyes said. "We need to restore the power. Is everything down?"

"Just this building and the manumed network. The NRT comms array and the living quarters are fine. We're on emergency power right now, running limited systems. No manumeds and very limited security cameras until the surveillance system reboots. We're still in lockdown with emergency lights."

"What about the fence?" asked Brian. The electrified wire topping the walls was the first thing that had come to Brian's mind.

Reyes cursed. "That's down too."

Brian could feel her anxiety as if it were his own. If power was off to the fence, the Sugians were now undoubtedly inside the walls.

"How bad is the storm?" Brian asked.

"It wasn't the storm. We've got a geothermal generator, and all of our cables are buried," Michele said. "But after a small flooding accident, the breakers got a little sensitive. It's possible something shorted and tripped them."

"Bad luck," Brian murmured.

Bel spoke up. "I think it's more than bad luck. What if Lithia was right? There's a Sugian inside the building, and now we know what the others were waiting for."

Michele and Reyes exchanged a look right as the surveillance system came back on. Brian was positioned so he could see the screens. They had been full of little squares before showing various rooms, doors, and hallways, but now there were only a handful working. He recognized the gate, the front doors, the main hallway, and the stairwell, but that was it.

"I'm not convinced, but we'll proceed with caution. The Sugians are still outside the walls, as far as we know, but that could change at any moment. We need to restore power and reestablish comms with Kai and Colonel Park."

"How are you going to do that?" Brian asked.

"The electrical closet is in the server room. We start there. I hope your friend was wrong about the Sugian and that it's just a short."

Reyes pushed back her chair and straightened her back. "Then let's go."

"No, we need you here," Michele said, putting a staying hand on the young woman's shoulder. "You have to be our eyes and ears."

The two women shared an intense look and a moment of silence, but Reyes bowed her head slightly in submission. "Yes, ma'am."

Brian could see the respect and trust between the two in that moment. They were in good hands.

Oberon stepped forward. "I'll join you, Michele. Shouldn't be hard to reset the breakers."

Brian felt Dione tense next to him. She didn't like that Oberon was volunteering, and she wouldn't like this either. "Me too," he said.

"Brian," she hissed. When she realized he wouldn't budge, she added, "Fine. Then I'm coming."

"No," Michele said. "You're staying here. Your leg."

Lithia also tried to volunteer, but Reyes shut her down quickly. "Not a chance. Stay here where you can do some good."

Brian knew Lithia well enough to know that she was furious. "There's a Sugian in the halls," she said through her clenched jaw. "Watch your backs."

After a few whispers to Bel, Zane also volunteered. "I'm good to go as well," he said. Brian wondered what he'd said to her. Those two were always scheming something up, but they made the perfect team. They were even more in sync than he and Dione, but they had the benefit of growing up with at least some shared culture.

"Any weapons proficiency after fighting all those Vens?" Reyes asked. Zane shook his head, but Oberon nodded. The Ficarans had trained the professor while the repairs were being made to the colonizer. Brian himself was already a good shot, thanks to growing up during a tense time between the Ficarans and Aratians. Oberon and Zane took pistols, but he took a rifle, the simplest one

Reyes had in the room.

Michele also took a pistol, which she handled with a comfort he would have expected from the security chief rather than the research facility manager. In no time, the group was out the door. The flashing red light blurred his vision and played tricks on his eyes, but no attack came after the door swung wide to release them. If there was a Sugian in the building, it was biding its time.

17. LITHIA

Lithia was sick of being treated like a delicate doll to be forgotten on a shelf. How dare Reyes interfere! Something was out there, a Sugian or a Sugian sympathizer. The Green Cloaks had been stupid enough to help the Vens, and stupidity certainly wasn't limited to Kepos. Maybe someone was helping the Sugians now.

And Reyes! The nerve. Following her outside, dragging her back into this building where they were completely trapped. *Who does she think she is? That bi—*

"Lithia," Reyes said. Lithia felt her cheeks grow hot. She'd never been great at hiding her emotions, and Reyes must have read the anger on her face. "Come sit with me." Michele's seat at the monitoring station was vacant. Lithia didn't want to sit with her, but she hoped she might get a little information out of the woman, so she took the open seat and crossed her legs.

"It's not enough to trap me in this room? You need to have me within arm's reach to keep an eye on me?"

To her surprise, Reyes gave her a grim smile. "You can hate me.

I don't mind."

"I'm not a little kid."

"I never said you were," the soldier replied. "Let me tell you a story."

"Wonderful. Complete with talking animals and a stern moral at the end, I'm sure."

She chuckled. "Sorry, no animals. And I wouldn't call the ending a moral either. I just see myself in you." Her tone grew more serious. "The fear. The anger. I survived a battle against the Vens too. Two years ago, before the attacks ramped up, when they still kept to the outskirts. I was there on a humanitarian mission. Disaster relief. This town had just been devastated by a hurricane. We were pulling survivors and bodies out of the wreckage, setting up a makeshift hospital, handing out food and blankets. It was terrible what happened, and then we got word the Vens were coming."

Lithia sat quietly, trying not to imagine it, but her own memories flashed through her mind.

"I was on the last ship to leave. We were tracking down the people who had left the main assistance area and gone back to their homes to rebuild. Communications were spotty at best, so we had to go get them."

Lithia's anger softened a bit. "But the Vens got there first."

"We were on our way back when I got the call that the Vens had arrived. We kept moving. Some people fell behind, I think, but we didn't have a choice. We walked into the middle of a slaughter. I—" Reyes stopped and took a deep breath. "I barely made it out. I left people behind. Those memories are places I don't like to go. I hope you understand. But for a while afterward, I found myself living inside of them every day. A sound, a smell, any little thing could set me off."

When Reyes paused, Lithia realized her breaths were shallow and her heart was racing. Somehow, this woman could see right through her in a way even Dione hadn't been able to. "So, what did you do?"

Reyes smiled gently. "At first, alcohol. Lots of it. Before I did anything too stupid, my commanding officer noticed, removed me, and sent me to therapy."

"That's good." Lithia thought back to the bottle of *vigo* that was sitting in her cabin on the colonizer. She'd had no opportunity to bring it unnoticed to Doran. She cocked her head and refocused on Reyes. "Therapy, huh?"

Reyes's smile widened to a grin. "I was so pissed. Screaming, throwing things, refusing to say a word during my sessions. All because I was completely fine, even if I knew that was a lie I was telling myself. This is my second mission back. I'm better, but I think Park still had his doubts. That's why I'm down here with you all, monitoring the camera feeds. He did something similar on our last assignment."

"He was allowed to do that? It really doesn't seem fair."

"I was annoyed at first, but I've come to a conclusion that I wanted to share with you. You don't have to be on the front line to help your team. This," she said, gesturing to the mostly blank screens in front of them, "might be the best place for me right now. So I'm going to do my best. The second they get the power back, I'll be here, ready to observe and advise."

Lithia nodded. "I don't think I was made for this kind of role."

Reyes squeezed her shoulder. "Neither did I. But the thing about strong, intelligent women like us is that we will always rise to the challenge."

They were silent for a few minutes while Reyes typed away, doing what little she could with the available systems. "Just promise me one thing, Lithia. When you get out of here and things go back to normal, or not normal, whatever happens, promise me that you will ask for help."

Lithia let the request linger for several long moments. "I promise." She wasn't sure if she really meant it, but she hoped she did, and that was progress.

18. BRIAN

Once the bunker door had been locked behind them, Michele took point and led the way up the stairs, all the way to the main floor. This was where they would find the circuit breaker. The things they'd learned about the Vens and Sugians in the past couple of months baffled him. Victory itself was not the goal of either species; rather the manner of their victory was key. They were locked into a centuries-old conflict, more concerned with the battles than the war. So far, it had worked to humanity's advantage. At least it had on Kepos.

Michele reached out a hand, and the door clicked open. She sighed. "This should be locked. Probably overlooked in the panic to get to the bunker."

Brian felt a small surge of adrenaline as he prepared for the worst. "It might not be an oversight." Life on Kepos had taught him never to take anything like that for granted.

"We'll proceed with caution," Michele said.

This room was especially cold, and Michele continued to lead the way back to the electrical closet though rows and columns of server racks. The door was nearly hidden in a corner of the room, not visible from the entrance thanks to all of the equipment. Zane had given him some basics in all of the tech he would encounter when he reached Lavinian, their home world, but it still always filled him with awe to see so much hardware.

Brian's fingers and the tip of his nose were already thoroughly chilled, especially now that they weren't moving. It made him uneasy. The closet door itself wasn't locked. He wasn't completely sure what they would find inside, but he imagined it would look similar to the power room back in the Field Temple on Kepos. His father had shown it to him once.

He had been right. It did look similar, though this setup was much sleeker—or it would have, except that wires and cables had been ripped from their fixtures and the pathways shredded.

Michele cursed under her breath, and Oberon pushed a hand through his hair. Brian didn't need Zane's expertise to know that there was no fixing that any time soon.

"Sabotage." Brian's voice was matter-of-fact. "Those look like claw marks. It has to be the work of a Sugian."

Michele nodded, but said nothing.

"Right now, we're on emergency power," Zane said. "Don't you have a secondary circuit?"

"We do," Michele muttered, leaning in to get a better look at the damage. "It should have switched over automatically once the primary circuit was damaged. The secondary circuit looks intact, though." She was talking more to herself than the others. "The Sugian must not have known it was here, but why isn't it switching over to—" She broke off midsentence and slammed a first against the wall. "Dammit, Jenkins! Was that what you were trying to do when you were supposed to be getting to the bunker?"

Brian recognized the name. The man that Kai had found dead.

"What was he doing?" Brian asked.

"We were in the middle of maintenance on the secondary power system. We were in the middle of it when nonessential personnel were evacuated. Jenkins was supposed to take over, but there was so much going on, he must not have finished putting everything back together."

"Can we switch it over manually?"

Michele cursed again before replying. "Yes, but it's in the comms array building. Someone will have to go outside."

"Maybe Kai or one his men can get there." Brian suggested.

"We have no way to tell them."

"But aren't we trapped inside this building now?" Brian said. "The front door is locked down."

"There's more than one way out."

"If not a door," Oberon said, "then what? I didn't see any windows."

"No windows," she replied. Her gaze was fixed on the tangle of wires in front of her, her mind elsewhere. Calculating.

"The roof," Brian guessed. Michele nodded. The hairs on the back of his neck stood on end. At first, he wondered why he should suddenly be afraid of heights, but then the uneasy feeling he'd had since they entered the server room made sense. He turned in time to see a Sugian coiled and tensed, like a cat ready to pounce. Its gray-white skin gave it a ghostly appearance. Once he made eye contact, the flaps around its mouth curled outward, revealing its sharp beak.

"Sugian!" he shouted. He raised his weapon and fired a shot, but the Sugian was already moving away from them toward the door. He hurried after it, but lost it behind one of the rows of servers. He was now exposed in the middle of the room, as were the others who had followed him. *Stupid move, Brian,* he chided himself. He needed to be better than this. People were counting on him. *His* people. Dione and the others were as much his as the Keposians by this point, and he wasn't going to die in some Sugian trap and let this monster prowl the building at will.

"The door must have given way," Oberon said, putting his back to Brian's.

"It's too soon," Michele replied.

"Lithia was right," Brian said. "There was a Sugian inside. They must have sent an advance scout to get intel and sabotage what they could."

Michele clenched her jaw but said nothing. She and Zane were back to back too. Each of them looked out in a different direction. He hadn't heard the door open. The Sugian was still in the room. Brian wasn't even sure which way the door was, and he cursed himself again for not paying better attention to his surroundings.

"We need to get back to the bunker," Michele finally said. "Warn the others. They think it's safe inside the building, but who knows if there are any more roaming the halls. First, we need to kill this one. We can't let it out of this room."

The emergency lighting made the room dark, and Brian's eyes started to play tricks on him. He recalled the strange shimmer he had seen at the gate. He'd thought it was heat from the car's engine, but now he was certain it had been a camouflaged Sugian.

"It hasn't been here long," he whispered. "And I think it's alone. More than one would attract attention. This one didn't even get in unseen. It just got lucky that we didn't believe the person who saw it."

Michele pressed her lips together and directed him and Oberon to check the rows and keep a look out for any hint of movement while she and Zane guarded the door. They'd been out of sight for less than a minute when Brian heard a wail of pain followed by three gunshots in rapid succession. These weapons were much quieter than the ones they'd used on Kepos, so thankfully his ears weren't ringing.

Zane lay on the floor, motionless. Michele was ignoring him, but for good reason. By the look of the blood spattered across the server racks, she had wounded the Sugian, and she was ready to finish the job at the first opportunity she got.

"I don't think it can camouflage well while it's bleeding," she said. "It ran off without disappearing." Michele's stance relaxed a bit, and she lowered her gun. "We just need to—"

Michele's gun was up again, and she was aiming at Oberon. She fired. The bullet hit flesh, and Oberon cried out in pain. Behind him, the Sugian collapsed, a hole slightly off-center between its eyes.

"Nice shot," Brian said.

"Kai's been training me," she replied. "Sorry, Elian." She tore a scrap of cloth from his shirt and pressed it against his arm. "I figured a little graze was better than having the Sugian rip out your spine with its claws."

Brian was already checking on Zane. He was conscious, but he didn't get up.

"You okay?" Brian asked.

"I feel a little sick," Zane said, closing his eyes again. "I hit my head pretty hard."

"Probably a concussion," Brian said. "Let's get you back down to the bunker so the doctor can check you out."

"Is everyone else okay?" Zane asked.

"Oberon got grazed by a bullet, but he's fine."

"I'm fine too. Mostly," Zane said, his voice a little shaky. "I think I need to lie down, though."

Zane was nearly as pale as the dead Sugian a couple of meters away. Brian and Oberon supported the young man, who limped along with their support. Zane grew heavier as they went, but Brian knew it wasn't his own fatigue. Zane was growing weaker, so Brian picked him up. Zane was as tall as Brian, but much lankier in his build, so he wasn't that heavy. Brian carried him down the stairs, just a few paces ahead of Michele and Oberon. Zane's head lolled against his shoulder, which only fueled Brian's concern.

19. DIONE

Dione was sitting while Bel paced. Zane was still out there, along with Brian, Oberon, and Michele. She wanted to join her friend, but some of the stiffness was returning to her leg after Dr. Philips's injection. Whatever they had here was a lot better than what they'd scrounged up on Kepos. The pain was still completely gone, and that was its own kind of miracle.

"I'm sure they'll be fine," Dione said. "If there is a Sugian in the building, it's probably moved on to wreak more havoc."

"I know. It's not that," Bel said.

"Then what is it?"

"I'm sorry."

"For what?" Dione asked.

"For being so difficult whenever you brought up the Sugians."

"You wanted something to stop the Vens. I don't blame you for that."

"Well, *I* blame me. I knew better, and I wasted time I could have spent helping you research the Sugians."

"I don't know if I discovered anything truly useful anyway."

Bel took a seat next to her and lowered her voice. "What did you find out?"

Dione drummed her fingers against the cot. "There was a lot of interesting stuff. I don't know if he told you, but Zane sent me some sort of index he generated of Sugian references. I didn't find some magical weakness we can exploit, but I did learn one interesting thing. Remember how the Vens used to growl before a battle? Apparently their growling interferes with the Sugians' ability to camouflage."

The information energized Bel. "If there really is a Sugian inside, maybe we can replicate the Ven sound and find it!"

"Brian said they were holding a Ven here until this morning. Think they have any audio samples?" Dione said.

"Or maybe another Ven hidden away…" Bel grumbled.

"No more Vens," a bald man said.

Bel shrugged. "Dione, this is Lars. He helped us rig up the paint trap."

He nodded to Dione. "Couldn't help overhearing. You need Ven audio? You really think it would reveal a Sugian?"

"It might. I don't think we have anything to lose by trying."

"I've got some recordings on my device. I can isolate some clips and make a Ven growl track. We'd need power to the whole facility to play it through the speakers."

"Where's your device?" Bel asked.

"This way," he said, beckoning them to follow. He led them to a makeshift workstation close to where Lithia and Reyes were sitting.

"What were you doing with a Ven anyway?" Dione asked.

"Can't tell you that. Here are the audio clips I have."

Lars played the first one, and Dione got goose bumps. Bel shivered next to her.

"Not that one," Lithia said, making her way over.

"Why not?" Lars asked.

"You need the sustained growling," she said. "That's what they do before attacking. That sound was just an angry growl."

"What about this?" Lars asked, playing another clip.

Lithia's lip curled, and she shuddered. "If any of their growling interferes with Sugian camouflage, that's it."

"Thanks," Bel said.

Lithia nodded and returned to sit with Reyes.

"I guess we just create a track of this clip repeated, then play it if they get inside the building," Dione said.

"If there's not one here already," Bel replied.

"Right," Dione replied.

The two sat nearby, and while Lars worked on creating a track of awful Ven noises, Bel stared at Dione.

Bel widened her eyes and subtly inclined her head toward Lars. What was the message here? Lars hunched over his computer a moment, scrutinizing something, and Bel mouthed the word "evidence."

Oh. That's a good idea. If they could get Lars away from his computer, maybe they could find something that would tell them more about what the scientists were researching. She could see he had a number of programs running. Maybe one of them could—

There was a pounding at the door. Dione recognized Brian's muffled voice, and now that she was paying attention, Reyes was already pushing it open. Several of the scientists and Ficarans rushed up, pulling them inside, checking the others for injuries, shouting words of concern or reassurance to others. There was chaos within the room, and Dione resisted the urge to rush to Brian as it unfolded.

Zane was injured badly from the appearance of his limp form.

Brian was calling for the doctor. Bel was already halfway across the room. Oberon was bleeding but still walking, and Michele was in quiet conversation with Reyes. Dr. Philips was in motion, directing others with barely a glance as she ordered Brian to lay Zane on a cot.

"Lars, the bandages are right there behind you. Bring them," Dr. Philips shouted over the concerned buzz of the few dozen people trapped in the bunker. "Maryn, get my scanner from the back."

When Lars, stunned, stood to obey, Dione came into sole possession of his device. She could close it and join her friends, or she could take this opportunity, as grim as the circumstances were, to get the answers they all wanted.

This facility worked with infectious diseases; that much they had figured out. They had been holding a live Ven here. Her father, the head of research and development for the Alliance, had sent a small team of soldiers to protect this lab, and whatever they were working on was valuable enough that the Sugians had sent a scouting party.

She was almost certain it was a virus of some sort that attacked the Vens or the Sugians. If it was a virus, then why was her father so closely involved? He mostly worked on agricultural innovation and other technology for the colonies, but Dione now had the suspicion that offensive tech played a larger role in his work than she'd originally thought. Even if the Alliance was planning to engage in biowarfare, how did that fall under her father's job description?

One good thing was that she wouldn't have to worry about covering her tracks. If Lars noticed, what could he do? She searched for a Ven virus, and her suspicions were confirmed. They were working on a virus that would infect the Venatorians, but the graphs that had come up didn't make sense. They were projections, and Dione tried to make sense of the lines. One showed a relatively steady upward progression on an exponential trajectory that shows the spread of infection. The other lines stayed near zero, each one spiking at a different point along the x-axis. Each of the spike lines was labeled as "Deaths if Event Day n," with n changing for each line.

She was too distracted to think properly about what it meant, so she snapped a quick picture of the graph with her manumed. Then she noticed that there was a link at the bottom, so she followed it to another graph. She snapped a picture of it, too, without really looking at it, before closing the graphs and deleting her search. If Lars wasn't suspicious, he wouldn't bother checking very hard for tampering.

Bel was glued to Zane's side, and Brian was there, too, talking with Dr. Philips. Lithia was with Oberon, who was sitting on the cot adjacent. Lars was on his way back. "Go check on your friends. I'll work on this myself."

"Thank you," she replied. Whatever those graphs meant, they were crucial to figuring out what was going on here.

20. BRIAN

Brian was glad when Dione finally made it over to join them. "I'm okay, really," he reassured her.

Everyone kept a respectful distance, but the scientists whispered to one another, stealing glances at Zane. They weren't used to seeing their children suffer like the Keposians.

While Dr. Philips assessed Zane and gave him something to relieve the pain, Brian gave a quick recap to Dione and Lithia. Bel and Oberon stayed by Zane, and Michele and Reyes were at the monitors.

"There could be more inside the building," Brian said. "Dione, did you find anything when you were looking into the Sugians?"

"According to the Vens, Sugians hunt in mated pairs," she said. "The Vens work in larger teams of three to five to combat them."

"So a pair of Sugians is an equal match for twice their number of Vens? Does that make them twice as deadly?" Lithia asked.

"I guess," Dione said. "Sugians might be easier to kill, but their camouflage and speed are deadly. We need to avoid head-on battles."

"There *could* be more Sugians in the building, but I don't think it's likely. If they hunt in pairs, wouldn't they have ambushed us as a team?" Brian asked.

Lithia shrugged. "Maybe this one came alone because its mate died or was killed," she said.

"I don't think we can rule it out. There's a lot we don't understand about the Sugians," Dione said.

There was more back-and-forth, but Brian's gaze settled on Zane, who was fidgeting on the cot under Dr. Philips's care. He knew he should pay attention to the conversation, but his mind lost focus. The minutes blurred past, and he found himself sitting on a cot with Dione on one side holding his hand, and his father on the other. Soon, Bel came over, a smile of relief on her face.

"Zane's going to be fine," she said. "The doctor just wants him to take it easy. It's a concussion. Not terrible, but not good. He needs to take it easy." Her update delivered, she returned to his bedside.

From their position near the security monitors, Brian could see Michele's face clearly, and that meant he could read her lips as she discussed something with Reyes. He watched her for a minute before standing up and tugging Dione after him.

"What are we doing?" she asked.

"The Sugians are inside the walls now."

"What? How?"

"That's what we're going to find out," he replied.

He didn't get to ask his question, though, because once they reached the security monitors, the conversation had dissolved into intense focus on the camera feeds.

Brian watched as Sugians came from nowhere, turning their camouflage into chaotic spasms of color. No doubt it had evolved to work best on Vens, but he felt a little disoriented just viewing it on-screen. The men outside in the rain looked unsteady. They must have been affected too.

"Oh my god," Michele said. "They were heading toward the comms building to restore power, but the Sugians were waiting. They got inside the walls and just waited for the gate tower's door to open."

"Two men down," Reyes said.

"Three," Lithia countered softly, as another man fell.

"We can't just leave them out there," Michele said. She took two swift steps toward the weapon stash, then turned on her heel and returned. "Can you lift the lockdown?"

Reyes studied the other woman carefully. "Yes, but I won't. Colonel Park wouldn't allow it, and Kai wouldn't want us to either."

"If we don't do something, they're all going to die."

Reyes pressed her lips together and kept her eyes on the screen. There was only one emergency camera in that area, and its coverage was limited, but Brian could see now that the rest of the fighters were retreating into the gate tower.

He called out updates. "They're retreating. They're barricading the door."

"And firing warning shots when the Sugians come in close," Reyes added. "That's good."

The crisis of the moment passed, but Brian's concern didn't disappear when the Sugians camouflaged and slipped out of sight.

For several minutes, he watched the limited camera feeds, searching for any hint of the Sugians. A muddy imprint, an odd shimmer, a failed bit of camouflage, but as it grew darker outside, it became harder and harder to see such details. Unfortunately, that level of scrutiny soon was unnecessary. The Sugians reappeared right outside the door to the main facility. Several Sugians, no longer bothering to conceal themselves, approached the facility's door. One of the Sugians brought forward an alien device and began cutting through the thick steel of the outer door.

"It will still take them a while," Reyes said.

"They'll get in sooner than expected," Michele said. "With Kai and Colonel Park pinned in the gate tower and no manumed communication, our only hope is if Marius gets here in time."

Brian glanced at Dione. She might have faith in her father, but he preferred to have a plan, just in case.

***

The Sugians had been working away at the door for almost an hour. The trapped soldiers fired short bursts whenever the Sugians made an attack on the tower, but they didn't have a line of sight on the facility's main doors. There was no one to stop the powerful aliens from breaking through.

Lithia left Reyes and Michele, who were locked in a tense debate from the looks of it, and approached the cot where Brian sat between Dione and his father. When Oliver noticed Lithia approaching, he gave Brian a kiss on the forehead and got up to give her a seat. "I'm going back to stay with your mother. We're glad you're safe. Love you."

Brian smiled. "Thanks, Dad. Love you, too."

"Sorry, Brian. Didn't mean to scare your dad away, but I couldn't sit there anymore," Lithia said as she settled in.

"What's up?" Dione asked, nudging Brian over to make room for Lithia on her other side.

"Michele wants to go rescue them," Lithia said.

"How?" Dione wondered.

"The roof. There's an emergency exit up there, and Michele is

114

trying to convince Reyes to open it. There's a fire escape or something she can use to climb down, then go rescue Kai and restore power."

The trio watched the two women talking and came to the conclusion that Reyes did not approve of Michele's rescue plan. The whispers grew more heated.

"What are Reyes's objections?" Brian asked. The plan sounded good to him.

"She can't lift the lockdown on just one door. She'd have to give the all clear, opening up the front door with it," Lithia explained.

Dione sighed. "That's not good."

"Reyes is just as anxious to help them. I think at least two of the people who died outside the tower were her fellow soldiers."

Brian shook his head. "They both want to rescue the people in the tower but can't figure out how," he said.

Lithia raised her eyebrows. "Michele's lost it, though. She wants to go ahead and open the doors."

Dione jerked her head up. "That's suicide."

Brian didn't agree. He could see it now. The bunker door was strong. Just as strong as the main door almost. The Sugians would get inside eventually, but Kai and the Alliance soldiers would still be stuck in that tower. Unless they could flank the Sugians guarding them while the others entered the main building. Then Kai and his men could go in behind them and clear them out before they got through the door to the bunker. Meanwhile, Michele could turn the power back on and give Reyes back the power of full surveillance and communication.

"Actually, it might be the best plan we've got." Brian explained his reasoning to the two. "If we take control of the situation—"

"Control? You call that control? Reyes doesn't think it's a good idea." Lithia wasn't buying it, but he could see Dione was coming around.

"I said it was the best option, not a good one."

"Then we figure out how to make it as good an option as we can," Dione said, giving his hand a squeeze before letting go. "I need to talk to Bel."

When she stood, Brian noticed her wince and shift her weight onto her good leg. Lithia closed her eyes and took a deep breath. Across the room, Zane was resting on his cot, and Bel sat silently next to him. Oberon was dozing off with his head leaning back against the wall. Their small group that had been through so much looked like it couldn't take much more, physically or emotionally.

The Ficarans looked afraid. The ones who had joined him weren't fighters, not truly, though all the Ficarans had been accustomed to danger and uncertainty back on Kepos. His father was keeping them calm. The Green Cloaks looked grim, sitting apart from the other Keposians. The scientists looked worst of all. They must have known the danger that was coming, but it was only hitting them now that they'd seen someone—a kid by their standards—come back seriously injured. The deaths of the soldiers and their colleagues were finally sinking in, and they were afraid.

Brian himself was pushing down the fear that threatened to overtake him, but fear was like water. Dangerous and unstoppable. Not to be underestimated. If he was going to be of any use in protecting everyone he cared about, he needed to embrace that fear and give it purpose, just like he had on Kepos.

He watched Dione hide her limp as she approached Bel. Sitting together on a cot in the back of the room, his parents embraced. He took a deep breath. Fear gripped him more tightly now that he had everything to lose.

21. DIONE

Dione's leg was starting to ache again, she wanted to have a private conversation with Bel. This was made difficult by the nature of the bunker, as well as by Zane's injury. She wanted his input on the graphs she had found. How she had ever treated him as inferior she couldn't understand, but she was glad they were on good terms now.

"Bel," she whispered. Zane's eyes were closed, and she didn't want to disturb him. "We need to talk about what I found on Lars's computer."

"Right," Bel said. "With all the commotion, I forgot."

"What?" Zane said, his eyes still closed.

"Let's get everyone over here first," Bel replied, beckoning to the other two.

Dione had hoped to look it over privately with Bel first, but she pulled another cot up parallel to Zane's. Bel kept her seat on the floor, and Brian and Lithia took the hint and sat on the cot on either side of her. Oberon gave them a look, but kept his distance and returned to his nap. He probably knew they were up to something but decided he didn't want the details. They kept their voices low and let the general conversations of the room disguise their meeting.

"Bel and I got a look at Lars' laptop. We all know there's something they're not telling us, so while we were helping Lars create a Ven growl track—"

"A what?" Zane asked, finally opening his eyes. They were bright blue and a little bloodshot, but he seemed to have a little more color in his cheeks than he had when Brian carried him in.

Dione quickly explained its anticamouflage potential before getting to the point. "In the chaos of your arrival, I got a few pictures. I searched for info related to a Ven virus and found this."

She removed her manumed so they could pass it around and look at the first graph. It took a few minutes for each of them to get a good look since she couldn't just send them a copy while the network was down.

"We were right about the virus," Bel said. "The exponential growth is what you'd expect with a viral infection. But the rest of it doesn't make sense. What are these spikes?"

"Why would death rates spike all of a sudden? Shouldn't they mirror infection rates or something?" Lithia asked.

Dione had her own ideas, but waited for a revelation from Zane; however, it was Bel who dropped the first bombshell. "This graph isn't for internal use. Look," she said, pointing to a line of cut off text in the corner. "*For inclusion in the repor*—. Report to someone. These graphs were made for someone outside the lab."

"You're right," Dione murmured. "Probably the Alliance." *Maybe even her father himself.*

"What does it mean by 'event'?" Brian asked. "It's set as day zero."

"Must be when the virus gets introduced," Dione said. "Which leads us back to Lithia's question. Why are the fatalities in spikes?"

Dione looked to Zane again, but he was lost in thought.

"Here's the other graph I found," she said. Dione had to take a minute to study it herself. This one wasn't for Vens, but Sugians.

This graph was nearly the same as the first, but with another set of data and projections added to it.

"This shows projected Sugian infections and fatalities too," Bel said. "The spikes on the Sugian lines follow closely after the Ven spikes."

"So there's a second virus?" Lithia asked. "One for the Vens and one for the Sugians?"

"That makes sense, I guess. But why put them on the same graph?"

"Because it's the same virus," Zane said, breaking his silence.

Dione cocked her head to one side. "I suppose that could be the case, but it would be very hard to get a virus to do exactly what you wanted in two species without the risk of it affecting more creatures than you intended."

"Not if it's a nanotech virus."

"I thought you told me nanotech was mostly illegal," Brian said.

"It is," Dione replied. "So that leaves us with two big questions: Why are they working with illegal tech, and how is the nanotech connected to the virus they've made?"

"Your father could probably tell us," Zane said. "But if I had to guess, I'd say they're trying to use the nanotech as a vector for the virus. Those fatality spikes on the other graph are a result of the activation of the virus. Activated one way, it affects Vens. A different signal or biomarker, and it switches to Sugian mode."

Dione gulped. She'd reached a similar conclusion but hoped she was wrong. If this was what her father was working on, either he was operating outside the Alliance's permission or the Alliance had sanctioned something even worse than biowarfare.

"How does that even work?" Lithia asked.

"I don't know," Dione replied.

Bel had been silent, deep in thought. "Things must look very bad if they're resorting to this. Virus-infused nanotech? No wonder your father would drop everything to come save this operation."

"Yeah," said Zane. "And no wonder they're using an independent lab and not a government facility. Plausible deniability."

"We can speculate all day about why they're using nanotech," Dione said. "One thing that we can be pretty sure about is that things are not going well. The war is just beginning, and humanity's prospects are bad. This facility was working on something that could change the tide of the war. Michele and Kai and everyone else here know the stakes. They know that they have to hold out until my father gets here with reinforcements, and that it's not just their own lives on the line."

"So you think we should leave Kai and the others out there to hold off the Sugians?" Lithia asked. Her voice was detached, and her gaze fixed on the empty wall behind Zane. No doubt she was thinking about Roy, the boy she'd left behind when evacuating the Field Temple. The Vens had killed him, and Lithia couldn't forgive herself.

"Not at all," Dione replied. "The opposite. We don't stand a chance if we just wait here. We can't even be sure that my father's coming, though I'm convinced if he has the means, he will. Even if he didn't get the message about us being here, this biological weapon they've developed is more than enough motivation. We need to rescue Kai and the men who are trapped with him because without their help, we're sitting ducks down here."

"You're suggesting we take the fight to the Sugians?" Brian

asked.

She heard his skepticism and could practically read his mind. Almost all of them were injured in one way or another. Her leg, Zane's concussion, Lithia's emotional state. Oberon was wounded too.

"We have a choice. We can lock ourselves up in here, wait for rescue, and hope that my father gets here before they kill all of the power and break our lockdown. If we change our minds once they breach the outer door, we don't have a chance. We're stuck in here until the end." Dione paused and looked over her shoulder at the forty or so people in the room. Most of them were Keposians. "Or there's option two. We can send a team to restore power, rescue Kai's group, put a few teams in the halls to kill the Sugians while they're bottlenecked at the door."

There was some more back-and-forth, but everyone, even reluctant Lithia, thought it was the best plan. Dione explained their plan to Michele and Reyes. She made it clear that they would be joining the teams, and to her surprise, received little push back. Apparently adults who didn't spend a lot of time around kids didn't mind a few seventeen- and eighteen-year-olds leaving the bunker. Or maybe they thought it would be safer to be outside the bunker and far away from the bioweapon the Sugians were after. Michele immediately agreed, and with a little more coaxing, Reyes was persuaded as well.

"The outer door won't last forever, and we need power back," Reyes finally conceded.

A man, one of the scientists, stepped forward. "You're sending a bunch of kids?"

"I was barely eighteen when I joined the Alliance Fleet," Reyes said. "No one cared then."

"I see your point, Jonas," Michele said, "but I don't see anyone else volunteering."

"Fine," Jonas replied. "I'll volunteer. I can restore the power."

Michele knitted her eyebrows together. "You don't have to do this to prove something—"

"I'm not," Jonas said.

Reyes nodded in respect. "As for the door, they know to focus their energy on the weakest points. Sometimes I have to remind myself how smart they are. Don't get complacent."

"You're staying here?" Lithia asked Reyes.

"Like I said before, there's more to this than firefights," she said. "Stay with me. Once we get power back and the Sugians are roaming the halls, I'll need another sharp set of eyes more than ever."

Maryn, who was now inching closer, chimed in. "Did I understand your suggestion? Hunt them? They're basically invisible," she said. "And they are designed to be hunters, not hunted. Even the Vens are losing their endless war against them."

"It's not going to be easy, but maybe we can do something about the invisibility. Turn the tables." Michele bit her lower lip, then peered at her group of frightened scientists. "Lars, how's that Ven growl track coming?"

"I've got something ready. Once we get power back, we can try it. It won't be fun to listen to, but if it works, it will be worth it."

Dione was curious, but there wasn't enough time to ask questions. Time to divide and conquer.

The doctor didn't want to give her a second shot so soon, but ultimately agreed when Dione made it clear that she was going, and it sure would be helpful not to be hindered by pain at a critical moment. After ten minutes, the pain was gone.

A team of Green Cloaks was allowed to take weapons and position themselves near the door. Brian was skeptical, but he had been speaking with them frequently throughout their journey from Kepos. They all understood what was at stake. Bel, who was also skeptical, muttered to Brian, "If they are still loyal to the Vens, killing Sugians is still in their best interest." That earned a dark chuckle from him. Dione didn't know what to think, but she trusted him. She was a little too trusting sometimes, but Brian didn't suffer from that defect.

The Ficaran team would guard the stairwell, hoping to catch the Sugians in a bottleneck if they made it past the Green Cloaks. The Green Cloak team had volunteered for the main door, the more dangerous location. They'd do as much damage as possible once the armored door was opened, and then they'd retreat.

"Are you sure you want the Green Cloaks in that position?" Dione muttered to Brian quietly so that no one else could hear.

"They understand the risk," he replied. "They asked Michele to put them in front. Jill and Asher are staying here, but the other five wanted to help."

Dione held back her concerns and mentally ran through the plan. The six of them who were leaving the safety of the building would leave through an exit to the roof. Oberon, Brian, and Michelle would take out or distract the Sugians guarding the gate tower. She, Bel, and Jonas, the only scientist who had volunteered, would reroute power from the NRT comms array through the secondary system. It wasn't a long-term solution, but it would get them through the current crisis, win or lose.

After that, they would all return to the building, coming in through the front doors and flanking the Sugians, who would hopefully be unable to camouflage once Lars got his Ven growl track playing over the sound system.

Lithia and Reyes were staying put. They would coordinate everything using the few camera feeds left until she and Bel restored power. At least the Sugians would get caught in the paint trap Bel and Zane had set up earlier. Even if the few cameras couldn't track them, they wouldn't be completely invisible.

Dione took the gun that was offered, a small pistol that reminded her of the one she and Zane had taken with them on their trip through the Keposian jungle to rescue Oberon from the Vens. When they'd learned Oberon was still alive, she'd felt a lot of things. Guilt that she'd left him on the Ven ship, thinking he was dead. Fear that they'd be too late. But also hope. Hope, because there was a chance they could save him.

Those same emotions flowed through her now, and she tried to focus on the hope. She and her friends hadn't survived the Vens, warring factions of colonists, and genetically engineered monsters just to fail when they were so close to home. They were fighters now, and they would see this through to the end.

Everyone was ready. Kai would see Michele coming and hopefully take the hint and join them while the Sugians were distracted. The teams were filing out the door, and once everyone was in position, Michele would give Reyes the signal.

They had a decent plan, but the next moment threw the plan into chaos.

Dione was already halfway down the hall, but with the door still open, she could hear Reyes shouting from inside the bunker.

"They've breached the main door. Go now! Run!"

Dione obeyed, following Bel up the stairs, hoping they could get past the main floor and up to the roof before the stairwell filled with Sugians. Without more than emergency power, there were limited cameras and no communications. Dione panted as she reached the next landing, trying to ignore the startled shouts below her. They needed power. If she could get Lithia and Reyes power, things just might be okay.

22. BRIAN

Brian sprinted up the stairs, ready to exit onto the main level and fire at the incoming Sugians. Instead, he found that Michele, who had been ahead of him, had jammed the door with a metal bar.

"We can't go in there. Getting Kai and restoring power is our best chance now," she said. She led the way up several more flights of stairs, and Brian had no choice but to follow. She was right. It was their only option. Get Kai. Flank the Sugians.

The Green Cloaks took up position at the door, and Dione and Bel trailed his team up the stairs. That door wouldn't hold for long, and every second mattered. The stairwell echoed with shouts, and even these quiet guns would make a lot of noise in the enclosed space. The six of them burst from the stairwell into the hallway on the top floor. A twist and a turn later, they were headed toward the rooftop door. Brian heard faraway gunshots, or maybe he was just imagining them. His heart was already pounding as they climbed the short set of stairs and spilled onto the roof.

The rain was a drizzle, but it was dark. A few emergency lights were still on outside, but if there was a moon, the clouds hid it. Even though it was a foreign world, the scent of rain, earth, and wet jungle smelled like home, and a pang of nostalgia hit him. His eyes adjusted after a few moments, and he could make out Michele striding along the roof's edge.

There was an emergency ladder up here that needed to be lowered to the ground before they could begin their descent.

"Here," she hissed, keeping her voice low. He and Oberon wasted no time.

They were still lowering the ladder, but it was close enough for Michele. She started climbing down the second it was locked in. Oberon was right behind her.

Dione was right there next to Brian. The adrenaline pumping through his veins thought for him in that moment, and he pulled her in for a brief kiss. "I love you. Be careful."

He grabbed the top of the ladder and made his way down. The bars were slick in the rain, and he practically slid down the last several feet. Thankfully, Oberon was out of the way. The second he hit the ground, he was running because Michele had barely waited for Oberon, and they certainly hadn't waited for him. Once they were closer to the tower, Michele slowed and stopped, taking cover behind a row of bushes. The gate tower was in view.

"They injured one earlier, right?" Brian whispered through quick breaths. "We might be able to see it if it can't fully camouflage. I can—"

"It's too dark. No time." Michele said. "We're going to cover the area outside and hope we get lucky. Once they come after us, Kai will have our backs. Get ready."

Brian looked at Oberon, whose alarmed expression mirrored his own feelings. There was no time to object, though. Michele stepped out and started firing in the general direction of the tower.

They were still at a distance, but when the first Sugian shimmered into view and charged them, even a "safe" distance didn't seem so safe anymore. A series of shifting colors and patterns designed to confuse and disorient shifted across its skin. The colors were barely perceptible in the low light, but the pattern changes hurt Brian's eyes. The Sugian became difficult to focus on, like the strain of staring at an optical illusion.

In the open space, the monster easily picked up speed, and their shots kept missing. The creature was nearly upon them when Brian had the presence of mind to wonder where the other one was. They hunted in pairs, so there must have been another. He never took his eyes from the one still charging toward them. There was shouting from the gate tower, a bright flash, and suddenly Brian couldn't see anything. He closed his eyes too late, heard a loud bang, then felt a shower of dirt.

He couldn't fire wildly in front of him because he wasn't even sure which direction he was facing anymore. A shuddering screech told him the Sugian was close, but it was also in pain. Kai must have used some sort of stun grenade. Brian had seen them in the movies Dione had shown him, and now he wished he didn't have firsthand experience. He could make out an outline near him. Oberon, maybe? He moved toward it. There were two more screeches, one closer than the other. He imagined one as a call for help, the other as a promise of providing it.

He reached where the outline had been, but it was gone. He blinked several times, recovering enough to see something leaping straight for him. He sidestepped the creature, but he wasn't fast enough. The Sugian barreled into him with enough force to knock him to the ground, even though it had been an indirect hit. Because it was so close, Brian could make it out as its clawed feet pressed down on his chest. The creature was heavy, and Brian struggled to breathe. The Sugian's mouth flaps were flared revealing its beak, and he knew it was over. One stab at his neck or some other vital area, and it didn't matter if it tried to eat him or not. He'd be dead.

He pushed against its abrasive skin, but his hands lost their grip on a patch slick from the mud. In protest, the Sugian, whose claws had been resting against his chest, dug those claws in, as if to hold its ground. Brian yelled in pain at the same time the Sugian screeched. They created a discordant harmony, one dying, one expecting death, until the Sugian's screech cut off, its sharp beak crashing into Brian's shoulder as it died on top of him. The weight of the monster collapsing on his chest knocked the wind out of him, and he couldn't so much as whisper, let alone wail in agony.

He was alive, but he still felt like he was dying with the full weight of the dead Sugian crushing him. More shouts, more figures. The stun grenade was wearing off, but he still felt disoriented. Just when he thought he'd pass out, the weight lifted. People were pushing the Sugian off him. He gasped in a breath, then coughed. He pressed a hand to his chest as he sat up, soaked with rain and blood that mingled in warm and cold patches on his torn shirt.

He could make out human-shaped figures obscured by the rain, so he gathered the others had been freed from the tower. His manumed, though powered on, was still unable to send or receive messages, and his thoughts turned to Dione, Bel, and Jonas. Had they had enough time to complete their mission, or had something gone wrong?

23. LITHIA

The team of Ficarans was still stationed outside the bunker, but rather than heading straight for them, the Sugians had spread throughout the building.

Lithia had made the mistake of feeling hopeful when her friends left the room. They had a plan. One group would save Kai. The other group would restore power to the main building, reestablishing surveillance and manumed communication. The last group would hold the Sugians at bay. But after the Sugians broke through, things went downhill fast. The one good thing was that the Sugians were covered in streaks of bright red paint, making it impossible for them to camouflage with their surroundings. They would at the very least be a visible target. Until the power came on and Lars could access the sound system, the red paint would have to do.

Their initial entry had been a bloodbath. Instead of the team being set up in the hallway, ready to unload on the Sugians the second Reyes opened the doors, the Sugians had broken down the door a couple of minutes too soon. They blew past the main hall and down the corridor toward the stairwell. Her friends had gotten out in time, but the Sugians had killed every single Green Cloak that had volunteered. There was only one Sugian body to show for it, though a few others had been injured. There was no love lost between Lithia and the Green Cloaks, but the carnage had still roiled her stomach. They had given the others time to get to the roof, and for that, she was grateful.

The Ficarans outside the bunker door had braced themselves, but the Sugians didn't come. Once the bloodshed was over, most of the creatures disappeared from camera view, though one pair hunched over the two bodies that were within the camera's angle. Once Lithia realized what they were doing, she looked away. No one deserved that.

When the pair of Sugians finished their meal, they trotted into the main hall. They were coated in red, and she doubted that much of the color could be attributed to red paint. Suddenly the Sugians started shaking violently.

"What the hell?" she muttered. "Are they having a seizure or something?"

Reyes was watching too. The red paint and gore that coated the creatures melted off and dripped to the floor. Lithia looked away, but the image was seared in her mind. No doubt it would come back and haunt her the next time she let her guard down to sleep. Soon they were out of view again.

"That's not good," Reyes said quietly so that only Lithia could hear.

"What do you mean?"

"The Sugians can somehow clean their skin. The paint—the blood, dirt, anything—that would cover their skin and prevent them from properly camouflaging can be cleaned away in under a minute. There's no way to tag them that will last."

The other Sugians were still somewhere inside the building. Lithia had counted ten total, but she doubted that number was reliable. Minutes passed, and she assumed they were coming for the bunker. The screams and gunfire she kept expecting to hear outside the reinforced door never came.

"What are they waiting for?" Lithia whispered to Reyes. "What are they doing?"

"Searching the place," came the soldier's reply.

"For what?" Lithia and the others already had a pretty good idea of what they might find, even if Michele had tried to keep it a secret.

"It's a scouting party. Anything they might find useful."

"Nothing in particular then?" Lithia asked pointedly.

"Hopefully not," Reyes muttered.

"Will they find it? Whatever secret weapon you've been working on?"

Reyes shook her head, confirming what Lithia suspected. The bioweapon was in this room somewhere, and above all else, the Sugians couldn't get it.

There was a commotion outside the gate tower, and she struggled to make out what was happening. At least two people were down, but it was impossible to tell who they were and impossible to call and check. She was voiceless. She was powerless. This was how she was supposed to help? How could she use her position here to provide warnings and tactical advice to help the people out there kill Sugians? She had no comms. No voice. She was trapped watching people get killed, powerless to stop it. She should have gone with them. She could be helping Dione or Oberon or someone.

"I should be out there," she said, clenching her fist.

"You're hurt," Reyes replied.

"No, I'm not. Zane's hurt. I'm just—"

The tightness in her chest cut her off, and she stopped speaking. She wasn't going to cry, not now. She wasn't a crier. At least she hadn't been until this disastrous trip had broken her. It had taken something from her, and she wasn't sure if she could name it, let alone recover it. She was about to lose control and cry anyway when Reyes saved her.

"Lithia, when the comms come back, you will be able to fulfill your role. I need you here, and more importantly, they need you here. Your friends know that this is where you will be the most useful."

One of the people on the surveillance screen was being helped to their feet. The skirmish outside the gate tower appeared to be over, and the humans had won. The bulk of the enemy was inside the building, and Lithia was certain another battle was on the horizon.

24. DIONE

There was no sign of Brian and the others by the time Dione, Bel, and Jonas made it to the bottom of the ladder. Jonas ran ahead toward the comms building. It was small compared to the main facility where the battle was now taking place, but it was still the size of a large house.

He had a small lead on them, eager to transfer power to the main facility. Once they got all of the cameras and manumeds functioning, Lithia and Reyes would be able to help everyone holding off the Sugians. If they were still alive.

As soon as Jonas reached the door, a Sugian popped into view, pulsing with a sickening array of colors and patterns. It charged him, tackling him onto the ground a couple of meters from the door. Bel fired a few shots, but nothing deterred it. Jonas screamed, and they kept running and firing, trying to kill the Sugian. One of Bel's bullets finally connected once they reached the door, and the Sugian wailed and reared back. Its claws and mouth flaps were coated in blood, and Dione realized that Jonas wasn't screaming anymore. He was dead.

"Inside. Now!" she screamed, pulling on Bel's arm and pushing open the door at the same time. The two ran in and immediately closed the door behind them. Bel leaned against it, as if her meager weight could somehow counter the force of the Sugian. Fortunately, Dione locked it in time, and the two of them stepped back as the door rattled under the Sugian's assault.

"This door isn't reinforced. We don't have much time," Bel said. "Come on."

Dione didn't have the luxury of wondering how they were going to get out of there once they rerouted the power. Jonas had been the one who was supposed to do the hard work, but they'd gotten a crash course, too, just in case. How naïve of her to think they wouldn't need it. The two young women ran past the jump chamber, tiny drones hovering inside like bugs. In fact, a blinking light indicated a message. *Dad.* It had to be from him.

"I'll catch up," Dione said, breaking toward the interface.

"That door isn't going to hold long," Bel shouted, hesitating.

"Just go!" Dione said. "We need manumeds back."

Bel obeyed, and Dione got to work. She'd seen one of these arrays before. Her father had taken her with him one day, and she'd gotten to see the massive array in Haisukia on Lavinian. She just needed to—

A particularly loud thump against the door made her jump, and she started pressing buttons. It had to be somewhat intuitive, right?

Seconds ticked by, and she struggled to concentrate on her task. Every time the door rattled under the Sugian's assault, she lost her train of thought. Having exhausted the selection of buttons to press, she despaired. There was no more time to waste. Bel would need her help.

A cracking noise indicated that the door was nearly compromised. She could stay and fight off the Sugian or find Bel—

hardly a choice. Despite the size of the building, it was almost entirely built to house the jump chamber. Aside from the main room, there was a single hallway with two small, narrow rooms, and a utility room in the basement. She went down the sole hallway and found the entrance to the basement room where Bel was working. She opened the door at the same time a bang echoed through the hallway, followed by a triumphant screech. The Sugian had made it inside. She closed the door behind her, hoping it was enough to buy them more time. She hurried down the straight, short staircase, and wondered how they would ever get out of this room alive.

She found Bel kneeling in front of several open wall panels, plugging things in. Rather than interrupt her, Dione tried to figure out where her friend was in the process of restoring power to the main building. Nearly complete, it seemed, but Bel looked grim.

"How long do you think we have to fix this?" Bel asked.

"The rest of our lives," Dione muttered.

Bel chuckled at the dark humor, but it was a bitter laugh. She checked all of the cables, pushing in one that looked a little loose. "Ready?"

Dione flipped a comically large switch, and a few green lights switched on. "That's promising."

Bel shook her head. "I've messed something up," she said. "I've transferred power to the secondary circuit, but manumeds are still dead."

"Did you launch the network?"

"It won't let me. See?"

Bel was right. The option was grayed out, impossible to select. The Sugian slammed into the door, causing the whole room to shake.

"Did you see that?" Bel asked.

"What?"

"When everything shook, the launch option became available. Something must be loose. If we can open up the wall and check the—"

"No time," Dione said. "Get ready." Dione pounded a fist against the wall right above the display with no effect. She did it again, and finally on the third try, Bel was able to select the icon and launch the manumed network.

Soon both of their manumeds hummed in harmony, alerting them that they were once again connected to the network. Or rather, that the network was back up.

Almost immediately, an emergency call came through. Kai had sent a general message requesting backup inside the main building from anyone who was available. He was alive, which meant that Brian and the others had succeeded, at least to some degree. A bang against the door at the top of the stairs reminded her that she and Bel had their own problems.

She called Lithia. Lithia had never failed them before.

25. BRIAN

The rain was falling harder now, and the visibility had gone from poor to nonexistent. Brian gritted his teeth as he propped himself up, clutching his right arm to his chest.

"He's alive. Cam, stay with him." A man Brian couldn't see was barking out orders. "You too. Everyone else with me."

Brian recognized Kai's accented voice. Oberon helped him to his feet, as did the stranger, presumably Cam. Once he was upright, the world spun, and Oberon steadied him until it subsided. He could walk, but his chest and shoulder ached. Cam limped next to him, and Brian realized why he'd been left behind.

"We need to get out of the rain," Cam said. "Come on. There are basic med supplies in the living quarters."

Brian nodded and waited for Cam to lead. In the downpour, he would have struggled to find his own way, even though it was a short walk.

His thoughts shifted from the others who were undoubtedly holding off the Sugians inside the building to his own condition. He was shivering uncontrollably, which made it hard to walk. The cool air inside the living quarters, once Cam ushered them in, only made it worse. Brian collapsed onto the couch in the common area and proceeded to bleed all over it, but it looked like the couch had seen better days.

"Check the cupboard by the sink for supplies. I'll get dry clothes," Cam said, hurrying off despite his limp.

Oberon opened a couple of cabinets before finding what he was looking for. Brian was grateful that it seemed to be a full kit rather than a few bandages. Oberon helped him remove his shirt. The professor seemed no worse than before, though the bandage on his arm could stand to be replaced. Cam returned with towels and dry clothes, and pressed a clean cloth against Brian's shoulder, which was bleeding more than the scratches on his chest. Now that they were out of the rain and he wasn't so disoriented, it didn't seem too bad. The Sugian had injured his right shoulder just underneath his collarbone. Moving that arm even a little sent pain snaking through his chest and arm. Holding a gun would be excruciating, and he didn't think he'd be able to aim with any reliable accuracy, but hopefully Kai and the others were making quick work of the Sugians that were now inside.

"Thanks for coming to rescue us," Cam said as he inspected his wounded leg. "I mean, you didn't even know us, but you did anyway. Thank you."

"What exactly happened?" Brian asked.

"We came out when one of the Sugians was charging you. The other ambushed us. Kai threw a stun grenade to slow the one charging you down so we could get to it. You got it full force too. Then the Sugian attacked you, and we got it just in time."

"By luck, I wasn't looking at the stun grenade," Oberon said. "But it dazzled Michele a bit. Luckily it slowed the Sugian enough."

Cam winced as he bumped his injured leg. "The other ripped

through Burke and got my leg before I could get off a second shot."

So that meant that with one dead and Cam here, Kai only had five people, plus Michele. "How many Sugians total?"

"We're not completely sure. At least a dozen. Two at our tower."

"There was one inside. No sign of its partner," Brian said.

"I don't think its partner was inside with it," Oberon said. "Maybe it was scouting another area inside the walls. Or maybe the original Sugian lost its partner in some other battle."

Cam nodded, but didn't offer any other suggestions. "We didn't get any of them before the power went out and they made it inside the walls. They kept slipping in and out of view, drawing our attention for long enough to seem like a viable target before disappearing again. They were trying to make us waste our ammo." Cam finished bandaging Brian up and gave him the dry clothes to change into. Through a window, Brian could see that the rain had let up and returned to a gentle mist.

"We should head back to the main building to help them," Cam said.

"Let me take a look at your leg first," Oberon said. "You'll be of more use if you're not bleeding all over the place." He rolled up Cam's pant leg, but Brian could see the young man's agitation and eagerness to rejoin his team.

"Make it quick. I've already been gone too long," he said.

Oberon obeyed and used a clean towel to dry off the blood. He applied an ointment that stopped the bleeding as quickly as it had for Brian and bandaged him up. They sacrificed another minute to put on some fresh clothes, too, since they were soaked and covered in mud, and while they were pulling on dry shirts, each of their manumeds crackled to life. While they had always been on, they had not been able to send and receive messages.

"Dione and Bel did it!" Brian exclaimed.

His relief at the sign that Dione must still be alive was short-lived because in the next moment, Cam received a frantic message from Kai. It was garbled and peppered with shouts and gunfire, but the meaning was unmistakable. They needed help. All that they could get. Cam was already limping toward the door when Brian got up to follow him. He grabbed his own gun, but it shook in his hand when he gripped it.

Oberon held out a hand to stop him. "Brian, stay here. You're injured far worse than we are. Don't be a liability."

Brian stopped in his tracks as the other two ran out the front door. Oberon had a point, no matter how much Brian hated it. He could barely hold a weapon. He'd seen it happen enough to know that they were right, and there was nothing noble in pushing past your limits to the point of failure when others were counting on you. It had been true on Kepos, and it was true here. He clenched his left hand into a fist, then tried to aim the gun at a picture on the wall. His chest ached at the effort, but everything about the pose felt wrong. He was not ambidextrous, and he had not practiced shooting left-handed. They were right to leave him, but accepting that didn't mean he couldn't feel bitter about it. He also felt guilty that he was tucked away in safety when others, including his own people, were at risk.

26. LITHIA

The power came back in full, and Lithia sighed in relief. Dione was alive. The flood of input was overwhelming as more and more cameras turned on. She went from monitoring just a few camera feeds to having access to dozens. She could see nearly every hallway, though the labs themselves did not have cameras.

Immediately, Reyes was fielding a call from Kai.

"The colonel?" she asked.

"Dead."

"Who else?"

"No time for that. I'm in charge now, and we're coming back."

Reyes continued the exchange, but Lithia's attention wandered. A pair of Sugians were feasting on human bodies. Reyes had already noted their location and called Kai. "Maybe they're vulnerable and distracted while eating," Reyes told him.

Lithia took in all of the screens, but the only Sugians she could see were the ones she was trying her best not to look at. Green Cloak bodies were draped at impossible angles in the stairwell, and there was no sign of the rest of the Sugians. They had ditched the paint and were able to seamlessly camouflage again.

"What can you tell me about their positions within the building?" Kai asked, as if on cue. "Do you have eyes on any of them?"

"There's a pair in the stairwell, but our paint ploy didn't work. They shed the paint from their skin in some kind of goo. I imagine they can remove any mud or other debris in much the same way, because I'm not seeing any sign of them." Reyes turned to her. "Lithia, see anything?"

She was about to reply with a resounding no, but Lars was scrambling in their direction, and that could only mean one thing. They were about to blast one of the most miserable sounds in the universe through this building.

"No, but give us a minute, and we just might have that information." Lithia said. "Lars is ready."

There was a brief silence while Lars got set up, during which Michele must have explained the situation to Kai.

"Ready?" Lars asked.

"Get on with it," came Kai's gruff response.

Lars pressed play, and it was everything Lithia imagined it would be. Loud. Grating. Horrifying. Goosebumps textured her skin, and images from her nightmares flashed through her mind like treetops thrown into relief by lightning.

"Focus on your breathing, Lithia," Reyes said.

She was right. Her breaths had become shallower. One glance around the room told her that she wasn't alone in disliking the Ven growls, though no one else seemed quite as affected.

Then Lars did something unexpected. He broke out into song. Using the rhythmic Ven growling as a baseline, he layered a slightly off-key melody over it. It was a children's song about cleaning the house after making a mess. Maryn joined in, and suddenly, the Ven growls were nothing more than a layer in a bizarre remix.

The pair had disarmed the Ven growls for her, but the Sugians were not so lucky. They were flickering into view all across the building like a light bulb dying in reverse.

"That's our cue," Kai said.

Reyes began giving them the positions of various Sugians throughout the building. "Let the hunt begin," she muttered.

In all of the excitement, Lithia almost missed a camera in the far left corner of one of her monitors, but movement in her peripheral vision caught her attention. It was the comms building. Her pulse, already racing, thumped faster. A Sugian was trying to break down one of the doors. That must have been where Dione, Bel, and Jonas were. Then she received a call from Dione.

"We're trapped in the basement of the comms building. There's a Sugian outside. It already killed Jonas."

"I can see that," Lithia said. "The Sugian isn't bothering to camouflage." Lithia's voice was strained, like she was debating what to do. "I'm coming to get you."

"No, Lithia." It was Reyes, who had apparently been listening. "I need you here."

"There's no one else out there who can help."

"Exactly. We can't open up that door either."

"You want me to leave them to die?"

"No, but there's nothing *you* can do from in here aside from help me track the loose Sugians. Focus. If we can secure this building again, we can send them help."

"Hang on just a little longer," Lithia told Dione. "I'll figure something out."

The call ended, and Lithia felt a new wave of helplessness wash over her. If Reyes expected her to let her friends die, she clearly had no idea what Lithia was like. Reyes was right about one thing, though. There was no way she was getting out of this room. What good was she here? She wasn't actually helping her friends. There was no one out there who could help. Kai and the others were in the middle of defending themselves. The Ficaran guards wouldn't make it out the door. Maybe up the stairs and down the ladder? She was about to send them when Oberon and another guy joined Kai to flank the Sugians. Maybe Kai would be available to—

"Wait a sec. Where's Brian?" she muttered to herself. "Oberon and that other guy just got back." He couldn't be dead, could he? Oberon would have said something. It was easy enough to find out. "Brian, where are you?"

"The living quarters."

"Dione and Bel need your help," she began, then hesitated. "Why? Why are you still there?"

"I got injured. But I'm fine, really. Where are they?"

She thought about asking for details and trying to judge whether he really was fine, but would it matter? If no one helped Bel and Dione, the Sugian would get them. Lithia linked her two other friends onto the call. "The three of you can manage the Sugian together."

"The four of us," Brian replied.

"No, just three," Lithia corrected him with a grimace. "Jonas didn't make it."

"It's still four," Dione said. "You're with us too."

Something about hearing the words come from her best friend made all the difference.

"All right," she said. "Let's get you out of there."

27. BRIAN

"Where?"

Of course he would go to Dione and Bel. He'd figure out a way to help them.

"Comms building. They're in the basement, and the Sugian is trying to break down the door."

"But they hunt in pairs, right?" Brian said. "Where's the other one?" He headed out into the rain. The light rain dampened his fresh clothes, but the downpour that had soaked him through just twenty minutes ago had ended. The storm had left its mark on the ground in the form of muddy puddles and slick patches of grass.

"We never saw a second one," Bel said.

"I think its partner was the one that got into the server room and cut the power," Dione added.

His shoes were still soaked, and they squelched against the saturated ground. He was running, albeit slowly, and the effort was dizzying. He lost his footing, slid onto his left side, and braced himself with his hands. Pain roared through his body, and he hissed. Their line was open, so everyone heard.

"You okay?" Lithia asked.

"Fine, just slipped in the mud," he replied.

"How injured are you?" It was Dione this time.

"It's not bad."

"Lithia?" Dione was asking for corroboration.

"I don't have eyes on him. I can't tell."

Dione sighed. "Brian, we need to know so we can plan around your strengths and weaknesses."

Brian grimaced again as he stood up, his mostly dry clothes now coated in mud down one side. "I hate it when you're right. Oberon and Cam left me behind because I'm not much use right now. My right shoulder hurts too much for me to hold a gun steady and fire more than one shot. I might not be able to shoot at all, or I'd have to use my nondominant hand. I don't think I could handle the recoil. Breathing hurts because of some shallower scratches on my chest, but that's bearable."

"Brian, you can't help us like that!" Dione fussed. "Trouble breathing?"

"Not trouble breathing. It just makes the scratches hurt. There's a difference." He tried to sound calm and confident. It was a persona he'd put on so often back on Kepos that he was pretty sure it was his real personality now.

"There's no choice," Lithia said. "No one else can come get you."

"I'm almost there anyway. I'll distract it, and then you can get out," he said.

"Then what?" Dione said. "It eats you first, then has us for dessert. We need a better plan than that."

"We'll be ready," Bel said. "The second it's distracted Lithia will tell us, and maybe we can get a few shots in before it leaves the hallway. It will be easier to aim if it has limited room to maneuver."

"We'll have to kill it immediately. It can close the gap between us in seconds," Dione replied.

"That's the plan then," Bel said.

"Brian, it must have heard you. It's headed in your direction!" Lithia said. "Bel, Dione, GO!"

Brian, who had just entered the comms building, reacted quickly. He slipped into the corner behind the door. The door itself was battered and barely on its hinges, but it was enough to act as a barrier between his body and the Sugian claws. The Sugian smashed into the door, knocking Brian's head back against the wall. The blunt force blurred his vision, and his shoulder screamed in pain as the door pressed hard against him under the Sugian's weight. He was sandwiched between the door and the wall, trapped in a tiny corner with his agony. Somehow, the gun was still in his left hand, but his arms were pinned back against the wall.

A shot rang out, and the Sugian screeched.

"Bel, you'll hit him," Dione warned.

They were here. That last attack from the Sugian had knocked the door completely off its hinges. The weight lifted from the door, and Brian pushed it off himself. They were under attack.

"Brian, get out of the way!" Dione shouted.

Barely able to think for the pain, he half crawled, half rolled over the threshold back outside. He heard the girls loose a stream of shots and crawled a few more feet from the door, hoping none of the bullets would ricochet. One of the girls screamed—Bel from the sound of it—but so did the creature. Maybe it was wishful thinking, but the alien scream sounded worse.

Suddenly, the Sugian staggered backward into view, framed by the open doorway. Brian didn't hesitate. He stabilized his gun the best he could and emptied the weapon with one continuous yell as he fought against the pain boiling in his shoulder and chest and head. He hoped it was enough. The Sugian staggered forward toward him, and Brian let the gun slip from his fingers. Maybe Dione and Bel would be able to escape after all, even if it was too late for him.

Then the Sugian collapsed a few steps away, splashing his legs with mud when it fell.

"Brian!" Dione rushed out and tried to help him to his feet, but it hurt too much.

"Just give me a second," he said. Dione got behind him and propped him up to a sitting position. He leaned back against her, catching his breath. "You're sitting in mud, and I'm bleeding all over you."

"I don't care. I'm just glad you're alive."

Dione was warm, and after another minute, that warmth gave him the energy to get to his feet. Or maybe it wasn't warmth. Maybe it was love. Could love do that? He chuckled, then groaned at the pain. No, that was probably just a side effect of getting the crap kicked out of him. With the Sugian dead, they took cover in the comms building to regroup.

"Here, sit down," Dione said, helping Brian into a chair by the controls. Bel was sitting there, too, bleeding from a scratch on her arm. It didn't look bad.

"I think I've got it," Bel said. "With Zane's help."

"Really?" Dione asked.

Brian followed her gaze to the flashing light. "Got what?" he asked.

"We're about to find out," Bel replied.

Brian really, really hoped that it was good news.

28. DIONE

Dione pushed the button that Bel had indicated, and a message began to play. She recognized her father's deep, authoritative tone immediately, and tears welled in her eyes.

"Kai, we'll be there in a few more hours. Keep my daughter safe. Keep yourselves safe. Keep it safe." The message cut out.

"That's it?" Bel asked.

"Is that not enough for you? He's coming. They need to know." Tears were streaming down Dione's cheeks, and Brian reached out a hand to her, wincing as he did.

"That's not what I meant. Just... details would have been nice."

"He got Kai's message, and he's on his way. Doesn't change anything."

"Actually," Lithia broke in on their manumeds, "it does. Now we have an ETA. Reyes heard the message. We're broadcasting it to everyone in the base. A little hope can go a long way."

Sure enough, her father's voice played again from their manumeds. Shortly after, Kai sent out his own message to everyone.

"Time to fall back to the bunker. Now that we know Marius will be here soon, we can wait it out until he arrives."

Then Reyes took over, giving out commands. "Oberon and Michele, pull out of the stairwell now while you've got the chance. The Ficarans can stay right outside until everyone comes back. Kai, your group needs to hold the main door so Dione can get back."

"She can take the ladder," Kai interjected. "Oberon holds the stairs, and we go support him."

"I don't think Brian can climb the ladder," Dione said.

"I don't think we can hold the door. We're a bit trapped here if I'm being honest."

"I'll climb the ladder," Brian said. "It will be fine. We'll come back in through the rooftop door, then back down the stairs."

"We'll keep the stairs clear," Oberon replied. "They can't get in here without opening a door and giving away their position. That, along with the auditory disruption to their camouflage, gives us the advantage."

Dione heaved a sigh. "They make it sound easy."

"Maybe we should hole back up in the basement," Bel suggested. "Might be safer than trying to get back into the building."

"Only if a Sugian doesn't find us down there," Dione said.

"We're better off with the others," Brian said. "I'm out of ammo, and I doubt you all have much left either, after all the bullets you put into that Sugian."

Bel nodded. "You're right about that. I guess it's settled then. We go back."

"We go back." Dione echoed her words, but her mind was far away. This was the right choice, but damn was it going to be hard getting back there.

The rain had stopped, but they were all wet to some degree.

Brian's whole back was covered in mud, and Dione wasn't much cleaner. Bel was more wet than muddy, but by the time they'd squished their way to the ladder, their shoes and calves were coated.

"Brian, you go first," Bel said.

He didn't even argue, as if he had a point to prove. Dione watched him grip the ladder with his good hand and keep his weak arm low and close to his body for stability, rather than climbing up normally, reaching with one arm after the other. Good arm, feet up, stabilize with bad arm, then reach up with the good arm again. He was nearly two meters off the ground and Dione was just about to follow him, when his foot slipped out from under him while he reached up. His weak arm was unable to take the sudden strain, and he fell back to the ground, splashing them with mud and groaning.

Bel cursed under her breath.

"This isn't going to work," Dione said, helping Brian back to his feet.

"I know," Bel said.

"We have to go in the front," Dione said. "I don't care what they say. There's no other option."

She called Kai. "We can't get to the roof," she said. "Brian can't climb the ladder. We're going in the front entrance."

"I don't recommend it," Kai said grimly. "We've already retreated to the stairs."

"The remaining Sugians are gathering off the main hallway. Kai's people caught them by surprise and killed three, but I think they're regrouping," Reyes said.

"Trying to. Some of them are trapped on different floors," Lithia said.

As they approached the building, the low, menacing Ven growls coming from inside grew louder. Even though Dione knew it wasn't real, every hair on her body stood on end. The reaction was visceral, and somehow it made perfect sense that the Sugians couldn't camouflage while the sound was playing. It made it impossible to think or concentrate.

Reyes's calm voice exuded authority. "There are four in the main hallway now, but a few are positioned by the doors on other levels. They know you're all in the stairwell. You've got to get back inside the bunker."

Oberon objected. "My students are not—"

"Not in immediate danger. You are. Retreat now," Reyes commanded.

Dione's heart pounded in her chest. She exchanged a look with Bel, who had the sense to ask Lithia what was going on.

"The Sugians are about to attack the people in the stairwell," Lithia answered.

"Give them a few more minutes," Oberon pleaded.

"Come on," Bel said, running away from the building's door in the opposite direction of Oberon and the others who needed their help.

"Where are you going?"

"To get an SUV."

"Why? A car isn't safe from the Sugians."

"We don't have a lot of ammo left on us. Those hallways looked pretty damn big to me," Bel replied.

"Oh," Dione answered.

"I'll drive," Bel said.

Brian kept pace with them, asking his question to Dione as they entered the vehicle. "What exactly are we doing?"

"I think we're driving into the building," Dione replied, buckling her seat belt.

"I was afraid you were going to say that." She heard his seat belt click in the back seat.

Bel's voice was calm. "Lithia, I need you to remote start our car. We're coming in."

"Which one?" she asked. "There are a bunch."

"I don't know!"

"I have an idea," came Lithia's reply. Moments later the engine of every vehicle in the lot vroomed to life, headlights illuminating muddy patches of grass. The lights made Dione realize how dark it really was.

"Here we go," Bel said, maneuvering them out of the lot along the gravel drive until she veered toward the building. The doors were already broken open, but it was going to be a tight squeeze. Bel didn't hesitate; she exceled at real-time decisions. She pressed on the gas, and the SUV burst into the hallway, losing both of its side mirrors in the process.

"The Sugians are in the stairwell!" Lithia said. "Hurry!"

"We're here," Dione replied.

Bel honked the horn, but that was unnecessary. Half a dozen Sugians appeared from around the corner, summoned from their battle in the stairwell. The Ven growling over the speakers filled the hallway, rattling Dione. She felt it in her gut, but the Sugians must have as well. Their ghastly white skin occasionally flickered with colors and patterns, but these were not disorienting. They were unable to hold their camouflage. Bel accelerated and rammed right into them. When Bel hit one, the airbags deployed, and the Sugian's body slammed into the windshield, sending a starburst of cracks across the glass. The vehicle was wedged at a slight angle in the hallway, but the driver's side had a clear pathway to the stairwell.

Dione felt dazed. From the back seat, Brian was shouting at

her. Bel was holding a hand to her own head. Dione remembered where she was and what was at stake. She unbuckled her seat belt, then Bel's. Brian was dragging Bel out of the vehicle and toward the stairwell. Dione scrambled across the front seats to Bel's open door, about to follow, when a Sugian leaped over the hood and blocked her only escape. She pulled the door shut, conscious of the fact it would only protect her for so long.

"Dione!" Brian tried to run back for her, but Kai and Oberon grabbed him.

Good. Brian didn't need to die too. Oberon had one arm around his waist and was pulling him back into the stairwell. Back in the direction of safety. The Sugians pursued them, and Dione sat frozen in the car, unsure of what to do. She couldn't follow them with the Sugians in between.

One especially ugly creature had flared its mouth flaps in frustration, revealing a bill strong enough to pry apart Ven plating.

"Di!" Lithia's voice grounded her. "Di! Di, listen!"

"Lithia."

"Run for that lab door. You can make it if you go now. Go!"

Dione's bad leg was stiff, but the adrenaline made the pain that had crept back up on her unnoticeable. From the stairwell, Oberon fired at the Sugian pursuing her. It stumbled and screeched, and her lead grew. She slid across to the other side of the vehicle, threw open the door, and sprinted toward the lab. She heard the Sugians scrambling to get around to the side she was on, and she chanced a backward glance. Oberon had fallen, but he was still firing, and she watched him take down one of the Sugians. The other he'd only injured had recovered and was closing in once again.

"Keep moving!" Lithia shouted. Dione looked forward and focused on just one voice: Lithia's. "Go, go, go, RUN!" Dione reached the lab and pulled the door closed just in time. She heard a mechanical sound, which she figured was Lithia remotely locking her in.

"Thanks," Dione panted. "Now what?"

"Brace the door," Reyes said.

"With what?" Dione looked around.

"We don't have eyes in the room itself," Lithia said. "Anything heavy that you think you can move."

Dione looked around. Near the door was a large cabinet, two meters tall, not attached to the wall. Without thinking, she began to pull it down. It wouldn't budge, so she pulled harder. She jumped back out of the way as the heavy wooden cabinet fell across the entryway, blocking the door from opening inward and preventing her from getting out. One of the cabinet doors swung open as it crashed, sending out a number of glass beakers and vessels that shattered from the force of their fall. Shards went everywhere. Dione stumbled as she tried to avoid the glass and ended up falling. While most of the glass containers had been empty, a few were not, and now the clear contents of one was soaking into her already wet clothes.

"What was in this cabinet?" she said. The stench made her gag, but she was more concerned about dangerous chemicals. She stripped down to her tank top and was about to remove her pants when the response came.

"Ven essence."

Dione refastened her pants. "That's it? Nothing dangerous?"

"No, just disgusting," came the reply.

"That's for sure." She sighed as she remembered the tracking squirrel that had marked her when they first landed on Kepos. That stench was a delicate perfume compared to this. She gagged again and stepped as far back from the broken glass as she could. There were a few scratches on her forearms and the palms of her hands from her fall, but she was okay. She collapsed into one of the chairs in the lab, her leg throbbing and heart pounding as the adrenaline began to wear off. She was safe for the moment. From the sound of the things the Sugians weren't pounding on her door.

Then the dread hit her. Of course not. Why would they chase her? They'd already combed the building for useful tech. They'd looked everywhere, except for one place. The bunker. She could hear the gunfire, but it sounded distant. She had mostly tuned it out during her own flight for survival, but now she needed to know.

"Lithia," she said, "did everyone make it back?" The last she'd seen of Oberon, he'd been on the ground, but still fighting. Brian and Bel had been dragged out of sight into the stairwell.

"No," came her friend's solemn reply. "Not everyone."

29. LITHIA

Lithia was still processing it.

The door had opened, and the muffled gunfire was suddenly louder. Her hands had started shaking, and they still hadn't stopped. A couple of Ficarans who had opted to stay in the bunker were at the door, ready to cover for the group of people retreating into the room. Michele came through first, propping up an injured fighter. Then Bel and Brian, followed by two more from Kai's security team. Then the Ficarans who had been guarding the door from the outside slipped in, followed shortly by Kai. The second he was in, he shouted for them to close the door. A Sugian paw blocked them, but Kai pulled a knife and stabbed it. The appendage and the knife were pulled back, and the door shut. Reyes sealed them all in the bunker. The front doors were still broken and wide open.

Lithia had been watching the door, not the camera, but it only took a moment for her to realize that Oberon had not made it back. She checked the screens and saw him, or rather his body, prone and eerily still. She didn't believe it, though. She had to be wrong.

She looked up again toward the door. Bel had her small, tattooed hand pressed against the door, and tears streamed down her face.

Brian reached out to comfort her, but Zane was back on his feet, looking pale as ever. He pressed his hand over hers, still on the door. He pulled her into an embrace, and that was when Lithia knew it was true. Oberon was dead.

"Lithia," Dione said, "did everyone make it back?"

"No, not everyone," Lithia said. She struggled to say the words out loud, and her voice broke in the middle. The shaking in her hands had become a tremor throughout her body. Then Brian was there, holding her hand, steadying her. He was good at that. He had held her in his arms after Roy and just let her cry. Tears wouldn't come this time, though, and she was denied that relief. Instead, all of the pain was caged inside her, pushing against her ribs and sending her heartbeat into a pounding fury.

"Lithia? Who?" Dione croaked. "Please." That last word was a whisper.

"P-Professor Oberon," Lithia said.

"Oh," Dione replied. "Oh. I just—I need a minute." Her friend ended the call.

Lithia imagined Dione sitting alone in a lab, drenched in Ven essence, trying to believe that Oberon was really gone.

"It's not fair," Lithia said. "He wasn't a soldier. He was our teacher. He never signed up for this. And we gave him such a hard time."

Brian shook his head. "He understood. He was so proud of you all. Everyone could see it."

Lithia didn't have the words anymore. Reyes was still monitoring the hallways, and Lithia convinced Brian to go get some medical treatment.

The Sugians took shifts assaulting the door. The pounding was rhythmic, and soon the pounding was in her head, like the sound was contagious.

Lithia pressed her fingers hard against her temples. "Why don't they use explosives or something?" she asked.

"It's not their way. They enjoy using their brute force and do everything in their power to force situations where they can use it," Reyes said.

"They don't need it," Kai said. "They used some device on the main door, but either they can't or won't use it now. They're probably enjoying the scent of our fear as they bang against the door."

"Brutes. Just like the Vens," Lithia said. "They were made for each other."

"We're getting a transmission," Reyes said, routing it directly to her earpiece. Lithia struggled to comprehend the grin that spread across the woman's face. Oberon was dead. How could anyone be smiling? Reyes called across the room. "Michele, it's Marius! He's making his approach."

"It's about damn time," she replied. Lithia found the source of the voice and watched Michele and a few of the others getting patched up by the doctor and other volunteers.

The door began to shake on its hinges. "Or maybe it will be too late," Lithia muttered.

Reyes took Lithia's hand in her own and fixed her with a stare. "When your hope is gone, the battle is lost. Hope is action. Hope is the fight."

"What do we do?" Lithia asked.

"We protect the virus with our lives. It's the only chance we have to stop the Vens and the Sugians, and if the Sugians get a hold of it…"

Reyes had finally confirmed what their group had suspected.

Lithia took it as another sign of how dire the outlook was. "The Sugians don't know what it is, do they?"

"Not exactly," Michele answered, approaching with a grim look. "That's probably why they've only sent a small scouting party. They might have come here hoping to find other tech. When they find a rich food source, they reproduce rapidly. They might have been looking for ship repair nanotech. We do some of that work here too. I'm worried they figured out what we were working on, or came here after hearing rumors to see if they were true. If they find out, our plan fails. We could go back to the drawing board, except there isn't time. If we fail, there will be a long, bloody war, and a lot of humans will die. Too many have already died. The Sugians will spread like locusts."

The door shook again and creaked under the weight of the massive monster trying to force its way in. Lithia felt the despair creeping in. The fear. The absolute certainty that the Sugians would break down that door before reinforcements would be able to get there. They were close, but not close enough. That made the loss even more bitter, the taste of false hope more acrid than if the Sugians had devoured them all by surprise.

Her manumed buzzed with a message from Dione. Instead of replying, she called her best friend.

"Dione, I don't think we're going to make it."

"What? My father's almost here."

"'Almost' only counts in horseshoes and hand grenades." It was something one of her old teachers used to say.

The door groaned again, loud enough that Dione must have been able to hear it. "Is that the door?"

"Yep. Everything tonight has been a waste."

"No, Lithia, no." She heard Dione sniff, and even though she couldn't see her friend, she knew she was crying. Tears pricked the corners of her own eyes, and she fought against surrendering to them. "Don't you dare give up. You are going to make it."

"This whole thing was pointless. The Sugians are going to break in here, kill us all, destroy the nanotech virus, and then destroy humanity. We're just the beginning." Brian was frowning at her, but she could see in his eyes that he agreed. He wouldn't say it, but she knew. Dione's optimism hadn't fully converted him. "I should have been out there with you. Maybe then…" Maybe what? Even if Oberon had survived, he'd be trapped in here with them now, his death merely postponed. Could she have single-handedly made the difference and killed the seven Sugians that remained outside pounding against the door?

"No, Lithia, it wasn't pointless. You saved me and Bel when we were trapped. No matter what happens, that mattered. You matter, and I'm not going to let you think like this. Not now."

"Di, I—"

"Shut up and listen to me. When you hang up, go get a gun and get ready to fight. If I have to come down there, I will."

Lithia chuckled through her tears. "We don't need you to come down here. You'll just die too. If you stay up there, the Sugians may even forget about you and let you live."

"I smell overpoweringly of tasty, tasty Ven. I don't think they'll forget about me."

The door groaned and buckled again.

"Tell my family I love them, Di," Lithia said. "You were right. The fight matters. Even when you lose, the fight always matters, and I'm not giving up."

30. DIONE

After Lithia ended the call, Dione felt numb. She didn't know what to do. She didn't even know what she *could* do.

She was just one person, unarmed and trapped.

No, not trapped. She could get out of here. Sure, there were no windows, and a heavy cabinet blocked the door, but Zane's words from months ago had stayed with her. She had to play to her own strengths in order to find a solution. She could unblock the door if she worked smarter, not harder.

Ignoring the glass and spilled Ven essence, she began to empty the cabinet, throwing heavy folders and books out of the way. The wooden frame itself was heavy, but once empty, it would be much easier to move.

She didn't know how much time was left before the Sugians got into the bunker or until her father made it to the building itself, but she wouldn't sit and hide while her friends needed her, no matter how much her hands had begun shaking. She pulled out one of the cabinet shelves that had come loose when she toppled it to the ground and used it like a lever to create enough space for her squeeze in between the door and the cabinet. The side of the door that opened was still blocked by the cabinet, but there was just enough room on the other side to squeeze in. Using the shelf as a lever, she braced her back against the door and pushed with her legs. The whole thing slid a couple of centimeters away from the door.

The shot the doctor had given her had all but worn off, and fire shot up her bad leg from her calf to her knee. Her whole body shook in response to the pain, and she had to rest a moment. It was working, though, and that was all the motivation she needed. Every centimeter she gained, the easier it got to push, and the more it hurt.

Dione was almost there. She only needed one more brief rest when she heard a few gunshots from deeper in the building, then nothing. Those were warning shots. Time was up. The Sugians were almost in.

With a scream of pain and desperation, she pushed again, forcing the fallen cabinet back. Her leg was throbbing. She opened the door as far as it would go, and it stopped short.

"I don't know how I'm gonna get my big head through here," she muttered to herself. The narrow gap she'd managed to gain would have to be enough. She sent one arm through, sucked in her stomach, and turned her head to the side as she squeezed through the gap. Her head did get stuck, but a few small adjustments later, she was out. The pain in her leg made it difficult to stay on her feet, but she stumbled around the SUV in the hallway toward the stairwell. She saw a large rifle on the ground near a dead man. One of Kai's security guards. There was so much blood on the floor, but she pushed the thought from her mind.

"Approaching facility," came a voice on her manumed. Her father's team.

She heard a few more cautious shots from downstairs and knew she couldn't wait. Dione heard Kai's voice give the reply. "If you don't bloody hurry, there'll be no one left to save."

Dione grabbed the gun and ran down the stairs, only one thing on her mind. *Distract them. Distract them just long enough.* Even as she accepted the fact that this would be the moment she died, she tried to convince herself that there was some hope. Maybe it would be quick.

Dione opened the door and stepped into the hallway just in time to hear a resounding boom. The bunker had been breached. The Sugians were visible thanks to the Ven growls over the speakers, and she saw several cross the threshold into the bunker. Gunfire, screams, and shouts erupted from the room. There was a moment of confusion in which two Sugians held back. They didn't have hackles like a dog, but their posture changed, as if they had perceived her as a threat.

The Ven essence. They must have smelled it on her, but when they turned to face the threat, they were halted by the fact that she didn't look like a Ven. In their moment of confusion, she opened fire. A few rounds hit her targets, but they rushed toward her before she could think to retreat. One of the Sugians tackled her to the ground. Everything hurt, and she closed her eyes, not wanting a close-up of a Sugian mouth to be the last thing she saw.

The sounds that followed confused her. A bang, another different bang, shouting, heavy steps, more shouting. Then the Sugian's weight was no longer pressing down on her. That weight was replaced by strong, human hands shaking her, pulling her. She opened her eyes to find a heavily armored man pushing her into the stairwell. From there, another pair of hands pulled her back, finally wrapping her in an embrace.

"Dione, you're alive!" The man's voice was thick with emotion, but she recognized it immediately.

"Dad?"

"I'm here. We need to get you out of here, though. My men will handle these Sugians."

He pulled her up the stairs, and whatever adrenaline her body had been using to keep going was fading fast. The battle raged below, and the inhuman screams sent shivers down her spine. They'd gone up several flights when a familiar shape captured her attention.

"Oh, god! Oberon," she whispered, collapsing to the floor next to the body.

"Dione, come on. It's not safe here." Her father tried to pull her to her feet, but she wouldn't budge. Instead, she sobbed over the body of the professor. Her mentor, her inspiration, was now a bloody mess. She was glad for the tears that obscured her vision, preventing her from seeing his wounds too clearly. After a few minutes, she wasn't just crying for Oberon. It was for everyone they'd lost, everything that had happened to them. It was finally over, but too late. Would this victory be enough? Had Oberon's life, and the lives of the other men and women who had died, served a purpose? She needed to know. She needed her father to tell her that whatever these people had been working on was worth dying for. She wanted to ask him, but she didn't have the breath to speak. Not yet. Only the shuddering gasps that broke up her sobs.

Voices crackled over her father's manumed, but she couldn't process it. She tried to steady her breathing, but in another few minutes, Lithia and Brian were on either side of her. Lithia wrapped her in an embrace, and the two of them wept together. Brian stayed close and radiated comfort like a fire on a snowy day. The Sugians had been defeated.

Her father crouched down to their level and lifted the two girls up. Brian stood as well. Her eyes stung from crying, but she could see the sorrow in her father's eyes.

"I'm so sorry that you ended up here for this," he said softly, pulling her into a hug and kissing the top of her head. He didn't show affection often, not like this, and it made the pain somehow sharper and duller at the same time. "We'll get you home," he replied. "We'll get you all home."

Not Oberon, Dione thought. Her father was looking at Lithia and Brian as he gave his promise, and Dione saw the confusion distort his features.

"Lithia, your parents will be glad to know you're safe. I've been keeping them up to date on every lead I had, but you"—he nodded at Brian—"you're not one of the students. And you're not one of the scientists who worked here."

Brian straightened and nodded at him. "I'm from Kepos. It's where Dione and Lithia ended up after the Ven attack."

"Kepos?" Her father eyed Brian with suspicion.

"It's a long story," Dione replied.

***

The next few hours were a blur. The Sugians were all dead, and they didn't have the nasty habit of coming back to life like the Vens. Apparently Colonel Park and Kai's teams had killed and wounded enough Sugians that her father's small team had been able to handle them in the bottleneck outside the bunker door. His men were elite soldiers, yet one was killed and another was injured. They all ended up on the colonizer, though her father was busy coordinating with his men and Kai and Michele. They all took time to clean up, but Dione didn't want to be alone. Brian, as if he could sense it, appeared at her door, his right arm in a sling. He wrapped her in a one-armed hug, and she felt like she was already home. When had that happened?

"I love you," The words came instinctively, but she meant them. She blushed. "I'm sorry it took so long to say it back."

"What do you mean?"

"You've been saying it a while now, and I never let you know how I really feel about you."

Brian laughed and pulled her in for a reassuring kiss. "I haven't been waiting for some grand declaration. I didn't know it was a big deal, though now some of those movies you showed me make a little more sense. Love isn't words. It's actions, and whether you realized it or not, you've been telling me you love me ever since we got stuck on Jameson's nightmare island and you helped me find my dad."

Dione thought about it a second, then shrugged. "Huh. I guess you're right."

"But it's still nice to hear out loud sometimes," Brian added, flashing her a silly grin.

Despite the uncertainty of the budding war and the profound loss she felt whenever she thought about Oberon, she was glad for this understanding with Brian.

31. DIONE

After a quick shower, Dione had passed out in her old cabin on the grounded colonizer. The battle had lasted through the night, and she probably would have slept through the afternoon if her leg hadn't woken her. Maybe Dr. Philips or her father had something for it.

She had no idea where the doctor was, so she headed outside to her father's ship. It was much smaller than the colonizer and could probably only carry two dozen men.

As she approached the ship, angry voices drifted through the humid air. She recognized Kai's accent and her father's frustrated tone.

"Take that monstrosity back home? You can't be serious, Marius!"

Monstrosity? Were they talking about a Sugian corpse?

"There aren't a lot of options," her father replied. "A Sugian warship is on its way. Those scouts got the word out about what's really here. This ship's too small to carry everyone. I'll take the kids. I'm not letting Dione out of my sight."

"I'm not the one who lost the Fleet ship that was supposed to come and get us!" Kai fumed. "You were supposed to bring a small army, not a handful of soldiers."

"You're damn lucky we managed to escape at all. Look around, Kai. You're rescued. I have the authority to commandeer that colonizer. The jump drive works. Take it to Pajyt and call for a transport from there. I'll tell the chancellor to expect your call."

"Pajyt? It would take three weeks, closer to a month, I bet, to get there."

"The colonists don't seem dangerous," her father said.

"I'm not worried about the colonists, fool! It's the Vens. The Sugians."

"Nothing as far in as Pajyt has been so much as scouted."

Kai gestured wildly. "Excuse me for thinking that might not be the case after a month's passed."

"Then stay here. I'll be advising whoever is the captain of the colonizer to leave before nightfall."

Dione saw her opportunity. "Oliver Caldwin, Brian's dad. He and Oberon shared the responsibility, but the ship belongs to the colonists. The Keposians."

"Dione—"

"You won't have to commandeer it either. I suspect he would happily offer passage to anyone who needed it if you asked nicely and gave him your word that the ship, their one valuable possession, would remain theirs."

"Then I'll try asking," her father replied.

"None of that changes the fact that I don't want passage on that old death trap," Kai said, pointing an accusatory finger at the ship.

"It's not so bad," Dione said. "In fact, I'd like to remain on the colonizer. I don't know how the others feel, but—"

"Absolutely not. That's not negotiable," her father said. "You're coming with me."

"Then so is Brian," she said.

Her father sighed. "I can see you're… fond of him, but he should stay with the other colonists."

"No. This might be the only chance he has to advocate for the other Keposians."

"I'll set up a time to meet with this Oliver fellow once the colonizer reaches Lavinian."

"Oh, let the boy join you, Marius," said a new voice. Michele was approaching, arms crossed. "He might surprise you. These colonists will be interesting companions, Kai."

"We're not flying that space junk, Michele," Kai insisted.

"Yes, we are. Our people are packed and on board, and if breakfast was any indication, our trip to—hmm, let me guess. Takuv? No, Pajyt!—will be the closest thing you've had to a vacation in a long time."

"Dione, get the other students."

"And Brian, if he wants to. The trip to Lavinian will be enough time to explain everything."

"We're not going straight to Lavinian," her father replied.

"Right. You've got to deliver the nanotech virus to the right people. I doubt we're going to use it ourselves, or you'd never insist on bringing me along."

Marius Quinn stiffened, then glared at Kai and Michele. "What on earth did you tell her?"

"Nothing. She and her friends put the pieces together, and when a band of Sugians is trying to kill you, priorities shift a bit." Michele shrugged. Dione admired the power in that one gesture.

"I'll get the others," Dione offered.

"And I'll join you for a late lunch, Kai. They have this delicious purple fruit you have to try." Michele led the grumpy man toward the colonizer, and Dione followed, trying to hide her limp from her father's scrutiny. Maybe she would find Dr. Philips before she told the others about their new ride home.

***

Medicated once again, Dione found Zane alone in his room.

"Oh, I thought Bel would be here," she said, staring awkwardly at Zane.

"She's not, but you can message her."

"I will, but I needed to talk to you too. How are you feeling?"

"Groggy. What's up?" She could count on Zane to avoid small talk.

"We're leaving on my dad's ship, not on the colonizer, so we need to pack up and go as soon as possible."

He furrowed his brows. "We're leaving the colonizer here?"

"No, the Keposians are going to take the scientists in the colonizer because my father's ship is too small. He's taking us." She gave Zane the few details she knew, including the part about the Sugian ship on its way to Doran and the rendezvous to hand off the virus.

"What if I want to stay on the colonizer?" Zane asked.

"Is that what you want?"

He sighed. "No, I'm just worried that things will get out of control again."

"The mission isn't dangerous. He's just handing off the virus to someone else."

"If you say so."

"Look, I know we've had our disagreements about the Alliance, but he's my dad. He wouldn't bring us along if he thought it was

171

more dangerous than sending us home on the colonizer."

"I guess that's true. Want me to message Bel?"

"Sure. I'll stop by her room, too, just in case," Dione replied.

She said her farewell and decided to try Brian next. If Lithia was sleeping, she wanted to give her as long as possible. She needed the rest.

Brian had decided to stay in his parents' cabin after the Sugian attack. When she knocked on the Caldwins' door, Oliver answered.

"Dione, I'm afraid Brian is still asleep. Can it wait a few more hours?"

"Sure, I can come back in a bit, but it's time sensitive."

"I'm awake," Brian called from one of the rooms. The Caldwins had a family cabin that was much larger than the ones she and her friends had been using. He was still pulling on a shirt when he emerged, his long hair clean but disheveled. "What's going on?" He rubbed his eyes and stifled a yawn. "Do we need to speak alone?"

"No, your parents should hear this. My father is taking us to Lavinian on his ship after he hands off the virus to another crew."

"Who is *us*?"

"Bel, Zane, Lithia, and you, if you want to come."

"Hmm. Just me?"

"To be honest, he didn't even want you to come, but I… convinced him. Oliver, I figured you would want to stay on the colonizer. The scientists will be asking to join you," she said.

Oliver offered her a tight smile. "Michele already approached me and warned me of the Sugian ship on its way. I'm a skeptical man, but I'm not concerned about the scientists' presence. Kai is pushy, but he has no motive to try anything. Nevertheless, I'm needed here, especially without Elian." He blew out a breath, and Dione realized how close Oliver had gotten to Professor Oberon.

"I was hoping that Brian might come along and help me explain Kepos to my father. This will be the best opportunity to catch him up to speed and see what he can do about all of you and Kepos."

"I'm not sure I'm the best one for the job," Brian protested.

"Why? You've told me yourself you feel like you're a link between Kepos and the Alliance. You're right."

"I get the impression our relationship might count as a strike against me," he said.

Dione bit her lip. "Maybe, but he'll come around. You really are the best one, other than Oliver, of course, to speak with him."

Brian shifted from leg to the other, and the gesture was so unusual for him that it took her a second to realize the problem. He was nervous, and something told her it wasn't about advocating for the Ficarans. He'd been doing that his whole life. Brian was nervous to meet her dad because he was *her* dad.

"All right. I'll go. As long as you don't need me here?" He addressed the question to both of his parents.

Brian's mother had linked arms with her son at some point in the conversation, though both she and Oliver reassured him that it was a good idea.

"We're leaving as soon as everyone's ready, so pack up and meet me at his ship."

On her way to Lithia's cabin, she ran into Bel.

"Hey, Dione! Zane told me your father is taking us. What's this mission?"

"He didn't confirm anything, but my guess is that we're handing off the virus. We're not going near the Vens or Sugians. Intentionally."

"You sure? I saw Reyes getting on his ship."

"She's an Alliance soldier, right? We're probably going to drop her off somewhere."

Bel looked down and rubbed the spiral scar on her cheek. "Do you really think this will work?"

"It's better than trying to introduce a predator higher up on the food chain," Dione joked. Bel didn't laugh. She wrung her hands. "Are you okay?"

"This isn't a battle they're preparing to win. It's the whole war. I feel like your father is limping to the next exchange to pass off a baton."

"We just have to trust that the people we meet can carry it across the finish line."

"I'm glad it isn't us," Bel said.

"Me too. I need to tell Lithia."

"Right. See you soon."

A few minutes later, Dione knocked on Lithia's door.

"Come in."

Lithia had dark bags under her red eyes. She was sitting on her bed watching a movie on her tablet. The small cabin was a mess, even by Lithia's standards. Clothes, food wrappers, and empty bottles were everywhere.

"Did you sleep?" Dione asked.

"No."

"Aren't you tired?"

"I couldn't sleep."

Lithia had to be exhausted. Dione glanced at the bottle on Lithia's nightstand. Dione raised an eyebrow. "Is that what was in the crate I saw you sneaking in?"

"Not exactly, that crate was full of *vigo*, but it's gone now. This," she said, lifting the bottle slightly, "is from the storeroom."

"*Vigo*? That stuff the Keposians drink to stay on watch? But why?"

Lithia hesitated. "I have nightmares. About Kepos. And the

Vens."

"I thought they went away back on Kepos."

"Being in space brought them back."

"And the *vigo* helped?" Dione's eyebrows pulled together.

"It helped me not sleep."

"Oh," Dione said. She looked past Lithia, forehead wrinkled with concern as she pieced everything together. "Lithia, why didn't you say something? No, never mind, you shouldn't have had to say anything. I should have known. I knew something was bothering you, but I thought you were just homesick and hated this ship. I thought you'd tell me if something was wrong."

"I didn't know how."

Dione embraced her friend. She didn't know what else to do, and she hoped that it was the right thing.

"Thanks," Lithia replied. "So, did you need something?"

Dione took it as a sign she wanted to change the subject, but Dione wasn't finished. Sometimes even things that were understood needed to be said out loud. "I'm here for you. You're my best friend, and I love you."

"I know. I love you too."

Dione filled her in on the details of their departure, and Lithia lit up at the news she would be leaving the colonizer.

"I bet your dad's ship will be warmer. What kind of ship is it?"

"You know better than to ask me that. All I know is that it's called *Starling*. Can I help you pack?" Dione glanced around the messy room, unable to keep the judgment from her voice.

"And you know better than to ask me that. I'm just gonna shove it all in a bag anyway. I won't take long."

"Then I'll help."

"If you insist."

Lithia really did just shove everything in a bag, so the packing was quick. Dione pretended not to notice Lithia pick up a bottle of *vigo* before setting back down.

"I think I'll leave this here."

The two then moved along to Dione's cabin, where the packing was more organized. As she rolled socks and pants into neat piles, Dione already felt the weight of the Sugians' impending arrival. They would not arrive until the next day, though, and she suspected the colonizer and her father's ship would be far from Doran before dinner. But there was something else pressing on her shoulders, something new that she hadn't quite adjusted to yet: the weight of worry for her best friend.

32. BRIAN

Brian was no stranger to disapproving fathers. Melanie's own father had taken a while to warm up to him, and she'd been his best friend. But the scowl Marius Quinn gave him as he approached the smaller vessel made him want to dip his head and shrink below his notice. Knowing that wouldn't make a difference, Brian did the opposite. He straightened his back and greeted him. Brian was tall with an athletic build. Marius Quinn was broader and had gray mixed in with his dark hair. This powerful man didn't want some backwater colonist dating his daughter. Brian recognized Dione's intelligent eyes in her father's face, but there was little other resemblance. Despite the challenges, this was his chance to explain to Marius Quinn what Kepos was.

"Mr. Quinn," Brian said, offering him a wide smile and an awkward handshake with his left hand. His right arm was in a sling. "Thank you for allowing me to come along and tell you about Kepos despite the many other pulls on your attention."

"My time is limited, and I can't make you any promises." Marius's lips formed a thin line that reminded Brian of Victoria.

She had become a harsh leader of the Ficarans during their food shortages, and he feared that the current crisis might have warped Dione's father beyond his daughter's recognition.

"I understand."

Dione and Lithia were approaching, so he waited. He felt Marius's eyes on him, but kept his own gaze fixed on Dione. He'd helped her navigate Kepos, and she was helping him navigate the Alliance.

"Bel and Zane are already inside," Marius said.

"Ooh," Lithia muttered. "A Harker model. This is going to be fun!" She winked, then headed inside.

"Let's go." Brian took Dione's hand in his. Relief flooded through him, and all was right again with the world. For a little while, at least.

***

Brian paused in the corridor to watch the camera feeds. Doran was far behind them, and the blackness seemed to go on forever. He tried to imagine where Kepos was, but there was no up and down or backward and forward in space. A moment of disorientation and homesickness welled up, but he pushed it down. He would return to Kepos one day.

Brian sighed and kept moving. Marius had invited them all to breakfast, and he didn't want to be late. There weren't many others on board: Marius's two remaining soldiers, Reyes, and half a dozen crew and technicians. This room felt much more like a dining room than a mess hall, and the food was also very good, though not as good as what his people had prepared on the colonizer.

Marius addressed the others as they gathered at the table. "I contacted all of your parents to let them know that you are alive and will be heading home soon. I'm afraid there was no time to receive any replies."

Brian realized Marius must have known a great deal about each of them, yet nothing about him. The man had been looking for his daughter, and therefore the others, so he had investigated every lead, every family tie each of them had. That still hadn't led him to Lithia's grandmother, Miranda Min, and her arrival on the planet Kepos. He had seemed genuinely surprised to hear the planet's name when Brian mentioned it.

"And you, young man," her father said, turning to Brian. "Where did you say you were from?"

"Kepos."

"The Alliance doesn't have records of a planet called Kepos. Does it have a proper name?"

"I'm not sure what makes something a *proper* name, but I don't know of any other name. We all call it Kepos."

"You've got records," Lithia said. "In the restricted archives. Would you like its catalog number?"

Marius raised his eyebrows at her. "And how would you know what's in the restricted archives?"

"I looked," she replied.

The frown on Marius's face deepened, and Dione stepped in. "Maybe we should just start at the beginning."

"That sounds like a great idea," he said.

Dione took over. She started with the Ven attack on the *Calypso*, but got choked up as soon as she got to the part about leaving Oberon on the ship. "I thought he was dead." Brian, daring Marius's disapproval, reached out to squeeze her hand.

Bel picked up the story, explaining her infection and what Zane found out about the planet Kepos from the space station that was orbiting it. Lithia and Dione took turns talking about what happened on the planet—meeting Brian, helping the Ficarans, Lithia getting kidnapped by the Aratians—though they left out a lot of the details. They also avoided any mention of Miranda Min. Then they got to the Ven attacks on Kepos.

"You flew a Ven ship?" Marius asked, incredulous. "How? Human physiology is incompatible with Ven ship controls."

"But Ven physiology isn't," Bel chimed in. "All you need is a Ven arm."

Brian suppressed a smile when the man gaped at Bel, a small teenage girl, who spoke so casually about Ven dismemberment. Apparently Dione wasn't the only one he underestimated.

"I'm sorry for everything you all have been through," he said. His gaze nearly burned a hole in the table as he was lost in his thoughts. He started to turn to his daughter but stopped himself.

"So you were trapped there, but found an old colonizer. Why wasn't it broken down? I've never seen one of these old models intact before. They're designed to be converted into integral parts of the settlement."

Dione and Brian exchanged a look, but Lithia rolled her eyes and spoke first. "Are you going to tell him about the dragons, or do I have to?"

"No, I'll tell him." Dione continued, once again leaving out some of the details. A lot of them, actually, but she hit the highlights: finding Brian's dad, the colonizer, and narrowly escaping the dragons with a bad burn.

"This is quite a bit to process," he said, shaking his head.

"Are you going to tell us about the mission?" Dione asked.

Her father wrinkled his forehead. "I have. We're handing off the Doran project to someone else."

He gave her a faint smile, but Dione's hand was balled into a fist in her lap. "And the nanotech virus?"

"What virus?" he replied.

Even Brian doubted himself for a few seconds. Had they really seen evidence of a nanotech virus? Was there an alternate explanation they'd failed to realize? No, Reyes and Michele had all but confirmed it. The corner of Marius's mouth twitched, and Brian knew. Her father was lying to them.

"The one you're going to use to infect the Vens and then the Sugians," Zane said. "We can show you the proof, if you want, but it doesn't change the fact that you're using nanotech illegally. It can't be used in any biological applications, and a nanotech virus is a violation of that."

Marius Quinn's jaw clenched for a fraction of a second before he went on the offensive. "I don't know what you think you've found, but this sounds more like a wild conspiracy theory than anything else. I can see how you feel about the Alliance, Zane. I wish you trusted us to do the right thing."

"Like you did the right thing for the Rim? Like you did the right thing for outer planets like Campos?" It was Bel this time.

"Zane, Bel, just leave it," Dione said.

"As little faith as you may have in the Alliance," her father said, "this plan is our best chance to minimize human casualties. Lithia, if you'd give me the designation for Kepos, I'd like to do a little research of my own."

Lithia complied, though she seemed a bit wary, as if she were seeing a side of her friend's father she wasn't used to. Brian's impression of Marius hadn't much improved, but he could see both versions of the man, the one Dione defended and the one Zane condemned.

As soon as Marius left the dining hall, Zane spoke. "He's lying. You know that, right?"

"I agree," Brian said. "He's trying to pretend it's all in our heads."

"I know," Dione said softly. No doubt she was thinking up excuses for her father—she tried to see the best in everyone—but Brian was glad she kept them to herself.

Lithia crossed her arms. "He probably wants us to pretend Kepos doesn't exist since, according to the Alliance, it doesn't. He'll probably make you dump Brian over there and send him and the rest of the Keposians back to Kepos, never to be heard from again. Plus, having his daughter nearly killed by Vens—and Sugians—doesn't exactly play well into the narrative of trusting the Alliance to protect everyone."

Protecting everyone was always a narrative, never a reality. Nevertheless, Brian thought that Marius Quinn was trying. With the vast array of resources available to the Alliance, even illegal ones like prohibited uses of nanotech, they could save entire worlds. Zane and Bel might question it, but Brian saw its potential.

33. LITHIA

It was late, but that didn't matter. Lithia and the others had important business together. There was a knock at her door. Dione.

"Come in," she replied. "You're late."

Her friend stepped inside and the party was complete. Dione took a seat on the floor between Brian and Bel.

"What are we doing tonight?" Dione asked. "Your message was cryptic."

"Yes, I think we'd all like to know," Zane said.

Lithia pulled a small bottle of Keposian booze from its hiding place. "We're going to remember the professor."

Dione shook her head. "Can't this wait?"

"It can, but I—" Lithia didn't know how to explain it. "It's this thing they did on Kepos. They celebrated the dead right after it happened. They celebrated life, and that's what I want to do."

"Okay," Dione sighed, taking a seat on the floor and stretching out her leg.

Lithia set her bottle on the floor and went to grab a small stack of cups, which she placed next to the bottle.

"We're gonna drink to the professor," Lithia said.

"Where did you get this?" Brian asked.

"The storeroom on the colonizer. It's not especially well guarded." Lithia pulled off the lid and poured enough to cover the bottom of each cup. "Just one drink." She hadn't been able to sleep after surviving the night with the Sugians, so she'd planned this memorial for the next opportunity.

"What is it?" Dione asked, wrinkling her nose.

"It really doesn't matter, does it?" Lithia said.

"I guess not."

Lithia raised her cup. "To Oberon."

"To Oberon," the others replied, clinking their cups against her own.

"He caught me skipping class once," Lithia said. "I went to get ice cream with Caden Reed and a few other upperclassmen. He gave me a zero on the day's assignment and told me not to skip his class again. I was so mad, but the next week, he brought our whole class ice cream and made a joke about having to keep us interested."

"Wait, that ice cream thing was because of you?" Dione asked, wide-eyed.

Lithia nodded, and the stories continued. Even Brian had fond memories to share.

"I've been thinking about it," Dione said, slowly rotating her cup with her fingers. "We were lucky to get the extra time with him when he showed back up on Kepos. What if we wasted it? I think he spent a lot of our time there mad at us. Or at least mad at me."

"No, Di, not mad. The professor was like a cicada exoskeleton."

Bel groaned. "Lithia, no. I see where you're going, but—"

"I'm going to use a biology metaphor in his honor, Bel, and you're not gonna stop me." Lithia's voice was firm, but the laughter in her tone brought a smile to the others' faces. "We were outgrowing him, and he didn't know how to cope."

"But he was proud," Brian said, staring into the bottom of his cup, as if deciding whether or not to pour himself another. "I promise you that. He was so proud of you. Especially you, Dione. I'm sorry you couldn't always see it like I could as an outsider."

There were tears in her friend's eyes, and then Brian started singing. Lithia had hoped he would. It was the same song they had sung back on Kepos at the Field Temple, the night that Victoria had returned with crates and crates of food stolen from the Aratians. The night they danced and drank and honored the dead from the first Ven attack. This was before the Vens had driven them to the Mountain Base and before she had left Roy to die. Before she had found her cousin, Cora, weeping over Will's body. Before they had found the Green Cloaks lying in pools of their own blood. Before the nightmares. That night had been one of civilized grief, almost as if it had been choreographed. It felt simple and manageable, and she wanted that feeling back, just for a few minutes.

She joined in with the melody, and he switched seamlessly to the harmony.

Sow their kindness with your hands
Plant it in the ground to bloom
Chirp their laughter from the branches
Sing away the heavy gloom
The loved are never truly gone
Let their light in you live on

Take the loaf and pass it 'round,
Then pour a glass to wash it down—
A toast to friends! A toast to blood!
We trees who all survived the flood,
Let's drain our cups; sate our roots;
Endure to bear tomorrow's fruits.

Lithia closed her eyes and felt the weight of her sadness pour out of her and into the song, like the release of a pressure valve. This was what she should have been doing all along. She opened her eyes at the end of the song. Zane's face was streaked with tears. Bel was pressing her small hand against the scar on her cheek, as if remembering Oberon through their shared spiral mark. Dione was sobbing silently into Brian's shoulder. Lithia wiped a few tears from her own eyes, suddenly exhausted.

"I think it is time to get some rest after all," she said. They cleaned up their modest memorial. Dione lingered after the others left.

Dione hugged her, pulling her tight and crushing her ribs uncomfortably. "Unless you object, I'm staying with you tonight. I'll pull a mattress from an empty room and sleep on the floor. I know I can't stop the nightmares, but I can at least be here for you now."

Lithia searched for the words to object, to demur, but they wouldn't come. She didn't want to be alone tonight, so she squeezed her friend back. "Thank you."

34. BRIAN

B rian woke to a loud noise that he eventually recognized as the door buzzer. According to his manumed, he hadn't slept through breakfast, and no one had messaged him. Plus, his friends usually knocked.

He opened the door to find Marius Quinn fully dressed and at least two cups of coffee into his day, if Brian had to guess.

"Hello, Mr. Quinn. Can I help you?"

"Dione isn't in her room," the man said, peering past Brian into his small cabin.

"She's with Lithia," he replied.

"Why is she with Lithia?"

"You'll have to ask her that. But since you're here, we can schedule a time to talk."

Marius frowned but said, "My office. One hour."

"Thank you."

Now that he was awake, Brian thought he might as well get dressed and get some food. His shoulder was already feeling a little better. One of the Alliance crew had smeared the wounds with some ointment that promoted healing. He wished it would work on Dione, but they'd given her an injection like Dr. Philips. He arrived outside Mr. Quinn's office a few minutes early and was let in promptly. The two exchanged polite greetings, and then Marius leaned over his desk. "Let's get to the point. Why did you want to speak with me?"

"Kepos would like to join the Alliance."

Marius shook his head. "I've looked into your planet, Kepos as you call it. It belonged to a biogenetics corporation, but the scientists were recalled due to the Ven threat. Unable to capitalize on the experiments it was running, the company went under shortly thereafter. There were also some ethical questions surrounding their experiments. The planet itself was deemed unsafe after they tampered with it, and it was removed from the general records so no one would ever colonize it in the future."

"Well, that didn't stop Jameson. One of the scientists came back," Brian said. "He brought a colonizer full of people and kept them in the dark about the rest of humanity."

"If there really are only a few thousand of you, we might be able to find you a suitable location. After the past few months, some places have suffered significant losses."

Brian held up a hand. "You misunderstand," he said. "Not many people want to leave Kepos. Despite its flaws, there's a sense of hope there that hasn't been so strong in a decade. People are rebuilding, together, with the wool finally pulled from their eyes. We took a risk leaving Kepos, but we want to join your Alliance as citizens, and we have the authority to petition for Kepos to be recognized as a protected planet."

"Kepos is outside the Bubble. We would have to evacuate its people."

"I was led to understand that the Bubble wasn't physical, rather simply a border you could enforce."

"That's true, but there's a lot of bureaucratic red tape holding that boundary where it currently is. Plus, with the looming war, our resources are already stretched thin."

The Keposian cocked his head to one side. "Looming war? Didn't you develop a nanotech virus on Doran that would prevent this tragedy?"

"There is no magical weapon. There is simply a plan, the tools to carry it out, and a good chance of saving lives." Marius peered at Brian, his eyebrows pulled together. "Your planet is full of hazards, is it not? Relocation could be a boon for your people."

Or yours. "It is, but there are hazards on any world."

Marius nodded. "I'll cut straight to the point. Until the Vens and Sugians are taken care of, Kepos will not be allowed into the Alliance. I doubt you could even get it recognized as an independent planet in the current climate. Unless…"

Brian crossed his arms. "Unless what? What could we possibly have to barter with beyond a few interesting crops?"

"There are a few technological and genetic feats accomplished by the corporation that was running experiments on Kepos, and their notes and any results would be of value."

Brian laughed. "You want the dragons? Or maybe the giant sundew?"

"It doesn't matter what we want."

"Of course it does." Brian felt the pit of his stomach drop. "You want to know more about Sam, the human turned AI." They couldn't legally perform nanotech experiments on people. Even though they were already meddling with a nanotech virus, they could justify it as necessary. He guessed human experimentation was too taboo. They might not be able to make their own human-AI hybrid, but he doubted there was anything to stop them from studying what they found.

"That would make bringing Kepos into the Alliance more of a priority," Marius continued. "Either way, we'll grant you and the others still on the colonizer refugee status and provide you with food, housing, and education while you get on your feet. With the exception of the two surviving Green Cloaks."

"What?!" Brian straightened in his chair, resisting the urge to stand. "What happens to them?"

"They'll be held in comfortable accommodations and given thorough evaluations. If they're deemed safe, they'll get refugee status as well."

"So you're going to lock them up?"

"Haven't you kept them locked up too? You don't trust them, yet you expect me to let them loose in my city?"

"We don't have the resources you do! And we've been relaxing our restrictions on them as we've talked to them more. Most of them died protecting others on Doran, as well as your precious weapon, during the Sugian attack. That has to count for something."

"It may count for something, but it doesn't count enough."

Brian steadied his voice. "What if they don't pass these evaluations?"

"They'll be sent back to Kepos."

"They're outcasts on Kepos. They have a chance to start with a clean slate on Lavinian."

"Yes, they do. A chance."

Marius folded his hands in his lap and looked Brian in the eye.

"Tell me more about these Green Cloaks. Traitors. Why did you bring them with you?"

"They would have been killed on Kepos."

"I gather that you were afraid the opposing faction on Kepos would kill you if they caught you violating their borders. Execution seems well within your customs."

"I meant killed by a family member wanting revenge, not executed. You think we're barbarians," Brian said simply, leaning back in his chair.

"I didn't say that."

"You didn't have to. Mr. Quinn, you wield more power than I can fully grasp and have access to resources and information I don't even know exist. I struggle not to hate the Green Cloaks. I saw what they were responsible for. But you have the chance to help them and educate them. Besides, only two of them survived. The others died fighting off the Sugians. You can get them evaluated, treated if necessary. We knew a lot of things on Kepos, but our growth was stunted for a long time. We brought them with us because we couldn't leave them, and Dione convinced me that they would have a chance in the Alliance. Where others have doubts, Dione truly believes in you. Don't let her down."

"She's going on to great things, you know."

Brian's smile widened into something genuine. "Yes, she is."

"I don't want her to get distracted."

Brian understood the dig, but brushed it off. "Then let's hope your weapon works. I can personally attest that growing up in a war zone has a profound effect on one's hopes and dreams."

Brian got up to leave, but stopped and turned at the door. "You should trust her with the truth. She knows you're lying about the virus, and all it does is hurt her."

Once Brian cleared the threshold of the office, he clenched his fists. There was hope for Kepos, and even the Green Cloaks, but Marius Quinn was too distracted to help. For now.

35. LITHIA

The vessel they were on, *Starling*, flew like a dream. It was warmer and cozier than the colonizer, and as a Harker model, it also held a little mystery Lithia planned to unravel later.

If she had to endure one more obstacle between her and home, she was glad it was this ship. She wasn't happy about it, but the devastation she had felt after their futile visit to Campos was not there. Being on *Starling* felt like she was standing on a threshold with the wild expanse of space on one side and the comfort of home on the other. She could hang on a little longer.

"Marius," she began.

"That's Mr. Quinn to you, Lithia."

"You're ready to tell us about some super-secret virus, and you're insisting I call you Mr. Quinn?" Whatever Brian had said to Dione's father that morning had made an impression because he'd summoned them to his office after dinner with the promise of the truth.

"Yes," he deadpanned.

"I'm beginning to think Zane has a point when he talks about messed-up Alliance priorities."

An elbow found its way into her side. "Lithia," Dione hissed. Lithia sighed. For the sake of Dione, her best friend in the whole galaxy, she would let it go.

"Fine, *Mr. Quinn*. What the hell is this nanotech virus master plan?"

Marius shot her an exasperated look, but they settled around the conference table. Everyone was grumpy and serious, but Lithia? She was just done. With all of it. With the Vens and Sugians and spaceships and government conspiracies. She wanted one thing, and that was to go home.

"I've decided to share a few details with you. I'm bringing you with me, and I want you to understand the impact that your actions—and sacrifices—here on Doran may have on the war.

"You all have been gone for four months now, but Lavinian and Alliance space are not the same places you left. The Ven attacks were ramping up when you departed, but things became extreme in the following weeks. We assumed that was what had happened to you, but we never found any wreckage. Then the Sugians showed up. We'd sent a team to rendezvous with them months ago, even before your trip. We received word the day you left that our delegation had been killed. I never should have let you go, but most of the attacks were on the Rim, far from your planned course. I was wrong.

"Soon after, the Sugians arrived. Really arrived. Based on our intelligence, we thought they'd attack the Vens. They did. And then they attacked a human colony. There have been countless attacks on the Rim and inside the Bubble in the past month. People on the core planets are starting to worry. The high-profile disappearance of my daughter and her classmates didn't help."

"But Lavinian is safe?" Lithia asked, suddenly far more

apprehensive than she had been just a few minutes ago.

"For now. But the outer colonies aren't. We need to protect them, but our resources are spread too thin. The Vens and Sugians design situations that force us to engage on their terms, which is largely hand-to-hand combat. The two species have evolved to slaughter each other, and one species is clearly more effective than the other. The Vens, whom we've always considered the hunters, are actually the prey. The Sugians, well, they're terrifying. They won't be satisfied with a few raids like the Vens. The Sugians are hunger incarnate. They are cruel and vicious, like the Vens, but they come with an appetite. We've managed to learn enough about them through Ven records and their own to discover that, centuries ago, there was a virus. It decimated the Vens, contributing to their low numbers today, and nearly spread through the Sugian population at a devastating rate."

"So you reproduced this virus?" Dione asked.

"In a way. We used it as a baseline and made modifications. For one, we've made it impossible for it to infect humans. It essentially self-destructs in the human body."

"Sounds like a great idea," Lithia chimed in.

"We can't effectively fight them. Their ships are capable of defending themselves, and the devastation that they bring in combat, well, I don't have to convince you of that. You've lived through it somehow. Many haven't. Alliance citizens and Rim colonists alike. If we don't take drastic action, and soon, we'll lose our window of opportunity."

"What's the plan?" Lithia asked. "You said it would only add a few days." She could handle a few days, but just a few.

"Yes. Very soon, we'll be sending a team armed with virus nodes to each of the two Ven Citadel ships," Marius said.

"What's a virus node?" Lithia asked.

"It's a small amount of the virus that will replicate, thanks to the nanotech aspect of its design, and spread widely before causing symptoms. The virus needs to infect the whole Citadel ship very quickly. By planting a few nodes on each ship, the virus will be able to replicate and then infect the Vens on a large scale. They'll also stop the Ven ships, making them an even more appealing target for the Sugians. The window on this operation is small. Once the window opens, it closes in a day or two."

"Why now?"

"There could be other opportunities, but the longer the Sugians have to get a foothold, the worse the outlook. If the Sugians experience such a decisive victory against the Vens, they'll come after humans even more vehemently. We've run hundreds of scenarios, and this is our best shot. The human cost if we don't is unacceptable. For all the grumblings from dissidents about the Alliance's callous attitude toward Ven attacks on the Rim, we do care. I can speak for myself when I say I care, and I wouldn't be here right now if I didn't think this was humanity's best chance. If this doesn't work, the war will be long and bloody, and I can't even promise you we'll win it."

His final words ushered in half a minute of silence as everyone, Zane and Bel included, processed the implications of his words.

"Why are you telling us?" Zane asked.

"It's clear to me that you all are bright young people who have been through more than your fair share of horrors, which is why I was brutally honest with you."

"And if we share this information?" Zane again. "Combining nanotech and a virus is extremely dangerous, not to mention illegal. We've seen what nanotech can do."

Marius sighed. "There's been an emergency exception."

"So you can change the rules whenever it suits you?" Bel said.

"Frankly, yes. We are the Alliance, and we will do whatever is necessary to protect humanity. I expect the vids will have worked it out before we make it home. That's the only reason I can tell you any of this. If they make me a scapegoat for this, I'll still have no regrets."

Lithia looked more closely at the lines that marked his face and felt bad for the man. The lines seemed deeper than she remembered, as if a few months had aged him years. She wouldn't point that out to Dione, though.

Were her own parents just as worn out? What about Grandpa Min? Lithia needed to get home, not sit around waiting for some virus to take care of the aliens that had invaded humanity's corner of the galaxy. This need to get home was programmed into her, and the closer she got, the stronger the pull. Talking to Reyes had helped, but as long as she was out here in space, unanchored, untethered, she wouldn't be able to heal.

36. DIONE

Brian hadn't told her much about the meeting with her father, but she could tell it hadn't gone well. There was still time before they got to Lavinian. They were close to the rendezvous point to deliver the nanotech virus. Once her father finished his mission, he would take them all home. They'd be safe in their beds in the capital city of Haisukia while the war wrapped up far, far away.

Even as she imagined spending the evening on her patio under a blanket with a book and a mug of hot chocolate, dreaming about getting into the right university, winning accolades in the scientific community, the fantasy seemed wrong. Hollow. How could she pretend that nothing was the matter when she'd survived the Vens and the Sugians? How could she rest knowing how much was at stake?

Even though her father had told them about the very real threat, and despite her own personal encounters with each vicious alien race, none of it had truly prepared her for the scale of what was going on. There had been battles, terrible showdowns among the Alliance, the Sugians, and the Vens, which left innocent human colonies in ruins.

"Dione?" Her father's deep voice on the other side of the door shattered her introspection.

"Come in," she replied.

She sat back down on her bed and rubbed her ruined calf. It hurt especially badly after the exertion of the Sugian attack. Her father crossed the threshold and scrutinized her.

"I know I've been dire and grim, but now that we've got the weapon, I have hope. Hope that we can save Lavinian and the Alliance."

"Just the Alliance? All of it? How many worlds have been attacked? We saw Campos for ourselves. Does this plan include saving everyone?"

"The plan doesn't concern you or your friends, Dione."

She raised her voice. "It concerns every single one of us."

He perched at the end of her bed. "Sometimes you can't save everyone. Allocation of time, energy, and resources is an essential component of government."

"Are you even going to try to save everyone? Or has a computer somewhere determined it's impossible?"

"The Alliance—"

"No, Dad, you. Have *you* tried?"

"Yes. That's what this weapon is all about. I fought for this," he said, gritting his teeth.

"What did you say to Brian?" she asked, hoping to catch him off guard.

"He has nothing to do with this. Is that why you're so hostile?"

"What did you say?"

"Nothing. I didn't give the Keposians the answer they were hoping for, but I offered them what I could both personally and

198

professionally."

"Sometimes our best isn't good enough," Dione said, staring at a scuff mark on his shoe. "Let's hope that in the case of the nanotech virus, the Alliance doesn't fall short." She pulled her legs up and winced.

"I'll have the medic teach you how to give yourself the injections for your leg. Once we're back on Lavinian, I'll schedule consultations with the finest surgeons in Haisukia."

"So I'll get a complete muscular reconstruction for my leg while the people on the Rim are decimated."

"Your pain won't make things on the Rim better, so I'm not sure why you're bringing them into it. Once you can walk properly again, you can move out to some dusty rock and pick bottle borers off Lernian squash plants."

Maybe she would. "Did you know that Lernian squash plants can grow to the size of a house if properly maintained and trellised?" It was the kind of factoid she often regaled—and annoyed—him with back home.

"I didn't, no." He gave her a proud smile, and for a moment, she forgot what the stakes were.

***

Despite being more comfortable and warmer than the colonizer, *Starling* lacked the older ship's charm. Her father mostly kept to himself, communicating with his bosses via a portable NRT comms box. They were so expensive that most ships didn't bother with them, but Dione guessed on a mission like this, the Alliance could afford it. The boxes weren't quite as fast as a proper NRT comms arrays, but they could still pass messages with an insignificant delay.

There were also two Alliance soldiers on board who mostly kept to themselves, though they occasionally entertained Brian's questions. The others had gone with Oliver on the colonizer, and one had been killed outside the bunker by the Sugians.

Dione had pulled Brian into her cabin to interrogate him about his meeting with her father.

"I really don't want to talk about it, Di," he said. "Your dad tried to help, I think."

"Then why are you so mad?" she replied.

"I'm not mad. Not exactly. He's not going to help us get Kepos included in the Alliance."

"Why?"

"The political climate. As long as the Vens and Sugians are a threat, they're not going to be extending their protection any further. I want to see how this mission goes. If things are looking up, he might be more willing to help. And Kepos will be safer if the virus really does decimate the Vens and Sugians."

"He did offer us refugee status, except for the Green Cloaks. Asher and Jill will be tested and interviewed or something to make sure they're not a threat."

"That bothers you," she said.

"How much faith do you have in him? Do you think he really means to help them, or will they get shipped back to Kepos no matter what?"

Dione bit her lip. "I don't know. I've been wrong before, but I think my father would have told you if he had no intention of helping Jill and Asher. He wouldn't agree to bring them all the way back to Lavinian just to send them back to Kepos right away."

"They still feel like my responsibility. I struggle with my feelings about them. The ones that died? I don't mourn them. I didn't wish for the Sugians to kill them, but I can't make myself miss them."

"No one says you have to," Dione replied, gently touching his forearm. "It's admirable that you're advocating for Jill and Asher, but it's not your job. You've been kind enough to take it upon yourself, and you're doing everything you can. They're not so blind anymore that they can't see and feel your kindness. That counts for something."

Dione gave him a reassuring hug, but Brian sat in silence, lost in thought.

37. BEL

Bel and the others had spent their days on *Starling* resting and recuperating. She was surprised by how quickly Brian and Zane were healing. Brian had been sling-free for two days already, and Zane's headaches had been less frequent and severe. Even on a small, fast ship like this, the trip took almost a week, and when they arrived, no one notified her. She only realized it when she was walking back to her cabin and noticed the large, red star, still small and distant, but much bigger than the usual pinprick of light. They were in orbit around a brown rock. This must be the rendezvous point, though there was no indication that anyone else was here yet.

Two hours later, Bel was in the mess hall, staring at the external camera feeds and into the dark void of space, when a small, dark-green ship filled the emptiness in an instant.

Vens.

She sprinted down the hall to the office where Mr. Quinn was calmly taking a call.

"Ven scouts!" Bel shouted, gesturing at the monitor.

He had been staring at the very same ship on his screen, but the look he now gave her was one of annoyance, followed by resignation.

"We recovered that Ven ship, Bel. Those are our people on board. I'm speaking with them now. I apologize. I realize that despite the secret nature of this mission, I should have told you to expect the arrival of Ven scout ships."

"Ships?" she asked, dumbfounded.

"Yes, one more will arrive soon."

"I guess this answers the question of how you're going to deliver the virus."

He didn't give her so much as a nod of confirmation before saying, "Tell the others that this ship will dock with us, and that another will be arriving shortly. The crews will join us for lunch."

Bel did as she was told, too shocked and relieved to ask more questions.

A few hours later, the whole gang was together for lunch, and nearly everyone on board was there too. One of the techs was eating at the next table over with Reyes, the other two soldiers who had come with them from Doran, and five entirely new faces. Four men and one woman, all with the same serious expression and tired eyes. They must have been the ones flying the Ven scout ship that arrived a few hours ago.

"The other team is late," Dione said. "I heard my dad talking to Reyes earlier."

"What are they late for?" Lithia asked.

"Isn't it obvious?" Bel said. "They're somehow using the scout ships to deliver the virus."

"Yeah, I mean, why are they late?" Lithia clarified.

"Coordinating jumps over such distances is bound to leave room for error," Dione replied.

"With so much riding on this, you'd think they would leave a few minutes early in order to make it on time," Lithia muttered.

Bel tried not to let this revelation worry her. "Zane and I were looking through some of the headlines from when we were gone. Things on Lavinian are mostly unchanged. People are hoarding toilet paper, but *they're* fine."

"But?" Dione asked, closing her eyes and breathing in.

"Things really have gotten bad. Lavinian is safe, but the Rim is a complete mess, and even Alliance colonies on the edge of the Bubble have suffered serious attacks. People are fleeing toward the core planets, though most never make it that far. They settle for other worlds that have better defenses than where they came from."

"That's good they're getting to higher ground, so to speak," Dione said.

"Yes, but to keep with your metaphor, so much is underwater, and it just keeps rising. There's nothing to indicate that the Alliance fleets are having much success against the Vens and Sugians. They've been attacking, then waiting for evacuation teams to come so they can decimate them too."

"Like an ambush?" Lithia asked.

"We already know they like fighting hand to hand, not via ships," Dione said. "It makes sense."

"The important part, the thing I'm trying to tell you, is that we are on defense, not offense. The Alliance is spread too thin to adequately fight off the enemy on this many fronts. When it was just Ven raiding parties and strike teams, they could manage the attacks and the narrative. Now, they're trying to plug a hundred holes at once on a slowly sinking ship."

"What's your source?" Dione said.

"Available data and projections. From the Malcolm Institute,"

Zane said, finally speaking up. He gave his manumed a few taps. "I just shared it with you."

"The Malcolm Institute? They're reliable."

"Yep. But the general attitude on Lavinian is that everything will get sorted out before it can really affect them."

"So no one believes how bad it is?" Dione asked, swiping through the various charts and projections.

"Not on the core planets where political power is the strongest. These outer and inner colonies have magistrates to represent them, but the power has always lain in the core."

"They're probably going to give us some fake story about where we've been to tell to the press," Zane said.

Bel crossed her arms, suddenly cold. "The Rim needs significant amounts of aid, and even evacuations in some cases, but they're not really part of the Alliance, so their needs are getting brushed off."

"Why are you bringing all of this up now? What can we do?" Dione asked.

Lithia, who had been mostly silent, spoke up. "We leave it to the people who can make a difference. We need to go home."

Bel shrugged. Truthfully, she didn't even disagree. "We just wanted you guys to know how bad it is and how bad it's gonna get. Lavinian will be safe for a long time, but if those projections are right, even being in the core might not save us in the end."

"Then let's hope that the nanotech virus will be enough."

Bel wouldn't put it past the Alliance to use the outer or inner planets as a human shield, but she was glad they were at least planning to bring the fight straight to the Vens and Sugians. If the Alliance was successful, she just might forgive them for all their previous failures. A life without the looming shadow of the Vens? She could hardly imagine it, but she hoped that others would fight for it just as much as she would.

The reserved camaraderie of the next table over was cut short when Reyes received a call from Mr. Quinn. She took it privately, but relayed information to her companions as needed.

"The other ship is here," she told the new crew, "so you'll be able to make the launch window we had—"

Reyes broke off, and her easy manner switched in an instant to high-alert mode. "One of the Vens on board wasn't dead. As soon as they initiated docking, it attacked. Come on," she said to the two other soldiers. "Everyone else stay put. You five included. You have your mission to carry out." The five new arrivals tensed, already out of their seats, but they didn't follow. They were alert and ready to respond if necessary.

"It's nice when we can actually leave this to the professionals, huh?" Lithia said, taking another bite of her sandwich.

"Lithia, now's not the time for jokes," Dione replied.

"I'm not joking. I'm tired of fighting. Bel ran into your dad's office an hour ago to tell him about the Ven scout ship outside, and he was surprised she'd bothered to let him know. He sent her away as if she'd been crazy to bother telling him, like, 'Why is it your problem if there's a Ven ship here? What are you planning to do about it?'"

Bel put a finger to her lips. "Shh." Lithia looked ready to shush her right back, but in the brief silence, they all heard it. The other table was getting updates.

"The Ven is down."

"And dead. Tripled-checked."

"Where's Fitzgerald? He called it in."

"Found him. No pulse."

"Marnet, Lee, and Tucker too."

"Rajan's alive. Come on."

The silence was easy to maintain after that. Mr. Quinn hurried into the mess and ordered them each into their cabins. The threat was over, but they were to stay put until after the mission launch in a few hours. Four of the five on the second scout ship had died. The fifth man was in bad shape from the sound of things. Could the mission be carried out by just one team? Bel hoped so. The Rim was depending on it.

38. LITHIA

Lithia had always wanted to explore a Harker model. They were spy ships in the early days of the Alliance but not anymore. Supposedly. That didn't stop Lithia from wandering around in the lower levels of the ship. She didn't expect to find anything. Secret panels and acoustics designed for eavesdropping were from a bygone era of ship design, but since there was nothing to do, she decided to nose around the ship anyway.

Mr. Quinn had told them to stay in their cabins, but he had known Lithia since she was five. He wasn't stupid enough to think she'd listen, was he? She figured she'd start by the engines. Her interest there was plausible. Plus, he'd be so glad she didn't break anything that he'd just send her back into her room and run a bunch of diagnostics.

Lithia proceeded to inspect the bulkheads for any tool marks or symbols that might give away a secret compartment. Maybe she'd find some long-forgotten booze stuffed away in a hidey-hole somewhere. The air was warmer here than anywhere else on the ship and hummed with energy. Invigorated, she kept searching for stray marks, tapping on wall panels, and generally looking like a total weirdo. Luckily, no one was around to make fun of her. The engine room didn't need constant attention, so she was alone. She had gotten a little too warm and was about to give up her dream of finding a secret passage when she heard voices. Someone was coming, and she and the others had been told to stay in their cabins. Glancing around for a place to hide before she got hauled into Mr. Quinn's office to explain herself, she noticed a tiny marking. A minuscule, asymmetrical X that looked like normal wear and tear or perhaps a stray tool mark.

Except it wasn't. Some people had a way with dogs or maximutes, but Lithia had a way with ships, and this was a sign. This ship had entrusted one of its secrets to her. She would honor that trust by using the space, assuming it was big enough, to hide from the voices. She quietly removed the panel, stepped inside the long, narrow space, and pulled the panel securely into place. Only once she was safely inside, now far too warm, did she realize the voices were not coming from the room. They were coming from somewhere else.

This wasn't just a hidey-hole. It was a listening space. That explained why she fit with relative ease. But whose voices was she hearing?

Please don't be Dione and Brian. Or Bel and Zane, she thought, scrunching her eyes shut as if in preemptive pain. A deep, familiar voice came through, crystal clear. *Holy crap, it's Mr. Quinn.* He must not have known about this secret panel. Hadn't Dione said it was a borrowed ship?

She quieted her thoughts and began to eavesdrop in earnest.

"Accurate report?" This was an unfamiliar male voice. Lithia guessed it belonged to an older man who wasn't very fun at parties.

"The second crew is dead, except for one man who is gravely

injured," Mr. Quinn said. "We suffered no further casualties on board, and the first crew is ready to go."

"Then that's it. Send the first crew and hope they succeed. Two successful missions were always statistically unlikely, according to my aides. One success is all we need to save the inner planets."

"Save is an overstatement. Two successes would significantly reduce the risk to the inner planets in our projections, but there's still the risk the Sugians will be able to reproduce too quickly with only one success. What about the outer planets? And the Rim? The very scientists who created this virus and made the mission possible were on an outer planet," Mr. Quinn replied.

"And I hope you bring them to safety as soon as the Citadel mission launches."

"Isn't there another crew ready to go?"

"No one close enough by a long shot. Everyone was deployed to other missions once both crews sent capture confirmation."

"What if we split the remaining team between the two ships?"

"It's a five-man mission for a reason. Splitting the team would make a double failure even more likely, and that's not an acceptable risk. We have reason to believe that if the Vens are unsuccessful in their next few encounters with the Sugians, they'll flee. If they do, the Sugians will have no distractions from attacking and feeding on humans."

"Understood."

"You're welcome to send your people, untrained for this as they are. How many soldiers do you have on board?"

"Three," he replied. "One of them, Captain Reyes, was familiarizing herself with the mission in order to join them, but three isn't enough, especially with so little mission training."

"You've got a couple of technicians, too, correct?"

Mr. Quinn scoffed. "I can't send them. They're techs, Patrick.

They can't fly a Ven scout ship. I know them well, and they aren't suited for a mission like this."

Lithia rolled her eyes. Mr. Quinn's assessment was reductive to say the least. With a little practice and Zane's translation program, the techs probably could.

"Marius, the timeline was tight before, but if the first crew doesn't leave within twelve hours, their window is closed. Every hour they delay reduces their chance of success by five percent. Send out the first crew, mourn the second, and be glad you live on a core planet. I want an update at the end of the day my time."

"Yes, sir. I'll dispatch the first crew at once."

The call was over, and she heard what sounded like a fist pounding against a desk. Mr. Quinn was a powerful man, but even he had masters to serve. Old, party-pooper masters.

Starling's secret compartments were awesome. This news, however, was not. She needed to tell the others and fast. She carefully left her hiding spot and hurried out of the engine room toward the cabins. She reached the hallway where their cabins were and paused. She told herself it was to catch her breath, but there was a more sinister reason.

No one else knew. She didn't have to tell them. If she explained the situation to the others, they'd want to do something. She could keep this information to herself and let the Alliance take care of everything. That was their job, right? There probably wasn't anything that she and her friends could do anyway.

Except she could fly a Ven scout ship. They'd all been on a Ven ship before. They had Zane's translation program. They weren't soldiers, but they weren't useless either. The outcome of this mission would have a huge impact on the length and severity of the war. As tempting as it was to tell no one, she knew that sharing the information was the right thing to do. They would make the decision together. She jogged the rest of the way down the corridor. Her face was still flushed when she burst into Dione's room without knocking. Dione was reading on her tablet, and Brian was watching a movie.

"Sorry to interrupt, but this is important. Where are Zane and Bel?"

Dione shrugged but put down her reading. "Why would they be here?"

"It's time sensitive," Lithia said. "We need Bel and Zane."

"I just messaged them," Brian said. "Said you needed them to come here urgently."

"Good."

"What's on fire?" Dione asked, putting her tablet down and sitting up straighter.

"Oh, just the inner planets," Lithia muttered.

"Did something happen?" her friend asked.

Bel and Zane walked through the door, and Lithia was finally able to spill. When she was through, she saw the exhaustion on their faces.

"So if both missions are successful, the war would be nearly over," Dione said. "But one failure would leave the outer planets vulnerable?"

"To say nothing of the Rim," Bel added.

"Yes," Lithia said. "And we already know that one of the missions has failed. Unless Mr. Quinn sends a team from his current crew, which he won't. It's suicide."

Her friends exchanged looks, and she could feel the tension in the air.

"You wish I hadn't told you," she said, "because now we have to do something."

Brian laughed. "A little. But that's normal, right?"

"We could talk to my father," Dione said. "There has to be someone around who can fly the ship and carry out the mission."

Zane crossed his arms, but Lithia jumped in first. "You didn't hear him. He's not going to do anything. I think he would if he thought there was a reasonable chance of success."

"We're the only option then," Bel said. "I won't give up on those colonies."

"Even if you die in the process?" Zane asked, taking her hand in his.

"I don't think I could live with myself if I knew I gave up the chance to stop the Vens for good. The Sugians too."

Lithia was certain she could live with herself. Happily. Despite the horrible images of raging Vens and wide-eyed corpses that haunted her nightmares, she would find a way to justify her actions. Even now, she regretted telling the others. "I'm tired of doing the right thing all the time," she said.

"You've done enough, Lithia," Dione said. "I'm going to talk to my father. Don't worry. I won't tell him we're thinking of going."

We've all done enough. It's someone else's turn now, isn't it? It has to be. It should be.

Lithia sighed. If only the universe worked like that.

39. DIONE

Dione believed she could help. Her father just needed another perspective to find the solution. There must be someone with military training in range.

When she neared his office, she heard angry voices in the hallway. Her father and Reyes were locked in an argument.

"You're going to give up, sir?" It was an accusation.

"There are no other options. We can't weaken the first team. If both fail, we're at square one."

"There must be someone," she fired back. "You can order the others to go. That would make three."

"I can't. You are the only volunteer, and I won't force any unexperienced crew members to go on this mission."

"What about yourself? I can give you a combat refresher on the way."

Dione tensed. Would her father volunteer?

"I'm not fit for this mission," he said.

"That's because you're a coward. Lavinian will be safe. Your daughter will be safe. That's all you care about."

Dione's shoulders relaxed. She was glad her father wasn't going on a dangerous mission, but she couldn't help agreeing with Reyes. He was a coward.

"Captain, if you'd like to go and get yourself killed, be my guest. Take the virus nodes and the ship. I'll start working on another plan that might actually work. I'm not giving up." He'd raised his voice, angered by Reyes's insult.

"How long will that take? How many more will die while you draw up another war map?" the soldier fired back. "My family doesn't live in the core, *sir*."

"I'm sorry, Reyes," he said, his voice almost too low for Dione to hear. "No one expects you to do this. It isn't your fault."

"No, it's not. But messes have to be cleaned up no matter who or what caused them. Have your crew deliver the mission supplies. I'll be busy prepping the ship. By myself."

The thud of boots was headed in her direction, and there was nowhere to hide. When Reyes rounded the corner, she locked eyes with Dione. The woman stopped once she reached Dione and muttered, "Hold him to his word, Dione. If I fail, make him find a solution."

Dione nodded, gulping as the woman resumed her march. She glanced in the direction of her father's office and heard his door close. There was no point. If Reyes couldn't convince him, nothing she could say would have any effect. She had to tell the others. If they were going to help, they'd have to hurry.

***

"The crew just left," Brian whispered. "I think that's all the mission supplies."

"Time to go," Dione muttered, leading the way.

The Ven vessel, a scout ship, was much smaller than the one that Dione had helped fly on Kepos. There were several crates that looked as if they were designed by humans rather than Vens. In the center of the bridge was a pilot chair with a large, mechanical glove shaped like a Ven claw, but black, not Ven green. Dione, Bel, and Brian stopped halfway across the control room, but Lithia headed for the chair. As soon as she reached for the claw, a voice came from behind them.

"Don't touch it." The captain was standing off to the side, obscured by one of the consoles. She hadn't looked up from her tablet.

"Reyes?" Dione called, clunking noisily into the ship. "Reyes, you can't do this alone."

"You can't be here. I'm leaving as soon as I hook up the jump automation program whether you're still on board or not."

Dione shrugged. "That was easy. We're here to help."

"I've changed my mind then," Reyes said. "I'll stun you and drag you out if you don't leave. I don't have time to waste."

"We're not wasting your time. We can help. We've been on Ven ships before."

"I'm not taking you or your friends with me. Marius would kill me." Reyes thought for a moment. "Though I suppose I might die anyway. I won't condemn you all too." Reyes drew a stun pistol and pointed it at Dione. "Please leave."

"No." Dione folded her arms. "We know what we're signing up for."

"Do you?" she said, scrutinizing the four of them. "We're going into a Ven Citadel ship. A hundred things can go wrong. The Citadel might raise an alarm, the Vens could board us, we could get killed planting the nodes. We could fail to plant the nodes. We might even get there too late to do anything about it."

"We know the most important part. The outer planets and the Rim need both teams to succeed," Bel said.

"Someone has to do it," Dione added.

"I wish it weren't us, but no one else stepped up," Lithia said. "You're the only other volunteer."

"What about the other two soldiers that came with us?" Bel wondered out loud.

"They weren't interested, and they have their reasons."

"We can stun you," Brian offered. "Then you couldn't be blamed. You'd have to let us borrow your—"

An alarm went off in the ship.

"What the—" Reyes glanced at the tablet she'd plugged into the console. "The hatch… Where's your other friend? Zane?"

Dione took a deep breath as fear settled in her stomach. Zane had closed the only way off this ship. There was no backing out, and the finality of it caused her resolve to waver momentarily.

"By the time you get the door open, it will be too late. You don't have a choice. You'll either be taking us unconscious," Bel said, nodding to the stun pistol, "or awake. We'll be much more useful awake. Do you really expect to do this by yourself?"

"Do you expect you can do it without any training?"

Lithia laughed. "At least we all agree that this is stupid and dangerous."

"But necessary," Reyes said, her voice low. She stared in Lithia's direction, then shook her head. "My family lives on one of the outer planets."

"Kepos, my home, is outside the Bubble," Brian said.

"The Vens destroyed my family and my home on the Rim," Bel said. "No one else should have to go through that."

Dione watched the emotion on Reyes's face as she glanced around at each of them. Then she clenched her jaw, cursed again, and lowered her stun pistol. She'd made her decision.

"Fine. We're probably going to miss the window anyway." Reyes paused to read a message on her manumed and clenched her jaw. "Marius is onto you. If he has the sense to check the security feeds, then we don't have much time."

Lithia snapped into action at the same time as Reyes, who reached for the glove. Lithia grabbed it first. "Zane, do you have the holo interface with the translation program?" He handed over their makeshift Ven translation device.

"You think you're flying?" Reyes said.

"No offense, but I spent time on Kepos studying the Ven ship that was still there. This one's a little different, but I can already tell what I need to do to undock."

"Good. Because I'm not set up for the jump quite yet." She didn't waste time glaring at any of them but stooped to pull a pair of goggles from her bag.

"Take these," Reyes said, offering them to Lithia. "Translation goggles."

Lithia put them on and gaped in wonder as she swept her gaze across the room. "Neat! This is a lot easier than using the holo interface."

"Good," Reyes said. "Hurry up." She pulled another pair of translation goggles from the bag on the floor, as well as a tablet. She rushed to plug the tablet into the navigation console.

Lithia inserted the claw into the base and tapped on the panel a few times. After a short delay, Dione felt their ship detach from *Starling*.

"So, have you ever jumped a Ven ship before?" Reyes asked.

"No. Where are we headed?"

"Just put some distance between us and Marius's ship, and I'll take care of the coordinates. All the mission gear is here. There's more than just the nanotech virus." She hesitated, glancing up at Dione. "How much did your father tell you about the mission?"

"He didn't give us the flight plan, but we know we're delivering virus nodes to a Citadel ship," Dione said.

Reyes nodded. "Lithia, when you see it, let me know."

"See what?"

"Something that looks like it would initialize a jump." Reyes tapped away furiously on the screen until Lithia reacted.

"Think I just found the jump button," she said. "Are we good to go?"

"Wait, what's that flashing thing?" Dione asked Lithia, pointing to a light on a wall panel.

"Incoming transmission. Probably your dad." Lithia gave a small shrug. "Want me to answer it?"

Dione shook her head. "No, it's better if we don't hear what he has to say and then ignore it. Just one more strike against us."

"You sure?"

Dione took the brief opportunity to remind herself that there was no going back to normal, to the way things had been. The future she had once painstakingly planned for herself, that her father had cultivated, too, was gone. The universe had changed. She had changed. She and her friends would see this through to the end.

"Yeah," Dione replied. "Let's go save the whole Alliance, not just the core."

Right before the jump, Brian stepped closer and intertwined his fingers with hers. Bel and Zane were locked in one of their meaningful gazes. Reyes had a hand on Lithia's shoulder, and Lithia was actually smiling. They could do this. They had to.

40. DIONE

The first jump felt less like the warm numbness she was used to and more like tiny, frozen needles puncturing her skin. By the looks on everyone else's faces, they'd been just as unpleasantly surprised.

"Ugh," Lithia said. "Everything about the Vens sucks, including their jump tech."

"Agreed." Dione shuddered, rubbing her arms to warm them up. "Reyes, how many jumps do we have to go?"

The young woman shrugged. "I don't know how many jumps, but our ETA is in a day and a half, according to this tablet. The jumps weren't programmed as set locations, just in case the plan was compromised, so Marius can't follow us."

Zane and Bel were already sorting through the contents of the supply crates. Bel pulled out a few more pairs of translation goggles and handed them out to everyone.

"These are nice," Zane said. "Way better than my translation program."

"What are you talking about?" Reyes asked. Zane showed her,

and she let out a low whistle. "Impressive for what you were working with. Maybe we'll pull this off after all."

"What exactly is the plan?" Brian asked.

"We have to plant four virus nodes on the Ven Citadel ship, one in each corner of the pyramid."

"How?"

"Stealth, Ven essence, and taking advantage of the fact that Warrior Vens don't congregate much in the lower levels."

Dione wrinkled her nose. "Ugh. Why did it have to be Ven essence?" It had taken days to fully rid herself of the stench from the jar she'd knocked over in the lab on Doran.

Bel, who was still going through the crate, pulled out a bunch of uniforms. The thick fabric was dark green, perfect for blending in on a Ven ship. "These are for stealth then?" She raised an eyebrow. "We'll have to modify them to fit some of us."

"They look warm at least," Dione said. "It was so cold on the Ven ship, especially in the vents."

"Vents?" Reyes asked.

"I assumed we'd travel through the vents. I guess Brian and Zane wouldn't fit. You might, but it would be tight with all your gear."

Reyes cocked her head to one side as if considering the idea for the first time. "That could work."

"What was the original plan?" Brian asked. "I won't be fitting into the vents, and I assume the original people assigned to this mission wouldn't have either."

"How much do you know about the Ven caste system?"

"We know about the different castes, Warrior and Worker, though we've only met Warriors as far as we know," Brian said.

"Good. There's another group, the Casteless. The sick, weak, and genetically unfit are typically euthanized, but some escape to the lowest levels of the pyramids to scavenge and die. That's why we'll be going in there. They'll be a lot easier to fend off than the Warrior Vens. The Ven essence will also make us smell like Warrior Vens, so as long as we don't get close to the Casteless, they won't want to get near us either."

Dione shuddered. She didn't want to encounter even a sickly Ven. Any Ven seemed like an insurmountable threat, and the Vens might have a very different idea of weakness than she did. She had to focus on the plan. "If there are four nodes, we'll have to split up," she said.

"This was really the plan?" Brian asked.

"The people chosen for this mission were elite. With the element of surprise and some luck, they would have been able to kill any Vens they couldn't avoid." Reyes shook her head. "They also knew it might be a one-way trip. I'm prepared to plant all the nodes myself. You didn't know the details when we left."

"I'm still in," Dione said.

"Me too," Brian said.

Lithia seemed to be zoned out for the moment. Bel and Zane nodded, but Dione wasn't completely sure if that meant they were in or out. Reyes rifled through the crate next to Bel's. At the very bottom, underneath packages of food and tools, was a briefcase. She opened it to reveal four, small metal disks, each the size and weight of a coin yet immeasurable in value—the delivery nodes for the nanotech virus.

"We need to decide who's going where," Brian said. "If we have to plant the virus nodes in each corner of the pyramid, some will be closer than others depending on where we dock."

Reyes provided more details. "Each side of the base is about six kilometers. Two of the nodes will be planted about three kilometers from where we dock, and the other two will be closer to nine."

"I can go to a far one," Dione volunteered. "I'll be able to take the ducts."

"Even with your leg?" Brian asked, his voice heavy with concern. "I'll take a far one instead."

"No, you'll be more exposed. I've got another injection for the pain I can take once we get closer. Plus, the vents may provide a shortcut. You take a closer one."

"How long would it take you to crawl nine kilometers? We might not have the time."

Reyes nodded. "He's right. Brian and I will take the other far corner. I'll be able to use the vents if necessary, and I have the most training. I assume Lithia will stay on the ship since she's our pilot." Reyes shot her a meaningful look, and Lithia nodded. She wasn't ready to face down another Ven, Casteless or not.

"I'll go," Zane said to Bel. "You stay with Lithia."

"No. Like Dione said, I can fit in the vents. I'll go," Bel said.

"Can we at least talk about it more later?" he asked.

"Sure," Bel said. "We can talk about it." Her tone gave Dione the impression that she was unlikely to change her mind.

"All right, we've got our runners mostly decided," Dione said. "We can modify the clothes, too, then get some rest."

No one wanted to go far. The ship itself was small, meant for just a dozen or so Vens. The main room was the bridge. There was another room on one wing that looked like it had been repurposed by the human soldiers who stole the ship to act as a dorm and a common area. The opposite wing had been Ven barracks, and the stench made it unbearable. They kept that section sealed. The lower deck contained the engine room and a few workstations, but Reyes assured them that they could control everything from the main room.

They decided to use the common room to get some rest. "That tablet basically has this ship set to auto, at least until we get there," Lithia said. "Then I'll fly us in and dock."

"You should get some rest too," Dione said.

"I couldn't sleep right now if I tried. Adrenaline," she replied, shaking her head. The bags under her eyes contradicted her words, but Lithia didn't look sleepy at all.

Reyes pursed her lips. "I only need a few hours of sleep. I'll relieve you when I wake and you can take a quick break, even if it's just to let your mind wander."

Lithia shrugged. "Can't hurt."

When it was time to sleep Reyes stayed on the bridge with Lithia so she wouldn't be alone. Dione and the others took some blankets into the adjacent room, each couple curling up in one of the corners. Bel and Zane exchanged heated whispers, probably arguing about which of them would be going on the mission, while Dione settled her head against Brian's chest and let his steady heartbeat drown out the whispers.

41. BRIAN

Brian awoke feeling a little stiff, especially in his shoulder, but well rested. Dione had already gotten up, and Bel and Zane were still curled together in their corner. Brian got up and went back to the bridge, where Lithia was dozing under a blanket. Her eyes fluttered open for a moment when he passed but closed again almost immediately. Reyes was sitting within easy reach of the claw glove, and she and Dione were whispering.

He lowered his voice to match their own. "Good morning," he whispered.

"How are you? How'd you sleep?" Dione asked.

"As good as can be expected. Reyes, want us to take over here so you can get a couple more hours?"

"No, I'm fine. Six hours out. I'm going to let Lithia sleep for four more if she can," Reyes said. "Go get some breakfast from the supplies."

Brian's stomach rumbled. *No objections there.*

The food was only a brief distraction, and he found that he had trouble eating as much as he normally would have. He was nervous. He'd faced so much back on Kepos, where nothing, not even the next meal, was guaranteed, but plunging into yet another life-threatening situation was not what he'd had in mind when Dione regaled him with the wonders of the Alliance and her home world of Lavinian. He'd listened to Zane and Bel's descriptions just as keenly because they saw their world differently. Their viewpoints provided balance, and he thought he knew what he was getting into. Still, Marius Quinn's refusal to help admit Kepos into the Alliance had surprised him, and his reluctance to help the Green Cloaks had angered him. Now here he was, trying to prove something so that his people could join an Alliance he wasn't even sure he wanted to be a part of anymore.

Lithia woke up long before Reyes planned to rouse her, but she still looked refreshed. Brian was surprised to see her so calm.

"Sleep well?" he asked.

"Strangely enough, yes." Lithia stretched her arms above her head and yawned. "Creepy as this ship is, the ambient noise or something is just right."

Brian shrugged. "Glad there's something good about it." Creepy was right. Everything was dark and eerily green. They had left the rest of the ship unexplored, sticking to the common room adjacent to the bridge. Even Reyes hadn't wandered far beyond her initial security checks.

Holding hands, Bel and Zane emerged from the common room and joined them.

"So, have you decided who's going?" Dione asked the pair.

"We both are," Bel replied. "We're going to do it together."

Brian could practically read Dione's thoughts as she processed their decision. She didn't like it. It was dangerous and inefficient, but in the end, she simply nodded and said, "Okay, so you're not taking the vents?"

"We're going to see if Zane can fit. It will be uncomfortable since he's tall, but he's not especially wide."

"I never thought my narrow hips and shoulders would be my best quality," Zane remarked.

"Oh, stop," Bel said, rolling her eyes. "Everyone knows your real best quality is your charming extroversion."

Everyone laughed.

For one surreal moment, Brian felt like they were back on Kepos, after the Vens had been stopped and while they were repairing the colonizer. Those had been some of the most carefree days he'd had in years. He would have them again. They all would, and this mission would give that gift to so many more. Suddenly, despite the fact they were in an alien spaceship an unfathomable distance from Kepos, he felt at home. He'd spent the hard times at the Field Temple smuggling food and people, making illicit deals and repairs, all to make life a little more bearable. This would be just like that, except now he wasn't in danger by himself. On Kepos, he had mostly worked alone, getting Melanie's help when necessary. But now? He had friends to help him.

"So Lithia stays with the ship, and we each take a virus node," Brian said. "We'll follow our manumed maps to our assigned corners, plant the nodes, and then book it back here."

"Yes, and there's more," Reyes said. "While we're on the Ven Citadel ship, we'll have to use the receiver on this ship like a switchboard. Lithia is the operator who can connect us by passing on the information. The other mission team has probably already finished, successful or not. We don't have a lot of time if we want this to work. The nodes will start replicating and spreading the virus as soon as all four are in place."

"How long exactly do we have to plant the nodes?" Brian asked.

"The window countdown says the Citadel will jump in four hours. We were behind to start, and the window wasn't large, considering the scale of our approach. But we can make it."

"What I still don't get," Lithia began, "is how the Vens will even make it to fight the Sugians. If we're spreading this virus among them, won't they start getting sick and dying?"

Reyes nodded. "The virus will replicate and spread, but it needs to be activated by a signal in order to switch on and start making Vens sick."

"How will that help? If the Vens die before the Sugians get here, they won't get the second-wave infection."

Reyes hesitated. "The nodes have another purpose. Once they detect the appropriate level of viral saturation, they will shut down the Citadel's ability to jump and leave it dead in the water."

"And the Sugians will come and find them," Bel said.

"The Alliance is helping that along too," Reyes replied.

"We should all get ready. Time's nearly up," Lithia said.

They all shuffled off to make their preparations, get dressed in their uniforms, modified or otherwise, and put on some Ven essence.

Reyes checked the tablet. "You're up, Lithia."

"No pressure," she said, getting into position in the pilot's chair. She brandished the black claw before putting it into the interface.

Brian had spent the past few years on Kepos taking risks, smuggling, to feed the Ficarans. Now he had the chance to help people on a scale he'd never have imagined possible a few months ago. That is, assuming things went according to plan.

42. LITHIA

Lithia exhaled. She felt clearer today than she had in a while. Maybe it was because she saw the light at the end of the tunnel. All of her disappointed hopes of getting home—first when they'd found Campos destroyed, then when Mr. Quinn had forced them to stay on his ship—had just extended the darkness. Yet now, as they were heading into the belly of the beast, her fingers didn't shake. This might have been better than seeing her family. This was saving her family and countless others, and she knew she could last a few more hours if it meant really and truly going home. Not to war-burdened Lavinian, but to protected Lavinian.

"Get ready," she said, clenching her fingers inside the claw. She triggered the jump mechanism with one hand and pressed a button on the console with the other. The tingling sensation started just behind her belly button and spread outward through her body like a firework, leaving numbness and pinpricks in its wake. She closed her eyes, and when she opened them again, they were in a completely new location, far away from where they had started.

A massive, green pyramid loomed on the camera feed. They

were still about twenty minutes out, and the closer they came, the more alive the massive ship seemed. The levels looked like layers of Ven plating, and all Lithia wanted to do was separate those layers and kill it. She could see a few other ships heading in: one large Invader class vessel and two smaller ones making their way toward the Citadel.

"Citadel Two," Bel said, shivering a little. "It's massive."

One corner of Lithia's mouth pulled up into a crooked grin. "The better to wipe them out. All of them."

"Let's do this," Reyes said, putting a reassuring hand on her shoulder and mounting the tablet in front of Lithia so that she could follow its directions to the correct docking station.

The Ven scout ship Lithia was piloting was precise but unforgiving. She moved them quickly toward the Citadel, and the ship obeyed so eagerly Lithia swore it could tell it was home. The bridge was quiet while she flew, and everyone's eyes were glued to the camera feeds. A small ship was getting closer, but it wasn't going to attack. Their cover was intact, and it wasn't until they were just eight minutes out that something went wrong.

"We're getting a message telling us not to dock," Lithia said, reading the incoming message as quickly as her goggles could translate it.

"Did they discover us?" Dione asked. "We can break away and jump."

Lithia kept reading, struggling to focus in the expectant silence. "No," she replied, her shoulders relaxing. "They're rerouting us to a different docking area."

"Where?" Reyes said, pulling up a 3D map of the ship on the tablet.

"Here's the designation," Lithia said, showing her the message. "Obviously, we're going wherever they tell us. Refusal would be suspicious."

"Do it," Reyes said. "We'll make it work."

Lithia shifted their course toward one of the corners of the pyramid, following the directions that the Citadel had sent. The tablet Reyes had plugged into the helm was flashing frantically, warning her that she was off course. After a minute Reyes made it stop, and Lithia was grateful for one less distraction.

The others were whispering in the background, but she tuned them out and focused on the ship she was flying. The docking would be partially automated once she got close, but she still had to make the ship respond at certain points. She'd read over the pilot instructions two dozen times in their day and a half on board, and after reading them, she'd understood why the Alliance hadn't wanted to send another team with a pilot inexperienced with Ven tech. The sequences were complicated and precise. How they'd ever learned them, she couldn't imagine, but who knew what kind of spy technology the Alliance had been using on the Vens? She was just grateful to be working with an Alliance-manufactured claw instead of a severed Ven arm. Without the prosthetic claw, she'd never have been able to make the precise movements required.

They were coming in a bit fast, but Lithia calmed her nerves and slowed the ship, bringing it in carefully. It felt precarious, but possible, as if she were stretching out her arm to set a fragile glass figurine on a shelf just a centimeter too high. She moved them forward until the Ven Citadel was a mere dozen meters away. "Initiating docking in five seconds."

Adrenaline coursed through her. She hadn't felt this alert since her last sip of *vigo*, but where the *vigo* drained her, this energy filled her, charging her up. She'd memorized the sequences, so when the first cue came, she responded. Then came the next and the next, like performing a new song at a recital. A loud thunk signaled the successful completion of the sequence.

"Is that it?" Dione whispered.

"Yes," Lithia replied triumphantly. "And you don't have to whisper."

She had done her part, and now she would help the others do theirs.

43. BEL

There was a slight change of plans. They were at a corner instead of centered on one side of the pyramid. Instead of two far corners and two close corners, they now had one very close corner, one very far, and two at a middle distance. Reyes immediately volunteered for the farthest point, which was twelve kilometers away now, on the opposite point of the pyramid. Dione and Brian would only go six kilometers while she and Zane had to travel less than one.

"How long do we have?" Dione asked.

"Three hours," Reyes replied.

"Can you make that?" Bel asked. She was strapping on her sword belt, hopeful she wouldn't need to use the thin, flexible blade. The Ven essence might be enough if the lower levels really were full of Casteless.

"If I keep moving. Set your manumeds with the time. We'll stagger our departures. I'll go first. After ten minutes, Dione and Brian will go down together and split up once they reach the lowest level. After that, Bel and Zane. You'll finish long before the rest of us, but hide out until we're on our way back. If someone gets spotted coming back to the ship and they figure us out, it puts everyone in danger. Plus, if someone needs backup, we want to be ready to assist. When everyone is in position, Lithia will call us back on board, and then we'll go. All communications go through her. If we need to relay a message, Lithia gets it and delivers it."

Everyone nodded and geared up. They each had a small spray bottle of Ven essence along with an unusual sword, which Zane had described as a glorified skewer. The long blades were thin but sharp. Despite their unimpressive appearance they were the best weapon Bel had seen so far for dealing with the Vens.

Reyes headed into the Ven ship. After an eternal ten minutes, Dione and Brian stepped forward. He kissed her on the forehead before they went through.

Then it was their turn. Bel and Zane stepped inside the Ven ship and took the ramp to the lowest level, passing no one. As they reached the lowest level, the stench of decay overpowered the Ven essence and the general sour smell of the ship. A Ven corpse lay off to one side, and a few motionless Vens were leaned against the walls. They barely moved in response to her arrival, and Bel didn't think it was the Ven essence or their dark clothing. The corridor was clear for the moment, and Bel chanced getting closer to one of the slumped Vens.

It was a lighter green, sickly and small. Its green plating, cracked in places, was thinner than that of the other Vens she'd encountered, and rather than towering over even a tall human, she estimated that it might not even be as tall as Zane. Suddenly, it flicked its eyes up to meet hers and acknowledged her presence with a weary stare. The creature didn't stir from its hunched position, attack, or raise the alarm. It lowered its gaze back to the ground, and Bel backed up into Zane, who steadied her.

A small group of Casteless scurried past them, back the way they came. She pulled Zane into another alcove, and the two headed toward their assigned location. They placed the node without encountering any Warrior Vens and retraced their steps.

All that was left to do was wait. They moved back toward the ramp they'd used to reach this level, finding a small room that may have once been used for storage. Half a dozen Casteless occupied it. Four of them slept while two huddled in the corner, softly growling to each other.

"Let's keep our distance," Bel whispered.

"We may not have that luxury," Zane replied, bowing his head toward the two in the corner.

They rose to their feet and began growling in warning rather than conversation. The sleeping Vens were stirring, and they had to act fast. Zane stepped toward the two, wielding the thin, sharp sword. With a swift stab, he sliced up at the closest one's leg. It buckled and fell, writhing and screeching. Bel turned to hiss at Zane to make it stop, but he was already sliding the blade under the hood plate and into the Ven's brain. Her attention turned to the others that were just waking. She dispatched two before they could stand, killed the third on its way up, and made short work of the fourth. By the time she returned to Zane, every Casteless Ven was dead.

"That was too easy," Zane said.

"In more ways than one," Bel muttered. She had a knot in her stomach as she glanced at the two still lying as if they were asleep.

"They're Vens, Bel. I don't care how pretty their poetry used to be, I doubt there's anyone on this entire Citadel ship who could recite a Ven haiku, let alone compose one."

Bel gave him an uneven smile. "Oh, I bet Dione could."

He smiled. "You're probably right. From how easy that was, I doubt these Vens can heal in the same ways as the others we've fought, but we should make sure."

She nodded, and they checked each other's work, flipping each Ven onto its front, inserting their blades, and slicing through anything that might be a neural connection. The effects of the adrenaline were wearing off, so she leaned against a wall and slid to the floor.

"This is the end, right?" she asked. *Lie to me. Be an optimist for once. One of us has to be.*

"I think it might be. The Vens and Sugians are so far from their home worlds after centuries of cat and mouse that I don't think they'd happen to find us again. And if this virus works the way the Alliance says it will…"

"We'll be free."

Bel had spent her whole life living in a hole left by the Vens. When she'd originally made her Ven hypothesis, she'd imagined a predator nothing like the Sugians. She'd dreamed up a race that sought to eradicate the Vens for their atrocities, not one that had squeezed the civilization out of them.

"Mother Nature is a real bitch. I almost feel bad for killing these Casteless Vens."

"Don't," Zane replied. "I'm sure it was a mercy compared to their lives here."

"I think I might feel bad for showing them mercy too. I can't win."

"Yes, you can," Zane replied, brushing her cheek with his thumb. He kissed her, something she had agreed was okay to do, but she was the one to break the kiss. Bel leaned into him, and his warmth made her hopeful.

"What if this works, and all of the anger and grief that have weighed me down are replaced with guilt?"

"Then I absolve you."

She laughed. "That easy?" Her eye caught the Ven corpses, and the smiled faded from her lips.

"Would you blame a wild boar for goring a pursuing leopard with its tusks?"

"No, but this isn't the same," Bel argued, pulling away and sitting up straighter.

"That's the trick. Convince yourself it is."

Bel hadn't found peace with the Vens alive, but what if she couldn't find peace after they were gone either? What if her future held no peace, only anger? Zane was right. Her mind was a powerful thing, and she would convince herself. *This will work. All of it.*

44. DIONE

The cold air and sour stench were familiar by now, but one thought mitigated her disgust. This could be the end of the Vens. No human would ever have to board a Ven ship again.

The hallway was clear, and they moved along until they found the nearest pathway going downward and inward. Footsteps. She and Brian exchanged the same warning with a look and dipped into a small alcove. She tightened her grip on the hilt of the slender sword, but the Ven kept walking without incident, wholly unaware of their presence. What Ven was expecting an enemy on board?

When the coast was clear, they continued down to the lowest level. Just as Reyes had said, the halls were empty. After a hard squeeze of her hand over his and a look that conveyed more than words ever could, they each headed in their own direction. Dione entered the vents and followed the map on her manumed. She was moving slowly, but it was the only way she could move in the enclosed space. The walls of the vents felt like they were closing in. Her heart picked up its pace, and she stopped to invest half a minute in calming herself. She kept going in the dark, trusting her map and the dim light of her manumed, reminding herself that she wasn't alone and that her friends were all doing their parts.

After twenty minutes of crawling, her injured calf began to ache. Her wrists and knees hurt, too, but the cold seemed to chill her bad leg to the bone and undo all the work of the painkillers. There was nothing to do but keep going. She considered leaving the vents and going on foot through the halls but quickly dismissed the idea. Even if she were warmer and it put less strain on her injured leg, the exposure was too risky. The others, quick and clever as they were, had their work cut out for them.

She got a silent message from Lithia: *Bel and Zane are finished.*

That was good news. If they stuck to the plan, things might work out. The happy thought distracted her from her pain for a few minutes, but a dark obstruction up ahead pulled all her worries back into her mind. She stopped, but the shape didn't move. She'd just passed an exit. She could back up, leave the vents, and chance the halls. The thought of being exposed in the Ven ship was enough to induce her to draw her thin sword and creep toward the dark shape. The light of her manumed was too dim for her to tell for sure, but the dark mass appeared greenish. *That doesn't make sense. A Ven could never fit in one of these vents.*

She approached the green mass and saw she'd been wrong. It *was* a Ven, but it was more dead than alive. Or perhaps just asleep. The miserable creature was small, and if it hadn't been for the green—as opposed to blue—coloring, she would have believed it to be a juvenile.

The creature stirred, barely more than a twitch, but quarters were close and Dione reacted. She slid her weapon between its plates with the ease of plucking a diseased leaf from a plant.

"What did they do to you?" she whispered as she dragged the Ven backward through the vent to the exit. *Was this creature a vestige of the Ven poets?*

While checking to see if the coast was clear, she noticed a trio of Vens huddled together in an alcove a few meters away. They saw her but didn't move. When she shoved the Ven into the hallway, they charged toward her. She frantically closed the door of the vent access and scurried away down the now-open passage, hoping those were too large to follow. A wet, ripping sound and low growls reached her, and she had to hold her breath to keep from vomiting. *No, there's no trace of poetry left in these monsters.*

They would not pursue. She kept going. A few minutes later, another silent message from Lithia lit up the screen: *Faster, Di.*

Why? Dione wrote back. Something must have gone wrong. Had Brian been caught? Had Reyes been seen?

The reply came after a short delay, and Dione understood. It was long, but she tried to keep moving as she read.

The tablet timer changed. Vens moved up their jump. You've got forty-five minutes left, not two hours. Brian is on his way back, and Reyes is planting her node. Use the corridors on the way back.

Got it. Dione shivered. Her perfect plan that maximized safety was shattered. She'd be exposed in the corridors, but if she didn't find a faster route back, she'd be left here, or worse, they'd wait for her and be stuck there too. And Reyes was already planting her node? Dione had been moving slowly, but there had been enough time. She'd been mindful of that as she proceeded.

The best laid plans. For now, she had to get to the next exit hatch, then plant her virus node. She pulled herself along more swiftly, the pain in her leg building minute by minute into agony. They could not fail. She could not fail.

45. LITHIA

L ithia's leg bounced as she monitored the progress of the mission on her tablet. Reyes and Brian were on their way back, Dione was almost to her location, and Bel and Zane were tucked away in a hiding place nearby. She'd nudged Dione along, and now she had to wait for the next check-in. A few minutes later, instead of getting the expected message from Dione, she received one from Reyes: *Trapped in a small room. Warrior Vens outside haven't moved in a while. If I don't make it back in time, leave without me.*

"Nope. Not gonna happen," she muttered to herself, getting to her feet. She'd find some gear and—

She wouldn't. She'd have to run there and back to make it in time. She would barely be able to get everyone back to the ship, and Dione still had to place the last node. What if she needed help? Lithia was her friend's only source of information and encouragement.

This realization didn't mean she'd given up. Not by a long shot. Brian was still close enough to Reyes. She messaged him.

Lithia: *Reyes is coming back down your side, but she's stuck. Needs a distraction.*
Brian: *Where?*

She sent him the details.

Brian: *What kind of distraction?*
Lithia: *Don't let them see you. Just get them to move.*

There was no response, but Lithia assumed he was too busy figuring out how to help Reyes. He would have to find something that didn't compromise their presence. If they got discovered, their mission—along with the other mission to Citadel One, not to mention their lives—was in serious jeopardy. Lithia let Reyes know that Brian was on his way, and the only reply she got was a terse *K*.

With nothing more she could do for them at the moment, she pinged Bel and Zane. They were holding position with nothing new to report.

Lithia looked over the tablet's readouts again, hoping that they would suddenly shift back to what they had been, but the timer stayed the same. When they'd arrived, they'd had three hours to complete the mission. Now, they had less than one. She'd noticed the change as soon as it had happened and wasted five minutes trying to fix the tablet before she realized it wasn't a fluke. Somehow it had detected the preparatory stage of a jump and had adjusted the clock accordingly. A ship this large would probably need a long lead time to complete a jump. Though she was glad for the notice, there was only so much she could do, and not because she was coordinating everyone. What change could any of the others make that would help them complete their mission faster?

She was about to check in with Dione when Brian sent her a

message: *About to try something.*

She held her breath and looked at the countdown clock once more. The minutes were slipping by, and a doubt stretched within her mind. Dione might not make it back in time. What then?

She sent a single word to her best friend: *Update?*

46. BRIAN

Brian had slipped through the ship, avoiding the sickly Vens. He'd found them wheezing, crammed in rooms, dead and dying in the corridors, united in their indifference to him. He'd avoided a few bands of larger Vens as they disembarked, and he'd killed a weak Ven that tried to grab him as he hid, but he'd planted his node without much difficulty. A great deal of planning and research had made this whole mission possible. Without the Ven essence and Ven ship, they never would have made it this far. Plus, a lot of Vens seemed to be returning to the Citadel ship, so their arrival was unremarkable.

He'd just started his return trip when Lithia told him Reyes was trapped. He cautiously picked his way down the corridor until he saw a trio of monstrous Vens loitering near one of the rooms. Most Warrior Vens he'd seen had marched straight for the ramps that led up to the higher—and presumably cleaner—levels of the pyramid. Having assessed his target, he retreated a little ways into a small storage room. A Casteless Ven slept against the wall, partially obscured by crates.

He didn't have much on him: his translation goggles, his sword, and an extra vial of Ven essence. He might be able to manage some type of diversion using the Citadel's systems, but that would leave evidence of their presence. When they left, the virus would keep spreading for days, maybe even weeks. If they were caught, the Vens might suspect something.

His sword would be useful, but he couldn't take on three Warrior Vens on his own even if Reyes came out to help him. That left only the Ven essence. He might be able to lure them away with it, but then they'd be chasing him…

His mind made up, he messaged Lithia, advising her that he was about to try something and that Reyes should listen for her chance. He sprayed himself once more with the Ven essence, gagging at the renewed strength of the odor. Then he stepped carefully toward the sleeping Ven, removed the lid from the vial, and dumped the remaining contents on the wretched creature. Brian left the room, hoping the Ven would be there when he got back. If he got back.

He was back within sight of the trio of Vens, but he stuck to the inner wall, wondering if they would catch his scent and if that scent would be enough of a challenge to make them pursue him. If the Ven essence was enough to keep most of the weaker Vens skittish, it might make a stronger Ven curious.

The Warrior Vens didn't budge. *The one time I want a Ven to chase me they stand around like gossips.*

The idea of Vens gossiping about the latest scandal amused him, so when he charged toward the trio, he had a smile on his face. The aggressive movement caught their attention, and just before he turned around to run back to the storage room, he called out to Reyes: "Now!"

Heavy footsteps pounded after him, but he was fast. He heard

Reyes's voice and a commotion behind him but didn't dare turn. Two Vens followed him into the storage room, tracing the strongest scent trail to the Casteless Ven that lay on the floor. One Warrior picked up the small Ven, which shrieked in alarm.

Brian slipped from his cover and plunged his sword between the back plates of one of the Vens. It fell to its knees, and he heard the sickening crunch of the other Warrior snapping through the thin carapace of his decoy.

His stomach clenched at the sound, but as the Ven he'd attacked fell forward, the other turned, tossing the Casteless Ven's corpse at him. The reeking body knocked him off balance, and he thudded onto the ground. He scrambled back, pushing the dead weight off him, narrowly dodging the Ven's claws.

The door opened, and Reyes swept in, her arm drenched in red blood. Even Brian could detect the metallic scent, so when the Ven whipped its head, he took full advantage of the distraction and sliced up into the Ven's knee. It howled in pain, and he exchanged a look with Reyes. If they didn't make this quick, he would attract others. If a Ven party docked and disembarked at the wrong place and time, they would be discovered and killed with little effort.

The two danced around the Ven, doing their best to flank it. Brian got another opportunity, but his weapon stopped short as he stabbed upward. "Third plate is fused!" he called to Reyes, who was growing pale. Her wound didn't seem life-threatening but provided one more reason to end this as quickly as possible.

He felt a presence at his back and shuffled to the side to get a glimpse in his periphery. A Casteless Ven stood at the edge of the room, but it kept its distance. Another Casteless appeared opposite him, far behind Reyes. Were they watching?

While Brian was distracted by their audience, the Warrior Ven swiped at him and gripped him hard, its claws ripping into the flesh of his newly healed shoulder. Encouraged by his howl of pain, the Ven moved forward. Reyes charged in for an attack, but the Ven batted her back.

The Casteless were restless. They got too close, and the Warrior Ven batted at them too. Brian maneuvered away, giving himself another meter, but the room wasn't very big. He'd moved close to a Casteless Ven who tried to scurry out of the way, but the Warrior Ven was too fast. It slammed the weaker creature onto the ground, giving Reyes an opening. She took it, shoving her sword between the plates in its back. The Ven turned, pulling the sword from her hand as it turned. The thin blade was still stuck in its back, and Brian acted quickly, adding his own weapon to the fray. He met tension that gave way with a gut-churning snap before the Ven collapsed. He grabbed Reyes's sword just before the Casteless, no longer interested in the two humans, descended on the dead Warrior Vens.

They left the hungry Casteless Vens to their feast and hurried back toward their own ship. Time was running short now, and they still had a fair bit of ground to cover. Reyes wrapped up her bleeding arm as best she could without stopping.

"The scent of our blood. Look," she said. The collapsed Casteless were stirring, and they were now too far from the scene of the fight for those bodies to lure these Vens. The Vens were hungry, and he and Reyes were starting to smell more like wounded prey than a Warrior Ven. She pulled out her own Ven essence and sprayed her haphazardly covered wound, wincing.

"It stings, but there's not much choice."

"I used all mine for the distraction."

Not waiting for further explanation, she sprayed him again, and the two continued, almost at a jog. They wouldn't have much time to react to arriving Vens, but if they slowed down, they might not make it back in time. Or they might have to fight off some very hungry Casteless Vens, who, despite their diminished state, were still predators in their DNA.

47. DIONE

Dione was in position. She slid the node from its secure pocket. The smooth, metal casing was the size of her thumb pad. Inside was a nanotech virus seed that would blossom into a Citadel-sized plague. Her numb fingers trembled around the node as she lifted it up to attach it to the wall, just over a line that stretched down like an artery, providing power to the lowest parts of the city-sized spaceship. The nanotech virus would feed off that power, then grow and spread until every inert virus activated simultaneously.

She adjusted the node in her fingers to get a firmer grip. The clock was ticking. Why was she hesitating again? The very first Ven she'd killed back on the *Calypso* had turned out not to be dead. It had woken back up and smashed Bel's face up against the airlock viewport. It had dragged her body out of view, leaving trails of bright red blood. The spiral mark it had carved into her friend's cheek was still there as a pale scar. Hesitation was a sign of weakness. The Vens and Sugians were guilty of the worst atrocities, and she had witnessed them with her own eyes.

Yet if the Vens were so guilty, why were there tears pricking at the corners of her eyes? Why had her stomach twisted into knots? The ancient Ven words she had found just weeks ago sang themselves to her:

Our homes are the citadels that chase the stars.
Our homes are the clans whose marks we bear.
But one day, our shells will once again be enough.

Their shells would never be enough, not after she planted her node. This was genocide. This would destroy not one, but two species. The Vens would get sick, and in turn they would infect the Sugians. Then the Alliance would finish them all off in their weakened state. Both species would suffer greatly, maybe even die out completely.

A message flashed across her manumed. It was Lithia: *Update?*

She wasn't supposed to call. The rule was messages only, but she had to risk being overheard. "Lithia," she whispered, "this is harder than I thought it would be."

"I know, Di, but you have to do it," Lithia said softly. "Humanity didn't ask for this. For all the mistakes we've made, and all the bills that will come due, this shouldn't be one of them."

Dione felt the truth of her best friend's words sink in. This preemptive strike was necessary. No matter how innocent they might have been long, long ago, when they got into an evolutionary arms race with the Sugians, the Venatorians were monsters. The Sugians were monsters.

That didn't make this right, but she knew beyond a shadow of a doubt that this was necessary for humanity's survival. She was prey, and this was the only way she and the rest of her species could survive the two predators that had invaded their ecosystem. This whole time she'd been trying to make herself more vicious, better adapted to survive, but she'd been overlooking the most important survival elements she'd had all along. Empathy. Camaraderie. Loyalty. Those were her greatest sources of strength. Her friends were out there risking their lives, too, and they were counting on her to fulfill her part of the mission.

She would plant her node, but that guilt that made her hesitate? It would stay with her. She would not learn to rejoice in killing like the Vens had. She would be quietly grateful for her species' survival, and she would continue to do what was necessary to get off this ship and see her friends and family again.

Dione placed the virus node against the wall and activated it with three gentle taps.

Heading back, she messaged Lithia.

She headed back in the direction of her friends. She hadn't been especially fast before her injury, but after her trip through the vents, she was exhausted. The way back was clear until she had nearly reached the pathway to the level where their ship was. The others must be close. Suddenly a deep, loud buzzing filled the corridor. She messaged Lithia her location. Lithia replied, and soon the others came out of hiding into the eerily empty corridor.

Dione was limping slightly, and her head was pounding, but she was fine. So were the others. No one had gotten lost or killed, and Dione was so busy counting her chickens that she nearly cried out in surprise when Bel's arm shot out, blocking her path.

Ahead of them, a deep green Warrior Ven with straight-edged plating stood facing a screen. She was too far away for the translation glasses to work properly, but it really didn't matter what the Ven was doing. It was blocking their path, and a darting glance revealed no places to hide. They were running out of time too. They had to move. With only an exchange of glances, hands moved to the thin, skewer-shaped blades each of them carried.

Bel stepped forward, her footsteps masked by the loud buzzing, and struck first. Unfortunately, the gap she had aimed for was fused, and her blade was stopped before it could do any damage. The Ven growled, and Dione hoped that the buzzing would be enough to mask the sound.

Bel was knocked back and slightly off balance. Brian and Zane moved in, keeping its attention, while Reyes positioned herself to flank it. The Ven swiped at the two young men, whirling in time to head off Reyes's attack. Dione feinted as well, giving Bel the perfect opening. The young woman thrust her sword through the next gap, and this time the silver blade disappeared as she put her weight into the attack. Dione listened for a snap but couldn't hear it over the noise of the ship. The Ven dropped to the ground.

"What do we do with it?" Dione asked.

"Leave it," Bel replied, wiping the Ven's fluids from her blade.

"It will distract any Casteless that might try to follow," Brian added.

The very floor was vibrating now, and the buzzing was only growing louder, like the ship itself was generating the noise.

"Let's go," Reyes said, glancing at her manumed. "Lithia's getting antsy."

At any moment Dione expected a team of Vens to round the corner and block their path, attracted by the commotion, but they didn't. The group made it to the ship with a few minutes to spare. Zane closed the hatch behind them immediately, and Lithia's hand was already inside the claw, preparing to detach.

"Oh no," Lithia said, swallowing hard. She looked from the tablet over to the hatch where the five of them were standing.

"What?" Reyes said, crossing the room in an instant.

"We can't undock. We're locked in."

"That's not right. They haven't jumped yet. We're back in time," Dione said. The words sounded foolish the moment they left her mouth, but she couldn't take them back now.

"They must have locked us in place. The countdown was to the actual jump, but there must have been a cutoff we didn't know about," Lithia said, pounding her fist against her leg.

"Or they discovered us," Bel said, glancing toward the door. "Do you think they blocked us?"

"If they knew we were here, they would have sent a team to kill us by now," Lithia replied, picking up the tablet with both hands. "This is jump-related, I'm sure."

"If you can't undock, can't you just use the engines and force it?"

"Even if I could, it would damage the ship. We might be free, but we'd be stranded, unable to jump," Lithia said, setting the tablet back down so that everyone could see the timer ticking down the last twenty seconds.

"Then what do we do?" Brian asked.

"Nothing," Bel said. "There's nothing we can do."

The six of them stood in a circle around the tablet, watching the numbers get smaller and smaller until a nauseating numbness pricked up the hairs on her arms and legs. The uncomfortable sensation was followed by dizziness. When her head cleared, Dione looked to Lithia.

"Where are we?"

"I have no idea," she replied.

48. DIONE

The camera feeds revealed nothing of interest. No planet, star, or asteroid. Granted, they had limited range on their view, but she wasn't optimistic. If they were near a planet, there could only be one motive, attack, and she didn't want that.

Reyes and Lithia were in discussion over the tablet, and Bel and Zane were at one of the readouts, peering through their translation glasses and frowning. She should go help them, but sudden exhaustion hit her and she wavered. She removed the goggles, and the sudden shift in her vision disoriented her, causing her to stumble.

Strong arms caught her. Brian steadied her, but her body refused to cooperate. "I need to sit down for a minute."

"You look terrible," Brian said, once he'd helped her into the other room and propped her against the bulkhead.

"I feel terrible. All of the exertion and the cold has my leg acting up, and my head is pounding."

"Where's your autoinjector?" he asked. "I can give you another dose."

She closed her eyes and shook her head. "There is no more. I didn't think I'd need more than one extra dose, which is all I had anyway. There was no time to get more. I figured if we failed, we'd be dead."

"The good news is that we're alive, and I don't think we failed. Not in the mission at least."

"We almost did."

"What do you mean?"

"After everything we've seen the Vens and Sugians do, I still hesitated. I didn't want to plant the virus node because I didn't want the blood on my hands, even if it was Ven blood."

"And that bothers you."

"It bothers me. Did you hesitate?"

Brian looked down a moment before replying. "I didn't hesitate. Maybe I should have. Maybe if we all did, the galaxy would be a better place. I love you, Dione. I love you for your hesitation. I love you for who you are."

"But do the Vens deserve compassion? They're not even human."

"Sometimes people don't deserve compassion, but that doesn't mean you can't feel compassion for them. I think that's how I feel about the Green Cloaks now that I've had to advocate for them to your father. Whether this compassion extends to Vens and Sugians, though? I don't know."

Dione winced and pressed a hand to her head. "Ugh, this headache is just getting worse. And you're bleeding." She nodded to his shoulder.

"I'll see what we have to take the edge off and get myself cleaned up," Brian said. He wrapped her in a warm embrace, kissed her gently on the lips, and headed into the main room. Brian's words had soothed away some of the pain and guilt that burdened her heart, but the physical pain remained, making it impossible to think or problem-solve. She was useless like this and hated her body for betraying her when her friends needed her.

But that was what friends were for. The balance of give-and-take wasn't necessarily even, but it worked as long as each carried what they could.

***

Dione was surprised she'd been able to sleep at all, but the analgesics Brian had found calmed the pain in her head and leg enough for her to get some rest for a few hours. She joined the others in the control room. Brian, Zane, and Bel looked like they were taking inventory, but Lithia and Reyes looked as if they hadn't moved since she'd last seen them. They were still hunched over the tablet, arguing. Lithia looked up when she entered the room.

"That beauty sleep did the trick. You don't look like a ghost anymore," she said.

Dione joined them. "Sorry, I guess the mission affected me more than the others."

"Don't apologize," Reyes said. "You did what was necessary and made it back."

"Not in time. Have you figured out what happened?"

"As soon as the tablet recalculated the countdown, we were out of time. No one except for Zane and Bel was finished by that point, so it wasn't you. There was no way we could have known and nothing we could have done. The original jump clock was based on intel and estimates," Lithia said.

"Frankly, I'm impressed by how close they were to the actual window," Reyes said. "Only off by about two hours."

"I'm less impressed," Lithia said, "since we're stuck here.

Literally."

"We still can't undock?" Dione asked.

"No."

"Is there a plan?"

"Kind of."

"Care to share?"

"Wait until we can undock, then flee," Lithia offered with a shrug.

"Hmm," Dione said. "That's not the greatest plan."

"Nope," Lithia replied.

Dione bit her bottom lip, but she was out of her depth. Sensing the importance of the discussion, Brian, Zane, and Bel joined them. "Do we have any idea where we are or where we're going?"

Reyes cleared her throat. "We're in clean space right now. No stars, planets, spatial anomalies from what we can tell. As for where we're going, based on what I know about the mission, wherever we're headed, it will end with this ship dead in space and teeming with Sugians," she said. "That's why the timing on this mission was so important. I don't know all the details, but the Alliance has been maneuvering ships and evacuating colonies for months. Doran has been working tirelessly for just as long, if not longer. The virus has begun spreading among the Vens, but it won't make them sick yet. It has to be activated, which should happen once their jump drive is disabled. Then infected Vens will pass it on to the Sugians before it kills them. The Citadel's exact destination never mattered for the mission, only its general range."

"Those graphs!" Dione said, recalling the evidence of the virus she'd found on Lars's laptop. "With the different start dates! This is why they had so many projected iterations. They were trying to figure out the best time to plant the virus nodes. Zane was right about the spikes all along."

"So we could be stuck here for days, maybe weeks," Zane said. "What if the Vens find us?"

Lithia shrugged. "We force undocking and hope for a miracle. I'd rather be torn apart by an ill-advised jump than killed by a Ven."

"If they haven't found us yet, I don't think they will," Reyes said. "They're not looking at the docked ships. Based on what I saw, I think they're all gathering for some sort of talk or ceremony. All the returning Vens were heading in and up, not sticking around the lower levels."

"I don't want to be here when the Sugians get here," Lithia said, "but I don't see how we're going to escape. There's no guarantee we'll be able to undock once the Citadel is disabled."

Reyes put a hand on Lithia's shoulder. "If the Alliance ships show up to broadcast the signal that activates the virus, we won't have to jump. We just have to get to them."

Silence fell over the group. The plan, if she could even call it a plan, was to wait. To do nothing. Dione should be happy that there wasn't another dangerous task ahead of her, but sitting in this ship for days felt like a prison sentence. Waiting felt like an invitation for disaster, but there was no better alternative.

"So we wait," she said. "Do we have food and water?"

"Water looks good, but food will be short. We'll survive, but it may be unpleasant if this goes on very long," Brian said.

"Unpleasant? This place?" Lithia said, gesturing in mock amazement at their dismal surroundings. "Surely not!"

Brian rolled his eyes, and even Bel smiled. Lithia yawned, and Dione realized that she was the only one who'd gotten any rest.

"I can take watch for a while. Everyone else should get some sleep."

There might not be much she could do, but giving her friends a chance to recharge was within her power.

49. LITHIA

Lithia was okay. Taking care of Dione kept her too busy to get caught up in her own thoughts. Neither of them could sleep well. Lithia would sleep for a few hours at a time and wake up sweating or shivering, sometimes from the nightmares, sometimes from *vigo* withdrawal. Dione tossed and turned thanks to her leg. Sometimes, they would sit awake together, and Dione would ask her to explain step by step how to land a shuttle, or she would ask Dione to teach her how plants turned sunlight into energy. They took turns distracting each other like taking turns carrying a heavy pack on a hike.

Dione's brace allowed her to walk, but unless it was right after she took her pills, she had trouble getting around. Everyone else seemed more or less okay, considering how long they'd been stuck on the Ven scout ship. Reyes and Brian's injuries were easily managed with the first aid available on board.

The Citadel ship was large and slow. It took nearly two full days for it to be ready to jump again, and it had jumped three times since they'd been on board. That meant they had been stuck on board for six days, and the timer had once again started its hourlong countdown. The six of them were awake, hungry, weak, and sitting together in the control room. If they couldn't undock after this jump, Lithia didn't think she could last two more days.

"How much longer?" Brian asked.

He was taking the hunger the best of all of them, probably because he'd had years of practice on Kepos. Lithia was cranky. Logically, she knew that eating less for a few days was nothing but an inconvenience. Her empty stomach, however, was ready to lash out at everyone.

"Ten minutes."

"This is going to be it," Bel said. "I know it."

Despite her optimistic declaration, the crew's overall mood was grim. They'd already done this three times, and Lithia was glad that it was silent this time. There had already been arguments, hopes, warnings, all of it. The exhaustion was palpable, like a thick blanket of humidity.

When the sickening sensation washed over her, she tried to regulate her breathing. Each jump felt worse than the last, and the only solace was that she didn't think she'd eaten enough recently to throw up. Bel squeezed her eyes shut so tightly Lithia could see the wrinkles at the corners of her eyes from across the room. Brian was gritting his teeth, and Dione had her arms wrapped tightly around her knees, scrunching herself into a ball.

Seconds later, the jump was complete. Everyone stayed put except for Reyes, who joined Lithia in scouring the camera feeds for any sign of a planet. She double-checked, looking for any sign that they were in a star system and not deep space, but there was nothing on their screens that gave her any hope. *Two more days*, she thought. *How are we going to last two more days?*

"Nothing," Lithia muttered, setting down the tablet to stop

herself from throwing it against a bulkhead.

The following hours were almost silent. Brian and Dione didn't touch. Bel and Zane didn't speak. Reyes muttered to herself, and Lithia thought she might be praying or perhaps reciting the digits of pi to herself. Lithia was just about to suggest something stupid, like breaking away and taking the odds of a jump in a compromised ship when Reyes darted to one of the camera feeds.

"Look," Reyes said.

"A ship." Lithia perked up. "A Ven Invader, undocking."

"What does that mean?" Dione asked.

"I don't know yet, but more Invaders are undocking. Marauders too." She reached her hand into the claw and tried the docking release. "We're still stuck," Lithia said, "but we might be able to release soon."

That was all that the others needed to hear. The torpor that had weighed them down lifted, and they put their new energy to use. They all put their translation goggles back on and waited.

And waited.

"Still nothing," Lithia said after twenty minutes.

"What if they never release us?" Bel asked. "This is a scout class ship. Do they ever use them in battles?"

Reyes frowned. "I don't think so."

"So we pry ourselves off and go find the Alliance ships in the area," Dione said.

"We still don't have tangible proof they're here," Zane said. "This could be just another colonial invasion the Alliance isn't here to stop."

"No," Reyes said. "There are too many ships leaving for it to be a regular attack. This is something big."

"It doesn't matter," Lithia said. "I ran some simulations, and there's no way a ship this small will survive a forced undocking. It's not an issue of not being able to jump. It's an issue of compromising the integrity of the ship and getting vented into space. I thought we could finagle something, but it just won't work. The only way off this Citadel ship is if they release us."

Everyone began talking at once, and Lithia tuned it out. This was a million times better than the last three jumps. There was action, hope, a chance to escape. If she could just find a way to get a better view of what was going on, they could figure out where they were and if there were any Alliance ships nearby. She picked up the tablet, overlooked in the midst of the argument, and checked to see if they had gotten any message. It was possible, right?

At once she noticed something was different. One of the icons had changed in color from red to blue. She tapped it, and it only took her moments to realize what it meant.

"Guys," she said. Zane and Reyes were in a heated debate, but Lithia didn't care. "Hey!" she shouted. "Shut up for a second. I have at least a little bit of good news." She held up the tablet. "Look. The virus has been activated. This is it."

"What good does it do if we can't undock?" Bel asked.

"*This* ship won't undock. I see a bunch of Invaders and Marauders out there. Clearly they don't have that issue."

"You want us to take over a Marauder?" Bel said. Lithia could tell by her tone that she was considering the idea.

"I want us to get the hell of this ship and go home. I don't see another way."

Reyes was examining the tablet, but when she looked up her face was full of grim determination. "The only way out is through."

"Are you up for this?" Dione asked.

"I don't have a choice. None of us do. We'll find out soon enough," Lithia said.

The next thirty minutes were a whirlwind of preparation. Along with the swords, they still had some of the Ven essence left, but the lower levels were bound to be busier than before.

She and Reyes had spent their time finding the perfect Marauder to infiltrate. They didn't have a lot of options available to them, but this ship had returned damaged. It had arrived a day ago, so they figured it was still jump capable. It was close, and many ships docked near it had already left. They shared their plan with the others.

"We don't know how damaged it is," Dione said. "Its life support could be failing, but it got back just in time."

"It's our best option. It's isolated, and if it was attacked, there could be fewer Vens on board," Lithia reasoned. "Or its crew could have left it to join other ships."

"If this is the best option, I'm in," Bel said.

"It is," Lithia said. Reyes nodded solemnly at her side.

"Then I trust you, Lithia," Dione conceded.

Brian and Zane voiced their assent, and then the group added the final touches to their plan. Dione with her limp was the slowest, so they'd keep her in the middle of the pack. She'd taken the last of her pills that she had rationed in case of an emergency. Lithia would stick with her and avoid direct conflict if they ran into the Vens. She still didn't trust herself after what had happened back on Kepos. That paralyzing fear pushing the air out of her lungs had been one of the most debilitating experiences of her life. She didn't know whether she feared the Vens or that feeling more. At least she could kill a Ven.

They packed up their gear, including the claw, and stepped cautiously out of their ship. The corridor was eerily deserted, and it set off all of Lithia's internal alarms, like she was watching a horror vid and waiting for a jump scare that never came.

They reached the Marauder, and she hoped it was abandoned, too, but the second they approached the entrance, a single Ven caught them by surprise. Or maybe they caught the Ven by surprise, because Brian and Reyes leaped into action and managed to take it down rather quickly. Brian slid his thin sword up between its green, scalloped plates, ensuring that it would not come back to hurt them.

The crew spilled into the Marauder and made their way to the control room. Before they could plan their approach, one of the two Vens in the control room caught sight of them and growled. Reyes charged forward with Brian, and Bel and Zane hurried for the second one. Lithia didn't have a weapon. She couldn't help.

She stood transfixed, but Dione tugged at her arm. "Lithia, the claw. Let's go."

Dione was right. There was no good reason they couldn't take control of the ship while their friends were fighting. With Dione right behind her, she went to the navigation console and inserted her clawed hand into the control post. There were a number of warnings on the screen that she flicked aside. With a few swift motions, she initiated the undocking procedure. She felt the controls respond, her heart fluttering as she heard the mechanical sounds of the ship detaching from the dock.

"Holy crap, it's working!" Lithia shouted.

A third Ven had found its way into the control room now, replacing one of its fallen comrades. It looked unsteady, and Reyes easily dispatched it while Brian distracted it. Lithia had never seen a Ven go down so quickly. Was it injured?

Something pulled her focus back to the navigation controls. What was wrong? There was a strange resistance she hadn't felt while piloting their smaller Ven ship. Was it the Marauder's size that made it feel so different?

No, just as there was something wrong with the Vens on this ship, there was something wrong with the ship itself.

"There's more damage to the ship than we'd hoped," Lithia said, taking stock of the various systems.

Dione was at the panel next to her. "Communications are down," she said.

"We don't need comms."

Dione glanced at the camera feeds. "Oh my god, Lithia, look." They'd moved away from the Ven Citadel and could see the battlefield. Hundreds of ships, Ven and Sugian, were joined in battle. Literally joined as Vens boarded Sugians and Sugians boarded Vens, battling in those close quarters both species preferred.

"Good. I hope they all kill one another. We've got a problem, though. The jump drive is working, but I can't access it," Lithia said. "Some sort of system safeguard."

"We've got to sweep the rest of the ship," Reyes said. "Bel, Dione, you stay here."

Bel obeyed, and from the corner of her eye, she could see Bel making sure that every last neural connection had been properly severed in the fallen Vens.

"I think these were Worker Vens, not Warriors. They weren't as fast or as strong," Bel said.

"Good," Lithia replied. "The Vens might not kill us, but this ship could still do the job. We can't jump."

"Why?" Dione asked. "I can't see a reason why not. Like you said, the jump drive is working."

Lithia swiped through the systems, looking for an explanation, until finally she found it. "The integrity of the outer hull has been compromised. That's why we can't jump."

"Maybe we don't have to. I found some Alliance ships," Dione said. "They're keeping their distance, like they're just monitoring things."

"We just find an Alliance ship and—" Lithia huffed in frustration. "The ship's comms are down."

"Manumeds?" Dione asked.

"Manumeds won't work on board," Bel said. "Our manumeds were all connected to the scout ship, remember? We couldn't even message each other during the mission. We had to send messages through Lithia, like a switchboard. We don't have anything like that now."

"We have no way to tell them we're friendly, and it's not like we're in the scout ship they'd recognize," Lithia said, summing up the problem. "Assuming we get close enough before hull integrity fails."

Reyes returned with Zane and Brian close behind. "Ship is clear," she said. "We found two more. One was still pretty sharp, but the other was slow, like the ones up here."

"That's nice," Lithia said. "The ship could rip apart at any minute."

"Wonderful," Zane said. "Anything I can do to help?"

"Fix comms?"

"I'm not sure what I can do in the next thirty minutes," he said.

"More like twenty."

Lithia changed their course. Hopefully, none of the Ven ships headed toward the Sugians would care.

"There are some Sugian ships on their way to the Citadel that haven't been intercepted," Dione added.

"But none of them are engaging," Reyes said. "Why aren't they shooting each other out of the void? They've got weapons."

"You know how they like to get up close and personal," Bel replied.

While there was no Citadel-sized ship among the Sugians, they had a greater number of vessels. Ven and Sugian ships practically crashed into one another as they engaged in the combat they enjoyed: boarding parties, face-to-face combat, and the brutality of predator hunting prey.

They passed within range of several Sugian ships without incident until an alarm started going off. "The hull?" Dione asked.

"The Alliance," Lithia replied. An Alliance craft was closing in on them.

"They're almost in range," Reyes said. "They can tell we're heading for them, so we're a threat. They're going to fire."

They couldn't take even one hit, not in their current state. If they couldn't explain they were friendly, they'd have to find another way to communicate. "I have an idea," Lithia said. "If it doesn't work, it will probably rip the ship apart faster."

"If it doesn't work, we're screwed anyway," Zane said.

"Here goes," she said.

There was a way pilots had communicated in dead zones early in the era of mass colonization. There were planets with lots of natural interference or failed communications infrastructures. And there were bandits and pirates and all sorts of wild cards who terrorized the frontier, so defensive pilots came up with signals and flight patterns to separate friend from foe. Lithia had read about them, but she'd never tried them. They were meant to be done in atmosphere where there was a definite up and down, not in space.

Lithia sent the Ven ship into a pattern of spins and flips, slowing and exposing their starboard side. It was a sign of trust, a declaration: *Here I am, don't shoot.*

"Lithia, what are you doing? They'll be on us in seconds," Reyes shouted from across the room.

"I know," she replied.

No one spoke. A second, louder alarm was going off somewhere, but they hadn't ripped apart yet. They hadn't been blasted apart either.

"They're not firing," Dione said. "They're... doing something like you. Some sort of spin."

"I've got to copy them. Hang on." Lithia took them for one more slow, careful spin, then slowed some more. "Come on," she said. "Get the message."

Truthfully, she didn't know if there even was a way to say, "Please rescue us," but she hoped that the miserable state of the ship would be enough of a giveaway once they established that they were not a ship full of Vens.

For a very long minute, the Alliance ship did nothing. Finally, it moved into position over top of them, matching their speed.

"Thank the void, I think they get it," Lithia muttered, slowing the ship even further until the Alliance ship could attach. They were not gentle about it, and the entire ship shook.

"They're going to board us. Put down any weapons, and don't make sudden moves," Reyes said, putting her sword on the ground and her hands up.

The others followed suit, except for Lithia herself, who kept flying the ship.

A squad of ten men and women came in, their leader shouting out the orders that Reyes had already given. Once they took in the sight—five young adults and one fellow soldier—they relaxed a bit. The dead Vens on the ground might have helped too.

"Your ship could go at any minute. Follow them out," said the leader. No one hesitated, Lithia included. She cut their engines entirely, counting on their momentum and the attached ship to carry them for the next minute or two. The Ven ship groaned even as they entered the Alliance ship's hatch.

The leader barked an order as soon as they were safely on board, though Lithia couldn't hear it all. Either way, the Alliance ship detached and sped away.

"My office," the man said, his voice as gruff as his manners.

No one spoke, and Lithia got that same feeling that she had at StellAcademy whenever she would get sent to the headmaster's office, except this felt somehow worse and better. Worse because she figured they were in big trouble. Prison-time trouble. Better because they were finally free of that miserable Citadel ship. She'd take Alliance prison over Ven prison any day. One soldier stayed outside, and two entered the man's office with them. It was stark. There were certificates and medals on the bulkhead behind his desk, which held one picture of a young man about Reyes's age. Everything else looked standard issue, completely devoid of personality.

The leader, a colonel she thought, did not invite them to sit. Dione was leaning on Brian, but she looked okay for the most part. So did the others, though Lithia finally had a chance to notice some light scratches on their arms and faces.

"Did you succeed?"

"What do you mean?" Lithia asked.

He addressed Reyes, not Lithia, when he responded. "I mean the virus, captain. Were you successful? Time is of the essence."

"Yes, sir," Reyes said. "We deployed all the nodes, and once we jumped here, the activation signal reached the Citadel ship we were on."

"You're certain? Lives are riding on the accuracy of this information." The man's jaw was clenched, his mouth a grim line.

"Yes, sir," she repeated.

Lithia nodded, as did the rest of them. They were certain.

He sent a quick message, presumably informing others of this new information, then sat and leaned back in his chair and took a few deep breaths.

"Do you have any idea what you've done?" he asked.

Lithia exchanged a look with Bel, perplexed. Dione shook her head.

"You've given us the chance to save a lot of lives," he said, his voice breaking. "A lot of lives. Would you like to see?"

Tears pricked the corners of Lithia's eyes. "Yes, please."

50. DIONE

Their ship joined a small contingent of Alliance vessels anchored at a distance from the battle. Colonel Wulf, which was how the gruff man had introduced himself, gave them the time to get cleaned up and offered them fresh clothes and some real food. To Dione, he offered additional pain meds, which she gladly took. Once they'd had a chance to recover, he took them to an observation station full of screens and camera feeds.

"Space battles like this take a long time," he said, "even though it's not really a space battle. The Vens and the Sugians have been working toward this major conflict. The timing of our missions to the Citadel ships had to be just right, and we thought we'd missed the window. When you didn't return to Marius, you were presumed dead, your mission failed. After all, how could a single soldier and five kids carry out a mission like that?"

The camera feeds shifted to more views of skirmishes between the Sugians and the Vens.

"Almost every Ven and Sugian will be affected by this battle. The survivors will return to their ships. The Vens will be easy to infiltrate. The virus has a high fatality rate, causing major complications weeks out if it doesn't kill them outright in a few days. The Sugians will feed on the infected Vens. The nanotech will mutate once it recognizes Sugian markers and then sweep through the Sugians too. Do you know what Sugians do when they find a rich food source? They reproduce in exponential numbers, enough to pose our Alliance a dire threat. This virus effectively sterilizes them, again causing long-term health complications for the Sugians. We've got soldiers searching out and destroying any errant Sugian ships. We'll be able to wipe them out more quickly with fewer casualties. They'll devastate fewer worlds, and more soldiers will go back home to their families. The outer planets won't fall."

"So the other team was successful too?" Dione asked.

"Yes, they were. That was its own monumental victory. With both Citadels infected and with high face-to-face engagement, our fleet is standing by. When the Alliance fleet arrives, we'll jump you to safety."

"To my father?" Dione asked.

"Yes," the colonel replied. "He's angry, but he believed you might pull it off. I'd thought it was wishful thinking, but now I'm not so sure. You all look like you need some rest." Colonel Wulf called in his assistant who led them to their quarters.

Despite her exhaustion, Dione's thoughts kept her awake. Was this really the legacy she wanted to leave? Was this her contribution to society? No one else around her seemed to have any doubts or guilt, but how could she go back to a classroom after everything that had happened?

A good night's sleep did not cure her misgivings, but by the end of the next day, they'd jumped to rendezvous with her father's ship. Brian held her hand on one side, and Lithia patted her on the shoulder before stepping over the threshold and into *Starling*.

"Home, Di. Can you believe it? We're finally going home!"

51. LITHIA

They'd arrived on Lavinian. Lithia had been poked, prodded, medicated, decontaminated, and debriefed. Dione was sitting with her as she waited for the car that would take her to her parents' house.

"We're home, Lithia. You seem… nervous."

"I'm afraid my parents won't recognize me."

"Despite everything that's happened, you are still you. And your parents love you no matter what."

"How can you be sure?"

"Because I love you. I can see that you are still Lithia, my best friend. And they'll see it too." Dione pulled her into a warm, tight hug. A car honked, and they both turned toward the sound. "Your ride is here."

"I just can't—"

"Tell them. Tell them the things that you didn't want to tell me and the others back when we left Kepos. Tell them the things that you and Reyes talked about. Let us help you," Dione said.

The car honked again, and Lithia nodded and got in. Her heart fluttered with nerves, but Dione's words had helped her breathe. And that's what she did on the ride home. She breathed slowly and let her thoughts get lost in familiar songs on the radio.

Once she arrived at her house, she stepped out of the car. Every member of her family—Mom, Dad, Max, and Grandpa Min—came out to greet her, and Lithia absolutely lost it in a snotty-nosed, gasping-to-breathe-through-sobs kind of way.

And she felt better. Not because everything was fixed but because, when she had hugged her parents, the burden that had been weighing her down felt lighter. She could carry it with their help, and she knew that they would help her. No matter how many exasperated moments she had caused them, the worry, the anger, she knew that they would listen and support her. All she had to do was find the words. Despite their high standards and strictness, they listened.

When she stepped into her house, it smelled like home. The scent was hard to describe, like a floral shampoo with a hint of cinnamon. Most of the time, she didn't notice it, but after months away, it filled her with unspeakable comfort.

Dinner was pizza, the kind of greasy takeout covered in toppings that she loved. She remembered how the chocobun had tasted like nothing, and the memory made her afraid to take a bite.

"Mushrooms, pepperoni, and extra cheese for you," Max said. "The other one is mine. Bacon and pineapple!"

"Gross," Lithia said.

"They're all to share," her mother corrected him.

"You can keep your sad little pizza," Lithia said. This felt normal.

How could it feel normal?

"Max has been eating your share of the food while you've been gone."

Lithia poked him in the stomach, and he swatted her away. "I can tell."

"What was the food like there?" he asked. "On that planet you guys crashed on?"

"Kepos? It was…" She trailed off, remembering her first proper Keposian meal. It had been with Michael and Cora in the Vale Temple. Evy had been dragged in to sit with her parents, Benjamin and Amelia. Lithia missed Evy. She missed Cora. She hoped they were both doing well.

"Lithia?" her mother asked.

"Hmm?" she said. "Oh, the food. It was different but normal. A girl I met there really liked *pollas*, a juicy, purple fruit with no seeds. Sweet, yet a tiny bit tart." Lithia took a bite of pizza, which threw her off since it tasted nothing like the *polla* her mouth had begun to water for. But it was good pizza, and that relieved her. It wasn't the chocobun all over again. There was hope.

"Did you spend a lot of time with the other children there?" her mother said.

"Children?" Lithia suppressed a laugh. Yes, they were all still children. No matter that they'd fought the Vens, stopped a Green Cloak coup, and survived the Sugians. She was still a child. "Uh, yeah, I guess you could say that. It was… different."

"Like the food?" Max asked.

Lithia shook her head. "Not at all like the food. Things there were not normal, at least not what we'd call normal. There was this scientist guy named Jameson that everyone called the Farmer, and he loaded up a bunch of people on a colonizer and brainwashed them when they got to Kepos. Wiped their memories." Her insides twisted in discomfort. "I need to tell you all something. About why we ended up at Kepos." She looked at her grandpa, who was cutting his pizza with a fork and knife like always. He was listening.

"Kepos isn't in the navigation banks. I don't know if Mr. Quinn ever told you how we found it, but it was me. I'd been researching different places that Miranda might have gone." Lithia didn't wait for a reaction. "When the Vens attacked, we didn't have any options, and we went to one of the secret planets I'd learned about, Kepos."

Her dad looked confused. "How did you find out ab—"

"Doesn't matter. I found her. At least, I found where she went. She'd passed away long before I got there, and so had her daughter Clara, but I met her granddaughter, Cora. She's the one who likes *pollas* so much."

The room was quiet. Grandpa Min had put down his fork and knife, and he seemed to be breathing faster than normal.

"Was she happy there?" he asked.

Lithia didn't know how to answer that. She'd read her grandmother's journal. She knew the pain and anger that Miranda had suffered when Samantha Meyers, back when she had been fully human and not an AI, had given her back her memories. The entries had gone from angry and defiant to remorseful. Ultimately, she'd taken her own life instead of living with the knowledge of who she was. But that was just a snapshot. Had she been happy while brainwashed, living with Jameson? Probably. The full truth wasn't necessary here.

"I think so. I think she had a pretty normal life with ups and downs. I also know that she regretted leaving you and Dad, for what it's worth."

Grandpa Min looked up at her, tears in his eyes. "I thought her memories were gone."

"She got them back for a little bit. When she remembered, she realized she'd made a mistake."

Silence fell over the room once more: her brother, confusion;

her mother, sympathy; and concern clouded her father's eyes as he looked at Grandpa. Grandpa Min's face held grief, but there was something lighter there, too, that she couldn't place.

Grandpa Min got up and came around the table to where she was sitting. She stood and fully met his embrace. "It's a relief to finally know. I was never able to stop loving her, and I never stopped worrying about her. She had a life, just as I did, and in a way, she saved you. If you hadn't found Kepos, you might not have escaped the Vens."

"I guess you're right. Without Miranda, we wouldn't have had a place to go." There were days where it felt like the universe was pulling strings.

"Do you have a picture?" he asked. "Of Miranda's other granddaughter?"

Lithia wiped away a tear. "So many pictures, Grandpa," she replied. She cast the pictures from her manumed onto the screen in the living room. The whole family got up to look.

"That's Cora. She's about a year younger than I am." Lithia stared at the image, taken shortly before her departure from Kepos.

"She looks just like you," her father said.

"I think she's ugly," Max said. Her mother shushed him, but Lithia threw her head back and laughed. The tension in the room broke, and her father cracked a smile.

"Maybe we should eat in here, if you have more photos to show us?" he said.

"Eat in the living room?" Lithia said.

Her brother joined in, and they said in unison, "You'll ruin the carpet!" Lithia and Max cackled at their unrehearsed impression of their mother.

"There are more important things than a clean carpet," her mother said.

"I hope that realization extends to my room."

"Don't push it," her mother replied, but when Lithia glanced over, she saw her mom's lips pressed tight, holding back a smile.

Lithia was home. *Home*, she thought, rolling the word around in her thoughts until it became a meditative ohm, centering her and bringing her peace.

She shared pictures and stories, leaving out the darker bits for the time being. There were no pizza accidents, and the carpet survived. After her brother and grandpa went to sleep, she sat back down at the table with her parents.

"Lithia, we're so glad to have you back," her father began. "We also heard about some of the things you experienced, like the loss of Mr. Oberon—"

"Professor," Lithia corrected quietly, thinking of Dione.

"Huh? Oh, Professor Oberon, sorry. Dione's father let us know what happened on Doran. We think you should talk to someone about it," he said.

"Losing someone close to you can be hard to process," her mother chimed in.

A knot formed again in her stomach. This was the hardest part because she knew that telling them the truth would hurt them. It would burden them. They loved her, and knowing the depth of her pain would wound them too. Thinking about all of this made her hesitate. She could just go to bed without telling them the whole truth. Did they really need to know? *Yes*, a defiant voice in the back of her mind answered. *You would want to know, and so would they, even if it's hard. They are your family.*

She was going to find herself again, and coming home had been the first step. Home was not a destination, but a starting point.

52. BEL

The car pulled up in front of Bel's aunt's house, and the front door was open before she even unbuckled her seat belt. Bel's tension melted away as she took in her aunt's features: the same dark hair braided like her own, the same dark eyes that had cried with her after her family's deaths. The same mouth that had found reasons to laugh with her in the years since—during science projects, and on long hikes and trips to the beach. The same strong arms that had held her then embraced her now.

"Sweetheart! It's so good to see your face," her aunt said.

"Aunt Sira!"

Her aunt squeezed her shoulders with slender fingers, then cupped her face and smoothed a worried thumb over the spiral scar on her cheek.

She pulled her aunt's hands away and clasped them in her own. "I'm okay. It's okay."

Aunt Sira clucked her tongue. "You've found your way back home again, Belen, and do not think I'll let you wander far for some time!"

"What about far enough for a birthday dinner with Zane tomorrow?"

"This is the boy you mentioned in your message? The one who took care of you when you were sick?"

"Yes, that one."

"I'd like to meet him very much." Her aunt smiled.

"Good. We're having a picnic after spending so much time stuck inside spaceships. His family will be there too."

***

The weather could not have been more perfect for a picnic. Her aunt packed a few finger foods including her famous butterscotch cookies, and off they went. The sunshine was warm, and not a cloud was in the sky to cast a gray shadow or threaten rain.

Zane's family was lovely, and her aunt delighted in meeting his little sister. The two families shared food and conversation, all of which was amiable and completely and utterly boring. Bel loved every dull, calming minute, drinking it in like iced tea on a hot day.

After the meal was over, Zane asked Bel to walk with him in the park. After assuring their families they would stay within eyesight, they were permitted to get up. Zane snagged a couple of butterscotch cookies on his way up, and Aunt Sira smiled at him.

They put some space between themselves and the picnic, walking in silence. Bel pulled at the edge of her shirt and kept tucking a stubborn stray hair behind her ear.

"What's wrong?" Zane asked.

Bel took a breath. For a while, she had hoped that she'd magically feel attraction the way that everyone else seemed to, but she didn't. She was coming to terms with that. "Things between us haven't been very physical, but now that we're home, I'm worried that will change."

Zane cocked his head. "I trust you to respect my boundaries."

Bel barely smiled. "I'm serious."

"You were up-front with me, and I'm being up-front with you. I won't pressure you. Relationships aren't set in stone. They change. For all we know, we'll break up next week after having a very intense fight about whether to get tacos or pizza."

"That's a silly reason to break up," Bel replied. "This isn't."

"I know," Zane replied, his tone growing more serious. "I feel doubts too. Like I've said or done the wrong thing. That I've messed everything up."

Bel arched her eyebrows. "Really? You feel that way too?"

"Yes. It's normal in a relationship, at least in the beginning when you're still figuring things out. But I've been happy. Have you?"

She grinned. "Really happy."

"Then let's see where this goes."

"How long do we take to figure it out?"

"I don't know. I don't have all my own answers either. But I do know that I love you. I love spending time with you, and I hope that we can keep spending time together. You've already told me how you feel about certain things, and I've done the same. We just keep doing that until it doesn't work anymore."

Calm settled over Bel once more, and she kissed Zane on the cheek. "Okay." He was right. Even on Lavinian, she didn't have every bit of information at her fingertips. Some answers would only come through experimentation.

The two of them stood close together under the trees, watching the picnic from a distance. Her aunt was exchanging recipes with Zane's father, and his little sister was giggling and hopping between two flowers while his mom watched with a relieved smile.

At the moment, that was how Bel felt. Distant. A stranger. Her aunt had looked and felt the same, down to the aromatic perfume she always wore. Bel was the one who was different.

"They'll never understand what it was like," she said softly.

"And that's wonderful news," Zane said. "I don't want my family to understand. For that, we've got each other."

He reached down and gripped her hand in his. "Things are finally looking up, Bel. You can let go now. The Vens have no power here, and after what we did—after what you did—they may never have power again."

Bel closed her eyes tightly, her lids the only dam against undesired emotions. The fury and the grief were both there, crashing into her consciousness like waves against a seawall.

In the turmoil, she felt Zane squeeze her hand. He was right. They had done it. Preliminary reports were good. Fantastic even. While she couldn't let it all go at once, Bel felt the ball of anger in her chest loosen a little bit more each day. This was how healing worked, right? Bel was patient, ready to put her energy to better use. She smiled, thinking of all she was capable of.

53. BRIAN

Brian and the other Keposians, including his parents, had been settled in the same apartment complex, though their units were spread throughout the building. On his way back to his own unit, he stopped by Jill's apartment. She'd taken in Asher after the two had bonded on the journey to Lavinian. Everyone had arrived over a month after Brian and were still getting their bearings. He was glad he was able to help them navigate the city that was still quite new to him.

"Jill," he said when she opened the door. "Need anything? I'm going out later."

"We're fine. Asher and I have been going for evening walks in Flores Park, and we get what we need on our way back. It's so different here. Much more transactional."

Brian knew what she meant. There wasn't that same sense of community that they'd had on Kepos, but the freedom from obligation was hard to describe. He'd been looking after someone for so long that the chance to figure out who he really was and what he wanted had brought him to tears more than once already.

"How's Asher doing?" he asked.

"They've got him attending school. The kids are nice from what he tells me. It's good for him to have a fresh start away from his legacy on Kepos."

He wished her a good afternoon, glad she and Asher had passed whatever evaluations the Alliance had required of them. As much as he'd been upset at first by Marius's decision, the man had kept tabs on the two former Green Cloaks and kept the other Keposians informed of their evaluation process. He'd been the one to make sure they were all settled in the same area.

Brian had opted for his own small apartment just a few floors down from his parents. The space was small and worn but clean. And his own. He stepped out onto the small balcony and took in the city. Tall, gray-and-black buildings gleamed in the sun. Patches of green dotted the city, and he planned to visit each park during his stay. His future was uncertain, but the possibilities were overwhelming.

He heard a faint knock and went to open the door. Dione greeted him with a kiss, and the two sat on his couch.

"Did you sign up for any courses yet?" she asked.

"I did. I'll be taking some intensive courses to catch up on requirements for a basic diploma. Do you know how many requirements there are?"

Dione laughed, and the sound warmed his heart. "Yeah, there are quite a few. But you'll knock them out in no time. What did your aptitude test say?"

"Here," he said, pulling the results up on his manumed. "I failed the first part, pretty much. I know very little about Lavinian history and the Alliance. Reading and analysis were okay, so was science. Math went well at least."

"Well, it looks like you know nothing but are capable of

anything," Dione laughed, looking over his shoulder.

"Do you really mean that?" he asked. Brian had always been confident. With girls, with his repairs, with smuggling stolen goods. Even with dealing with Victoria. But that was on Kepos. There, he had been Brian Caldwin. People knew him, looked up to him, and counted on him. On Lavinian, he was just another refugee. It was hard to hold on to his self-worth here.

"Of course I do!" she replied. "Do you doubt it after everything you've done?"

"I'm the same fish, but the pond is so much bigger. If that makes sense."

Dione stared off for a few moments before nodding. "It makes perfect sense. Have you thought about finding a smaller pond, so to speak?"

"Like what?"

"Find a profession or a group where you can focus your efforts and stand out."

Brian sighed. "I already have that. Kepos."

"Good. But don't be afraid to test the deeper waters. You never know what you'll learn about yourself."

Brian held her close. He was glad she'd be here to help him navigate the strange new world he was living in.

54. DIONE

Dione sat in the back of the class. There had been open seats in the front, but she didn't want to sit there anymore, not with all of the stares and whispers that would be directed toward her back. She still wore her knee brace, but her first surgery had gone well. They would be able to repair nearly all of the damage, and by graduation, she'd be walking pain free and limp free. There were rumors about dragons, and she let them stay that way.

Dione had wanted to finish the year virtually, but Lithia, Bel, and Zane had convinced her to come back to class. Brian was currently taking some accelerated classes along with the other refugees. Dione and her friends had only missed two months of school and had very understanding teachers who got them up to speed.

"Ugh. Mr. Huang keeps trying to get me to fill out med school applications," Lithia said on the way to lunch. "I'm not going. I think my parents have given up on me becoming a doctor like them, but Huang won't let it go."

"You should apply. You don't have to accept any admission

offers," Dione replied.

"Oh, and where have you applied? Your dad's worried you haven't applied to Haisukia University yet."

"How do you know that?"

"Our parents talk. I eavesdrop."

"I'm not going to apply."

"Really? I thought it was your first choice."

"It was. Back when I wanted to do more theoretical research."

"But you don't want to do that anymore?"

"Not really."

"Then what do you want to do?"

Dione stopped walking and pulled Lithia to the side of the hallway, out of oncoming student traffic. "I haven't told this to anyone yet. Not even Brian."

Lithia's tone grew serious. "Got it. Lips sealed. What is it?"

"I want to apply to some apprenticeships on the Rim and focus on agricultural intervention in the colonies."

"How long are the apprenticeships?"

"Usually two or three years."

Lithia whistled. "That sounds intense. Are you sure you want to go live out there? The Vens and Sugians still aren't under control on the Rim."

"They will be by graduation, according to the projections, but the risk is acceptable."

Lithia was silent for a little while, and Dione could see that her friend was grappling with her revelation.

"If that's really what you want to do, then I support you."

Dione hugged Lithia, who, despite being a self-proclaimed non-hugger, seemed to be relaxing her stance on the display of affection.

"But you should still probably apply to Haisukia, just to appease your dad."

Dione smiled at Lithia. "Will do."

The two young women resumed walking to lunch, one a little lighter, the other a little heavier, as things often are in the imperfect balance of friendship.

EPILOGUE: THREE YEARS LATER

The ship had run out of coffee days ago, but Dione was wide awake. She was stuck in orbit waiting for shuttle clearance. When you were nobody, these things took time. Especially when it was this busy. She was expecting a call from Brian, but it was Bel whose message reached her first.

"Dione! You made it!" she said. "We were beginning to worry you'd miss it." Bel was sitting outdoors on a small patio in front of what Dione recognized as the main math building on Haisukia University's campus. Even though her choices had taken her on a different path, she'd spent her teenage years studying HU's brochures.

"We?" she asked, furrowing her eyebrows.

"Yes, Brian's here. We've been working on a few things together." After getting his basic diploma, Brian had enrolled in Haisukia University, and she was glad he had a friend like Bel there. It blew her mind that, in another few years, he would have more academic credentials than she did.

Brian called from off screen, "One sec. Let me just finish…"

He trailed off but soon appeared next to Bel. He looked rested, happy, and handsome as ever in a blue T-shirt and jeans. Academia suited him. She and Brian had broken up shortly after she left Lavinian, but they stayed in touch.

"So, how did things turn out with the bean fungus?"

"A lot of work. And some heartbreak. It managed to spread to some other legumes too. Blights don't mess around." Dione paused, reflecting on her time on the Rim. "Everyone out there is a fast learner, though. They have to be."

She had been doing the work that Bel had aspired to, helping the farmers on the Dappled Rim combat infestations and blights by introducing predatory species and breeding stronger hybrids. She was also making slow progress toward a degree through virtual classes. Now, most of what she did directly related to solving farming problems at real colonies.

"I'd love to hear about it over dinner," Brian said, his grin lighting up his eyes.

"I doubt I'll be down in time for dinner. With all the traffic for the festival, I'm sure we'll be up here for another day or two."

"We've got that taken care of," Brian replied. "See you tonight." He winked, then ended the call.

Right on cue, she received another call.

Lithia. Pilot extraordinaire.

Lithia had started making a name for herself in solar races, but those were just for fun. The real money came from her freelance gigs. She'd gone straight to flight school, graduated in record time, and, as far as Dione could tell from her frequent vid-letters, was doing well.

"This is an absolute rust bucket, Dione. Did it really make the trip back here?"

"Took us two weeks, but we—wait. You're here, aren't you?"

"Ready to escort your shuttle down. You're welcome, by the way."

"Thank you," Dione said, her eyes stinging with tears. She hadn't been home in over a year, and she physically ached to see her best friend in person again.

When they finally landed and got everything squared away, Lithia pulled her into a hug. "You look exhausted."

"It was a long trip."

"Want to catch up over dinner?" Lithia asked, leading Dione to her car.

"Oh, I have dinner plans with Brian," she said. "You should join us."

"Nope," she said. "I'm not third-wheeling your reunion date."

"It's not a date," Dione protested.

"Sure it's not. And how many serious relationships have you had out on the Rim?"

"I've been working nonstop. No time for dating. Plus, I did date Miles for a while. I told you about him."

"Di, he was a footnote in a love letter about that weird species of frog you imported to take care of some crop-eating bug."

Dione opened her mouth to protest but closed it again and sighed. "That's a fair assessment. He was nice, though."

"Well, as I pointed out in my last letter, Brian is not seeing anyone at the moment."

"I just—can we get coffee? I'm shuttle-lagged. You can tell me about Max and your parents and show me the latest race footage."

"Yes, but please don't be offended if I don't want to look at pictures of fungal growths and wasp galls."

"Deal," she replied.

As they waited for their drinks, Lithia regaled her with some of her recent photo finishes.

"How's the treatment going?" Dione asked.

"Haven't needed to adjust my meds in a long time and the meditation almost practices itself."

Dione raised a skeptical eyebrow.

"Okay, okay," Lithia conceded. "I have to work on it every day, but I've got a good thing going. It works. I'm doing well. Really, Di, I promise."

"Then I'm glad to hear it." The two enjoyed their coffee and caught up as if it were a weekly, rather than annual, tradition.

***

Today was the day. The reason she'd come back a few months early. She'd considered skipping it, but it felt important to be there in person.

Lithia picked up Dione from her father's house.

"You didn't have to wear black, you know," Lithia said. "It's a celebration, not a funeral."

"It just feels right," Dione replied.

"How was dinner?" Lithia asked, tone suggestive. "Did he show you his apartment?"

"No, he canceled. Last-minute something or other. We're going out for lunch after the dedication."

"Oh, I'm sure it's no big deal."

"Yeah," Dione agreed, though her heart ached. As much as she'd tried to keep her expectations low, she still had feelings for Brian. Real ones. Strong ones. Ones that had never faded like all the songs and vids had promised her they would. Moving so far away had broken her heart, but she knew it was something she'd had to do. She promised herself she wouldn't let a relationship get in the way of her dreams. She was too young to be pinned down.

It was the right choice, and she didn't regret it, but she'd been excited to see him again.

"Got your speech ready?"

"Memorized."

"Typical." Lithia shook her head, but she was smiling.

"Are you going to be okay?" Dione asked.

"Yeah, my parents are coming. Max will be there. He'll be graduating next year."

"I'm glad. My dad claims he'll be there. He's making a special trip. Coming straight from the port and going straight back out. My uncle is coming too."

"You're sticking around for a whole month this time, though," Lithia said.

"Yeah, and they're taking some time off next week to spend at home."

When they reached StellAcademy, aside from the clockwork growth of the trees and bushes, the grounds looked unchanged. Today marked Dione's first return since her graduation three years before, and though she'd loved her time here, this place would always hold bittersweet memories for her. Memories of Oberon were an ever-present ghost in these halls, especially today.

An eager pair of student guides gave them the tour as if they were old and disconnected from the building, and in a way they were. Behind the main building was a new one. The stone facade and white trim matched the other buildings, but it lacked the distinguished weathering the others had. The sign out front, white and navy blue, read "Oberon Biology Wing." Off to the side a newly planted garden with gravel paths and stone benches tempted her. A small greenhouse was visible near the back. She wondered what flowers and trees they'd selected.

One of the student guides cleared his throat, snapping her out of her thoughts. "Over here we have refreshments while we wait for the dedication ceremony to begin."

"Thanks," Dione said, giving the boy a warm smile.

"Look!" Lithia said. "There's Bel and Zane."

"I thought they broke up?" Dione asked.

"They may not be *together*, but they're like us. Separate but inseparable," Lithia replied.

The two were talking to their old physics teacher, who was gesticulating wildly. "Some things never change, do they?" Dione said. "Let's go."

"Dione!" Bel said, pulling her into a hug.

"Good to see you," Zane said, also offering a hug. "How's the Rim?"

"It's…" Dione took a breath and held it for a moment. It was hard to describe. "It's incredible. And humbling." She still didn't know the right thing to say, but that apparently satisfied him.

The group caught up over the light refreshments, but Dione kept looking over her shoulder for a sign of Brian. He was supposed to be there, but he still hadn't arrived by the time the dedication was beginning. Dione took her seat on stage behind the podium and to the left. Next to her was a trustee whose name she didn't know. The headmaster was giving the opening remarks, and soon the Chair of the Board would thank the benefactors who had funded the new building. She was giving the keynote address, a heartfelt speech from a former star student about a stellar teacher.

Her old headmaster introduced her and shook her hand when she reached the podium. Her uncle whistled, and she cast him and her father a smile. She scanned the crowd for her friends. Bel, Zane, and Lithia all sat near the front, and there, next to Lithia, was Brian. He'd made it after all. Seeing him there brought a smile to her face and gave her the push to start her speech.

"Elian Oberon came to StellAcademy from Haisukia University because he wanted to share his passion for science and discovery. He modeled his love of learning for all of his students. He saw the best in each of us even when others didn't."

She took a deep breath and looked up at the silent crowd. "More than that, he had a compassion and humanity that few can claim. He risked his life to save me and the other students when the Vens attacked his ship, and months later, he died fighting to save us—and everyone—from the Sugians. He was a good man, and he is missed. But his legacy lives on through his students, who remember his curiosity, kindness, and support, and that spirit will live on at StellAcademy."

Dione had practiced her speech so many times that she managed not to cry. She struggled to focus on the closing remarks from one of her old teachers, who attested to Oberon's worthiness as a scholar and colleague. Soon, the ceremony was over, and her old headmaster invited her and her friends to take a walk in the new garden. The young trees were small.

"This garden was built in your honor," he said to them. "There's no ceremony, but toward the back you'll find a lovely stone bench with a plaque. I'd better get back to the reception. Take your time here." There were more wrinkles at the corners of his eyes than she'd remembered, but the kindness in his smile was unchanged.

"Thank you," Dione said softly, starting off along the path, gravel crunching beneath her feet. Lithia was at her side the next moment, with Brian, Bel, and Zane close behind.

"A plaque," Lithia said in mock wonder. "The honor! The dignity!"

"I think it's nice," Bel said. "Plus, this is a beautiful garden."

In a quiet corner just off the path, she found it. Set before a young tree was their bench. The plaque was simple:

Courage is a choice.
Zane Delapont
Lithia Min
Dione Quinn
Belen Sangha

"I like it," Dione said.

"It fits," Zane said.

"It's a *polla* tree," Lithia said, ignoring the plaque and bench. "Brian? Was this you?"

He grinned. "There were viable seeds on the colonizer. We've managed to grow a few."

Dione met his gaze at last, and everything she'd expected to feel was there. He wrapped her in his arms, and it finally felt like she had come home.

***

The whole group had gotten lunch together, but after a few hours, she and Brian were the only two left.

"Want to take a walk? They've put in a new art installation at the park."

"Sure," she replied. "You can tell me all about school."

"There's not much more to tell. I study and work almost constantly. I see my parents for dinner twice a week."

"No hobbies?"

Brian raised his eyebrows. "Aside from cultivating and selling *polla* trees to rich people? Not really." Dione laughed. "How has the Rim been? I expected you to be tan, but you look the same.

You actually do the real work, right?" he teased.

"A lot of picking bugs off cabbage leaves and genetically modifying their appetites."

"To eat what?"

"A local plant that poisons the occasional lost sheep. You know, kill two birds with one genetically modified stone."

"I know it's a saying, but I still have to ask. Are you killing the birds too?"

Dione laughed, and so did Brian. The corners of his eyes creased with the very beginnings of wrinkles like his dad had. He was looking at her, calculating.

"What is it?" she asked. "What aren't you telling me?"

"We finally got approval. That's why I canceled yesterday and why I was late today. It happened all of a sudden."

Dione's eyebrows went up. "Oh, wow. I guess it has been a little while. No Ven or Sugian sightings for six months either." The virus had done its work, and within two years, there were hardly any vestiges of the alien races that had plagued them. The Vens and Sugians had either fled, succumbed to the virus, or killed each other.

"There's a lot of bureaucratic stuff that still has to happen, and I plan to go back to Kepos for it."

"That's good, but what about your degree?"

"I'm finishing it early."

"How is that even possible? You've only been working on it for three years."

"Like I said, I don't do much else besides study."

"Do you think you'll stay there? I thought you wanted a PhD."

"More school can wait a few years, or I can do it remotely like you've been doing it."

"And it's taking me a lot longer this way. I've still got two more years."

"I wanted to ask you to come to Kepos with me."

He caught her by surprise again. "When? I might be able to carve out another week or two later this year. I'll need a faster ship, though. I can—"

"Dione, let me finish. I want you to move there. You can finish up your internship while things get finalized, your other classes are already remote, and you know there are more than enough struggles to occupy you out there. Plus, it's a paying job."

"Move to Kepos for a few years?" she said. It was a bizarre thought, but it sounded even stranger coming from her own lips.

"I've heard from Moira. Some of the creatures on Jameson's nightmare island are finding their way to the mainland."

Dione pulled on a stray thread of her dress and swallowed. "The dragons?"

"No, thankfully, but they need help putting a stop to it, and who better than you?"

"There are plenty of qualified people."

"But those qualified people aren't you. If you aren't interested in the opportunity, no hard feelings. But I want you to understand the whole opportunity."

"What are you talking about?"

"There's the removal of invasives, a long-term solution to the creatures on the island, as well as studying the progress of the phytoremediation efforts. Moira tells me that she's discovered a plant that can cut the anticipated time to clean up the soil in half. She's has been digging into the research done by the other scientists, not just Jameson and Samantha."

"That is a very appealing set of problems to solve," Dione said. "But why ask me?"

"You know why, Dione." He reached out and tucked a stray

hair behind her ear, his fingertips brushing gently against her cheek. "I love you. I want to give us a real chance without you having to sacrifice the path you chose.

"Are you part of the benefits package?"

"Only if you want. The job offer stands. Kepos needs someone like you, and I personally hope that it is you. For selfish reasons, of course." He stepped closer and rested his forehead against hers. It was a question.

Dione looked up into his earnest, dark brown eyes. "I still love you too." Her work on the Rim had been meaningful. She didn't regret it, but it had also been lonely. Courage was a choice, and even though the thought of returning to Kepos filled her with mixed emotions, she knew the answer.

"Yes," she said. "But only if you promise we can get our doctorates after."

He laughed and kissed her. "I promise."

Dione put her hand in his, ready for the next adventure.

Thank You

Thank you for reading! If you have a minute, I'd appreciate it if you could leave a review on Amazon or Goodreads. Every review helps me get the word out about my books!

If you want to receive updates on new releases and deals about my books, sign up for my mailing list. I send out emails when I have news: subscribe.ericarue.com/

Acknowledgments

Thank you, **Jacob**, for your endless support. Thank you to my parents **Ralph** and **Jane** for letting me bounce some early ideas around that helped me solve plotting issues. Thank you to my wonderful beta readers: **Maggie Burnside, TR Dillon, Jane Eickhoff, Donna Royston, Bradford Karl Slocum,** and **Martin Wilsey.** Thank you to *The Hourlings* for the blurb feedback, especially from **Emma G. Rose**. I'd also like thank **Jessica Hatch** of Hatch Editorial Services for cleaning up an especially poorly punctuated draft and brainstorming a specific issue with me.

Finally, a special thank you to the readers who made it to the end of the series! Your support is much appreciated.

About the Author

Erica Rue is a reader and writer of science fiction and fantasy, especially YA. Her abandoned biology major and handful of astronomy classes have prepared her well for writing sci-fi. She enjoys learning new words and promptly forgetting them so that she can rediscover them. When she's not writing, she forgets to water her garden, completes every side quest she triggers, and boosts her dog's self-esteem.

Also by Erica Rue

The Kepos Chronicles

The Kepos Problem
The Ven Hypothesis
The Island Experiment
The Predator Analysis

Short Stories

Last Ship Home

www.ingramcontent.com/pod-product-compliance
Lightning Source LLC
Chambersburg PA
CBHW031549240626
47153CB00002B/432